A Grand Murder

A NOVEL BY

DAVE VIZARD

ALSO BY DAVE VIZARD

A Formula for Murder

Edited by Christina M. Frey, christina@pagetwoediting.com
Cover photo by Joey Lax-Salinas, joeyblsphotography.com
Design by Susan Leonard, roseislandbookworks.com

ISBN 978-0-692-45222-6

Printed in the United States of America

Acknowledgements

This novel would not have come to life without the help of some great people who made many significant contributions.

I extend my sincere thanks to all the good folks on Mackinac Island who helped in many different ways. Ken Hayward and his gracious staff of the Grand Hotel and former Police Chief James Marks were very accommodating. And a special thanks to the Gang at the 'Stang.

Pharmacist Kendal Truemner was a great guide through the examination of drugs and helped me discover the wonderful world of animal tranquilizers.

I can't say enough about my editor, Christina M. Frey. Christina's advice and suggestions were invaluable in turning an interesting tale into a novel that I'm truly proud of. Working with her was a joy. She became a true partner in the development of this work of fiction.

Hats off to Susan Leonard of Rose Island Bookworks for coming up with a terrific cover design.

Thanks to all of my proofreaders: Teresa Calkins, Sherry Mocniak, and Tom Glide. Your help and support are much appreciated.

Developing this story was a special delight because I had the early help and support of my son, Michael D. Vizard. Mickey and I traveled to Mackinac Island together to do the initial research for the story. He also was terrific at helping develop the storyline. When you're trying to figure out how to commit murder in one of America's great playgrounds, there's nothing like collaborating with your son. This was so much fun, I'm looking forward to our next opportunity to create mayhem together.

Chapter 1

Sunday morning

Nick Steele took a deep breath as the mortician reached for the corner of the sheet nearest the body's right ear. Identifying the dead was a task Nick had done a few times during his reporting career, but it always made him sick to his stomach.

"Wait, I'm not ready," said Jake Zimmer, the brother of the stiff under the sheet. Jake steadied himself by holding on to Nick's shoulder. "I feel light-headed. I never thought this day would come."

The embalmer nodded at both men, indicating he understood their discomfort. Cool, damp air flooded the back room of the St. Ignace funeral home. Two filled caskets rested on carriers in the darkest corner of the room. A single string of fluorescent lights hung from the ceiling, illuminating the sheet that covered the corpse.

The body under the sheet had crashed onto the hard flooring of the famed covered front porch of Mackinac Island's Grand Hotel a day earlier, just missing one of the white rocking chairs on the porch. It looked like it had fallen from a third-floor balcony room early Saturday morning.

No witnesses to the crash had come forward. A security guard had discovered the lifeless body during routine rounds.

The balding male appeared to be less than six feet tall, fit, and trim. The body had no ID on it, but a wallet was found in the room, which was three doorways to the Mackinac Bridge side of the Grand's Governor's Suite.

Mackinac Island police said the room was registered to a Zeke Zimmer. A wallet in the room held Zeke's credit cards, a scrap of paper with six numerals on it, and eighty bucks in cash. Nothing else.

Police, at the urging of image-conscious hotel officials, had declared the death the result of an accidental fall. In no time the dead man was scooped up and whisked off Michigan's most famous Lake Huron island. County sheriff's deputies escorted the body by boat to St. Ignace in the Upper Peninsula. After initial examination revealed a cracked skull and broken neck, the body was transported to the nearby Dodson Funeral Home.

Nick had been alerted to the death when he received a call from the newsroom of *The Bay City Blade* Saturday evening. A reporter on weekend duty had called to tell Nick that Zeke Zimmer, a noted Boys & Girls Club volunteer in Bay City, had died on Mackinac Island. Nick had written a lengthy feature story about Zeke a year earlier, describing the retired autoworker's fundraiser to help establish the Burn Center at Bay Medical Center. The article had run in *True North* magazine's May 1998 issue. Zeke was quoted saying he felt it was his duty to help kids whenever he could.

Jake Zimmer was the deceased's only living relative. When Nick had called Jake to express his condolences, Jake had blubbered and wailed on the phone.

"Why, Nick, why?" he cried. "He was the best brother anybody could ever want. I just can't believe he's gone."

The *Blade* reporter had tried to console Zeke's younger brother, but failed. The shock was too great. The sudden acknowledgment that death had knocked at his family's door was too stunning. He had begged Nick to help him identify the body.

"I can't do it alone," he said.

"Absolutely. I'll talk to my boss, but I'm sure he'll okay a run to Mackinac. Your brother was very well known around Bay City. I bet my editors will want a story on what happened to him. Let's take off first thing in the morning."

The Straits of Mackinac are about 180 miles north of Bay City, almost directly north on I-75. That's a long way for a small newspaper's coverage to stretch, but *The Bay City Blade* was Up North

Michigan's largest daily. Editors of *The Blade* sent reporters into the wilderness to cover big breaking stories frequently. Assigning Nick to this story was a cinch because the victim was a prominent Bay Cityan whom the reporter had profiled before.

The three-hour drive from Bay City to St. Ignace had given Nick and Jake plenty of time to recall fond memories of Zeke. Cool spring air during the third week of May meant that the two drove north with the car windows closed. Being so confined with a distraught man made Nick uncomfortable. When they stopped to get coffee in West Branch and Gaylord, breaking the monotony of the solemn ride, Jake was so upset that he opened up to Nick all about the Zimmer family—inside, personal information that few outsiders had been privy to.

To say the least, Zeke had lived a full, and sometimes wild, life. Married four times and divorced three times amid a handful of sordid affairs, he often confused love with lust. He was impulsive and couldn't resist a game of blackjack or five-card stud. He smoked like a locomotive, and a rock glass of iced Kentucky bourbon was never far from whichever hand wasn't holding a lit cigarette.

"I hate to say this, but if his time was up and he had to go, I'm glad it was a sudden death," Jake had said on the ride up. "I would have hated to see him suffer."

"Yup," Nick had agreed. "Suffering is something only editors and publishers should have to endure."

Now the funeral director at Dodson Funeral Home reassured them that death appeared to have come quickly for Zeke. Nick and Jake could take all the time they wanted, he said, to view the body.

Both men took deep breaths, looked at each other for support, and nodded at the undertaker. The mortician pulled back the sheet.

Nick gasped for air.

Jake's eyes rolled back into his skull. He fainted, falling drop-dead style to the floor.

"Oh my," the mortician said. "I was hoping that wouldn't happen again. I guess the shock was too much for him."

"Well, yeah, I guess you could say that," Nick said. "Especially since the guy on your table there is not Zeke Zimmer."

"What?"

"Nope. That's not him. Might look a little like him from a distance, but that's definitely not Zeke," said Nick as he knelt over Jake's twitching body on the floor. "I don't know who you've got on that slab, but it's not Zimmer. That means ol' Jakey here will be very happy—once he comes to—that his brother's whereabouts are unknown."

Chapter 2

Late Sunday morning

When the elevator door dinged and opened in the newsroom of *The Bay City Blade* at 11:30 a.m., all activity stopped. Second-edition papers had arrived from the newsroom.

An editorial clerk grabbed an armload of future puppy trainers and distributed them to the editors and reporters in the newsroom. The papers were still damp. The smell of drying ink hovered in the air as staffers opened pages and scoured each column, looking for bad headlines, errors, omissions, and the other general screw-ups that typically occurred in the rush to deadline. Corrections could be made for the third, or bulldog, edition of the paper, but they had to happen fast.

Dave Balz, a retired police reporter who now worked part-time on retainer for *The Blade*, waited for a paper like a starving man watching for a slice of bread to get tossed his way. The veteran scribe pushed his shoulder-length hair, once mostly sandy but now speckled gray, away from his creased, weather-beaten face and reached for a paper with his other hand.

Dave, pushing sixty-five and shaped like a sturdy fire hydrant, stood at the desk and unfolded the paper. He scanned the front page, searching for the story Nick had written in his notebook and called into *The Blade*'s rewrite desk between morning editions.

Headlines for May 9, 1999, included "Bay City searches for new city manager," "Yeltsin survives Russian impeachment," "Thumbs-up for recipient of first human hand transplant," and "Walters scores interview with Monica Lewinsky."

In the bottom right corner of the front page, Dave found the Mackinac Island story. He devoured it.

Mystery Man Dead from Fall at Mackinac's Grand Hotel

By Nick Steele

A Bay City man who authorities believed died from a fall at the Grand Hotel on Mackinac Island was misidentified.

"It's not him," said Jake Zimmer, the youngest brother of Zeke Zimmer, the man originally thought to have died after falling from a third-floor balcony and landing on the famous front porch of the legendary hotel.

Jake Zimmer had been summoned by Michigan State Police to the island to identify the body of the man believed to be his brother. He arrived on the island early this morning to view the body.

Authorities said the room at the Grand was registered to Zeke Zimmer and one of his credit cards was found in the room. Police and hotel officials are not revealing what other items were uncovered during a search of the room after the body was discovered. The railing of the third-floor balcony was not damaged, police said.

"Kind of looks like him, but that definitely was not Zeke," Zimmer said today. "I can't tell you how relieved our whole family is that it wasn't my big brother."

The younger Zimmer said that Zeke's wife told him her husband had planned to attend an electricians' conference on the island that weekend. She has no idea where her husband is, and has not heard from him since he left Bay City last Thursday afternoon, Jake Zimmer said.

Mackinac Island and state police are trying to identify the body of the mystery man now.

The county medical examiner initially ruled the death a result of head injuries and a broken neck from an accidental fall. Since the misidentification, authorities have ordered an autopsy of the body, which has been removed from Mackinac Island and is at Dodson Funeral Home in St. Ignace.

A spokesperson for the Grand Hotel expressed surprise this morning.

"Of course we were stunned by the misidentification," said Steven Fordson, a public relations specialist with the hotel. "The safety and well-being of our guests is our first priority. Naturally, we were saddened and disheartened by the accidental passing of a guest. We are working with police to help identify the deceased."

The "mystery man" is described as white, average build—about 5'-10" and 160 pounds—and in his late 50s or early 60s, with dark, receding hair. The man wore dark slacks and a dress shirt with open collar. His shoes apparently fell off during the fall. They were found on the porch, not far from where the body landed.

Hotel officials told police that the body was discovered during a routine security check of the front porch at about 1:30 a.m. Saturday. No witnesses reported seeing or hearing the man fall, police said.

Dave sat down and read the story a second time. He whispered out loud to no one in particular, "Nick, Nick, Nick, my man. This baby has got the stink of good story all over it." The two had been buddies for nearly twenty-five years, working on stories together whenever the opportunity arose. Dave started to salivate at the idea of heading to Mackinac Island to jump on this piece with Nick.

"B-a-l-z," boomed Drayton Clapper, the local news editor, across the newsroom. "Get in here now!"

Like a schoolkid heading for recess, Dave scooted across the newsroom to Clapper's office. But his hopes were dashed after he walked through the door.

"Don't even ask. Don't even think about it. You're not going up there," Drayton said, taking a huge load off his feet and slumping his massive body into the chair behind his cluttered desk. "The last thing I need is you two cavorting all over Michigan's playground, ticking people off, drinking, and getting in trouble."

"But Drayton," Dave said, pulling up his sagging jeans and squaring off to argue his case. "You gotta send me up there. Are you kidding? A dead body? A misidentification? A missing Bay City man? A . . ."

The news editor held up his hand like a traffic cop halting cars in the middle of the street. "Stop, no more. I need you here to work the story from this angle. Make the calls, find Zimmer. Start with the jails and hospitals. Check the bars, the whorehouses, the gambling joints. You know what to do."

But the former police reporter did not give up easily. "Look, I'm a part-timer, a newsroom bottom-feeder. I want to go on vacation, take a little time off. Just a few days. I gotta get out of town."

Drayton rolled his eyes. "Please don't make me fire you again. Be a team player. Help us cover the story on this end. It will all be over in a couple days, Zimmer will pop up, and then you can go wherever you want."

Dave retreated to his desk like a spanked puppy. It would almost be worth getting fired again, he thought, to join Nick on the island.

Firings and suspensions weren't foreign to Dave or Nick. Dave had become Nick's mentor. They'd been canned at least a half-dozen times over the years. Their corporate crimes? Felony disrespect for authority, criminal disregard for *Blade* management—sometimes bordering on insubordination—and high misdemeanor violation of the dress code.

In the big scheme of things, their transgressions were relatively minor. Nick and Dave were simply nonconformists, working for a company that wanted—no, demanded—good foot soldiers.

Dave once wore the same loosened necktie for two years straight. It started out as a fashionable plaid, but soon took on a yellow, red, and brown hue, the result of too many collisions with chili dogs and mustard.

Finally it had all come crashing down on Dave when he wore the chili-dog tie with a fading, rumpled sport coat to a Ronald Reagan press conference in Flint. Dave asked the GOP presidential nominee a question about welfare reform. In response, the Gipper looked the frumpy reporter up and down and then turned the question back on him. "Are you collecting welfare checks?"

It probably would have blown over with no problems, but the whole exchange was caught by TV cameras, and Dave made the nightly news. He was canned the next day.

After a week or so on the sidelines, he was reinstated. What always saved Dave and Nick was this simple fact—the two were excellent reporters and skilled writers who had a knack for digging out great stories. Bottom line: their work kept readers engaged and sold newspapers.

Nevertheless, it was the end of the road for the chili-dog tie. To get his job back, Dave agreed to ditch it for good. The tie went up in flames outside O'Hare's Bar & Grill to the sound of clinking beer bottles in a final, rancorous salute.

On this day, Dave's necktie was a bright-green clip-on job that dangled just below the top button of his untucked burgundy shirt. He pulled the tie off and tossed it on his desk in frustration.

Within minutes, however, he snapped out of it, grabbed the phone book in his desk drawer, and pulled his Rolodex up close, ready to chase down the missing electrician. If Zeke was in Bay City, Dave was going to find him.

As Dave reached for his phone, it rang. Nick was on the other end of the line, calling from the Upper Peninsula.

"Clapper is an SOB," Dave declared.

"Really? I guess that means you're not coming up here," Nick said. "But Drayton wants you to work on this with me, doesn't he?"

"Yup," Dave said. He updated his buddy on the latest developments in the newsroom, but he was more interested in what had happened after Nick and Jake Zimmer realized that Zeke was not the dead man stretched out in St. Ignace.

"That's all everyone is talking about," Nick said. "I've got a ton of ideas to kick around. Have you got a few minutes?"

"You bet. Shoot."

Nick unloaded. Word of the misidentification had raced across the Straits of Mackinac. The mystery body had prompted a slew of questions: If the dead man was not Zeke, then where was the electrician? If Zeke was still alive, then who crashed onto the deck of the Grand's front porch? Why was a room registered to Zeke if someone else was using it? Why was Zeke's credit card in the room if he was not there? What about the numbers on the scrap of paper—did they mean something? And was the death an accident? Did a man simply fall over the rail of the third-floor balcony and crash to his death?

Dave wondered if the tiny Mackinac Island Police Department was equipped to deal with a case like this.

"Not sure—all six members of the force will no doubt work on it," Nick said. "I think I'm going to have to stay up here for at least a few days. Could you clear that with Drayton for me?"

"I'll mention to him that we talked, and what your plan is, but I can't guarantee anything with him," Dave said. "I'm not on his best side right now. When I talked to him this morning, he tossed around that 'Don't make me fire you' line again."

"Well then, I really don't want to talk to him now," Nick said. "I'll catch up to him later. Just tell him I'm chasing this story like crazy right now, which is the truth. I've got to get over to the hotel as soon as I can."

Chapter 3

Early Sunday afternoon

Nick arrived at the Arnold Transit dock just in time to catch the 12:30 ferry to the island. He paid cash for his ticket and boarded the ship with a mix of passengers who were as varied as the faces normally seen entering Disney World—mostly families young and old, hailing from a wide range of middle America.

Though it was chilly, Nick opted to sit outside in the sunshine. The reporter relaxed in his seat and took a deep breath. He was a tad winded as a result of his walk from the funeral home. He'd had to hoof it because Jake Zimmer, elated that his brother might still be alive, was already on the road back to Bay City. Family members had been alerted that *The Blade*'s final edition that day would include a story about the misidentification, and Jake had wanted to be with them.

When the ferry docked at the island, Nick found himself in a mass of tourists unloading—some with their own bicycles—and scrambling toward the main thoroughfare. Nick saw a sign pointing to the Grand. Soon the massive hotel, perched on the side of a high ridge, came into view.

"Wow," Nick said to himself. "I guess I know how the resort got its name."

More than a hundred years old and constructed almost entirely of Michigan white pine, the four-story hotel stretched as far as the eye could see. Its forest-green roof accented the long, ranch-style white building. Bright-yellow awnings hung over its windows. American flags flapped in the wind across the length of its covered front porch. Fire-engine-red carpet greeted visitors at the front entrance. The mighty Mackinac Bridge, spanning the Straits of Mackinac and linking the Upper and Lower Peninsulas of Michigan, stood behind the hotel in the backdrop of Nick's view.

The Grand was a top-rated hotel and a renowned world-class resort. People from across Michigan took pride in Mackinac Island and the Grand. The vacation destinations were viewed by most as special places, unlike any other location in the world. It was almost as if hotel developers created the word elegance just for the Grand and then had it struck from the dictionary.

Nick, who was still in pretty good physical condition for a guy nearly fifty, hiked up the steep hill leading to the famed hotel with ease. The resort's landscaping was precise and lush. Bright yellow and red spring flowers bloomed everywhere he looked. As he approached, polished horse-drawn carriages passed him in both directions.

Part of Mackinac Island's mystique is the fact that no motorized cars or trucks are allowed on the island except for emergency vehicles. Most visitors view the lack of cars as part of the island's Victorian charm. Dodging a few horse nuggets in the street is a small price to pay to slow life down a little and enjoy some time without noise and exhaust.

The *Blade* reporter found his way to the Grand's front desk. Normally reservations would be a must, but the Grand was just awakening from its long winter hibernation. The hotel, which is shut down and closed except for security personnel during Michigan's harsh, severe winter months, was now beginning to yawn and stretch from a four-month slumber.

"Please repeat—how much is a room?" Nick looked at the registration clerk in disbelief. Drayton Clapper would give birth to kittens when he saw the bill. "$300 a night? Well, okay, just charge it to *The Blade*. What time do they serve dinner around here?"

"Are you aware of the hotel's dress policy?" asked the clerk, a dark-haired young woman, probably in her early twenties. "After six o'clock, we require guests to dress for dinner. Jacket, tie, and slacks for men—no blue jeans."

"Dress code? Neckties? Why, that's what almost got me fired from *The Blade* last fall," Nick said, remembering the close call he had with *Blade* management during the development of a ground-breaking story. "I think that means I'll be staying in my room after six. Have room service send up your best steak, all the fixin's, and some ice-cold beer to the room. I want the chow and suds to arrive at the door when I do—5:30 p.m. on the dot."

"How many nights will you be staying?" the clerk asked.

"Don't know. I guess as long as it takes, or until my boss finds out what my tab up here is—probably whichever comes first," Nick said. "And put a nice tip on the room service for the person who brings it up, and one for yourself."

"No tipping," the clerk said in a flat, even tone as she jotted a note into the registration chart.

"No tipping? Why, that's almost un-American," Nick said, trying to keep himself from laughing out loud. "I'll just slip you a twenty and you can split it with my waiter."

"No, you won't be slipping me anything," the woman said, her voice rising slightly. "We have a no tipping policy throughout the hotel. Everything is included in the cost of your room. And if you receive anything less than excellent service, please let one of the hotel managers or me know. We will take care of it immediately."

"Wow, policies on top of policies. What's your policy on having a little fun? Is it okay to whoop it up a little in this place?" Nick asked, eyeing a bellman who stood at attention, dressed in a red uniform with gold trim and shined shoes. A small, round hat sat squarely on his head.

"You can enjoy yourself and have fun as long as you don't disturb our other guests," she said. "Our guests are ladies and gentlemen."

That gave Nick an idea. "Tell me, did you happen to be on duty when the body fell on the front porch the other night?" Nick asked. "I'll bet that disturbed a whole bunch of ladies and gentlemen."

"I worked that night, but did not see anything," she said. "Most guests had retired for the evening when it happened. You should really speak with the hotel manager about it."

Nick signed the registration form and headed for the elevator. He decided to spend some time roaming the hotel to get a feel for the place. As he turned to walk away, the clerk hailed him.

"Sir, just noticed you have a message. It came about an hour ago."

A note arriving at the desk even before Nick checked in surprised him. Only a few people knew where he was or what he would be doing. Nick took the note and nodded his appreciation.

It said simply, "Knew you'd be at the most expensive place on the island, you dog, you. Have a beer for me, but call before you do.—Dave Balz."

Nick tucked the paper in his pocket. It would be good to talk with his newsroom friend after he did a little investigating. Bouncing ideas off of Dave always resulted in good ideas on how to chase a difficult story.

Plus, Nick hoped that either Dave or Tanya Johnson, Nick's girlfriend, would drive up north to provide taxi service back home. Nick decided he would call Tanya and Dave later in the evening. Right now he wanted to check out the hotel's front porch to see where the body had crashed. He also wanted to meet the hotel manager.

Nick turned to the bellman in the tricked-out suit. "Excuse me, do you know how I could find the hotel manager?" he said. "I really need to speak with him."

"Yes sir," the bellman answered, looking over his shoulder in the direction of two women talking. "*She's* right over there talking with the police chief."

A pair of distinguished women, dressed in pantsuits and high heels, stood nose to nose. Both looked very officious. Their discussion was intense, but not uncivil. Nick could see the veins sticking out in their necks as they rattled back and forth at each other. For now, he decided, it was best not to break into their conversation. Instead he casually sauntered past them, hoping to eavesdrop a little inside information.

"No uniformed cops in the hotel," said the taller, heavier woman. Nick guessed that she was in her mid-fifties. She was blond, with hard blue eyes. Big bags hung under her eyes like purses slung from forearms. "You can conduct your investigation and we will assist in every way we can, but I do not want any more spectacles on the porch or in the hotel. Have your cops blend with the guests. You look fine. Just have them dress like you."

"Well, my cops are men, and if they run around your hotel dressed like me, that's really going to be a spectacle," said the auburn-haired cop, who looked old enough to be watching the mailbox for her first Social Security check to come any day. She wore no jewelry, and only faded traces of makeup. "We'll blend, but we've got to interview your employees and the guests who were here when the body hit the deck," she said. "We have to move fast. We've got to find out what's going on here."

Both women paused to check the pagers on their hips, and Nick decided it was the perfect time for an introduction. He stepped closer to them.

"Hello, I'm Nick Steele. I'm a reporter with *The Bay City Blade*," he said, thrusting his open right mitt in the direction of the two women. At six foot two and 220 pounds, Nick was the size of a small linebacker. The women were physically smaller, but yielded no ground.

They both looked at the hand dangling in the air and then up at Nick. Then they replied in unison, almost as if someone had choreographed the reaction, "Oh shit, a reporter."

"We have no comment at this time," said the taller woman, who introduced herself to Nick and shook his hand firmly. Nick thought he'd stuck his hand in a vise. "I'm Sylvia Shane, day manager of the Grand Hotel. I know you've got a job to do, but so do I."

"Nice to meet you, Sylvia," Nick said, and turned toward the other woman. "Do you not want to meet me, either?"

The smaller woman smiled at Nick and grabbed his outstretched hand. "Why, no, I don't hate reporters. Actually, I despise them. Just kidding. My name is Lucille Calkins. I only despise lazy, sloppy, dumb reporters who cut corners."

"Oh, well then, I think we're going to get along just fine," Nick said.

Sylvia Shane told Nick that he was welcome to visit the hotel and ask questions of authorized personnel, but that he could not invade anyone's privacy or upset guests in any way.

"I am a guest," Nick said. "I just checked in. I hope I will receive the same kind of personal attention and service that all guests receive. When can we meet to talk?"

"I have some business to attend to," Sylvia said, turning sideways. Her left eye blinked. Nick believed it was a wink. "I will be available first thing in the morning. Just ask for me at the front desk."

Nick winked back at the hotel manager as she turned to leave. He then faced the chief. "Are you going to run off on me too?"

"No, but as you can imagine, I am a little busy," she said. "I've got an unidentified body over in St. Ignace, a missing hotel guest, and a lot of island employees and visitors feeling a little bit spooked. I can give you five minutes right now, but then you're going to have to catch me when you can."

"Sounds good," Nick said, pulling a notebook and pen out of his hip pocket. "You've already answered one question. The body in St. Ignace that landed on the porch is still unidentified? Do you have any leads on who it might be?"

"Not yet, but we have some ideas that I can't disclose now. The medical examiner is going to do an autopsy, including a tox screen," she said. "We'll see what that turns up."

"Why a tox screen if the fall was accidental?" Nick asked.

The chief paused to check her watch before replying. "The first examination of the body didn't include one, so we decided to look at everything—including what foreign substances might have been in him when he fell. We're simply covering all the bases."

Nick scribbled notes in his pad, then cleared his throat before asking a question he was afraid might rile the chief.

"Don't take this the wrong way, but I have to ask, is your department equipped to handle an investigation like this? My guess is that you spend most of your time chasing around fudge filchers, not tracking down murderers."

"Who said anything about murder?" the chief said, her eyes flashing. She stepped closer to Nick, leaning into his space. She was so close that Nick thought he detected a hint of mint or peppermint schnapps on her breath. "Don't jump to conclusions—that sounds like a lazy reporter cutting corners. We're still looking at this death as accidental—there's nothing to indicate otherwise at this time."

Nick's question clearly had agitated the chief. "And furthermore, I've been a cop for thirty years," she said. "I've handled every kind of investigation you can think of. Don't worry about what we can handle and what we cannot. If we need help, and I will be the one to determine that, then I'll call the state police for assistance."

Nick knew the chief had had a distinguished career in law enforcement long before she took the ferry ride out of Mackinaw City to the island for her first interview.

He figured that she had taken the island's top cop job to pad her retirement income while escaping the madness of everyday life. In that case, the last thing she'd want was an unidentified body landing on the porch of one of the world's great resorts. That might screw things up for the aging cop. Under her breath, Calkins was probably praying for the death to be accidental.

But Nick already had his doubts. "Chief, I'm not making assumptions. The whole thing just sounds so odd to me. An older guy with no ID on him comes flying over the railing of a third-story balcony room in the middle of the night and lands on the porch. No witnesses. Does that really sound accidental to you?"

"I will tell you more when I know more," the chief said. "Your five minutes are up." She turned to leave, but then glanced back at Nick.

"By the way, that wasn't a wink Sylvia gave you," she said. "Sylvia has a little twitch when she's stressed. You run a hotel with hundreds of employees and thousands of visitors and see what that does to your nervous system. Then add a mystery body and a missing guest on top of that—it's a wonder her whole body isn't convulsing."

"Oh, yeah. I can see that," Nick said, feeling slightly ashamed for thinking the hotel manager had the hots for him.

"Again, don't jump to conclusions," the chief said, wagging a finger at Nick. "That's only going to get both of us in trouble."

Chapter 4

Late Sunday afternoon

The room Nick rented at the Grand was the least expensive available. Even so, the brightly colored room was luxurious by his standards, which varied from roadside hole-in-the-wall to No-Tell Hotel. It was nicely appointed with distinctive but not gaudy furnishings. A polished mahogany desk with a soft executive chair was the focal point of the room. Hand-painted green and white stripes adorned the main wall behind the tall, fluffy double bed. Yellow and blue florals accented another wall. Of course the floor covering, bedspread, and pillows were all color coordinated with the other décor. Way more comfort than Nick needed or was used to, but it was nice to feel how the side with money recreated.

As Nick poked through the desk drawers, he heard a soft tapping at the door. "Room service."

Like almost all hotel rooms, the entry door had a peephole. Nick did not use it. Instead he whisked open the heavy wooden door, salivating slightly at the thought of the thick, juicy steak, salad, asparagus, and fresh bread that would be coming across his threshold.

"I have your dinner, sir," the young woman said. Instantly the aroma of sizzling grilled beef filled the room. Nick closed the door, hoping to trap the delightful smell and keep out prying eyes.

"Where would you like me to set you up?" The woman rolled the table into Nick's room as he motioned to a spot in front of a sturdy overstuffed chair in the furthest corner from the door. She positioned the table and locked its wheels in place. After quickly unfurling Nick's linen napkin, she reached under the tablecloth and pulled out a bucket of iced Heineken, wiping away large droplets of water from the green bottles.

"If you would be so kind as to sign for it, sir," she said.

Nick scribbled his name on the room service tab, quickly noting the $90 charge. "I hear there's no tipping—is that right?"

"Yes, sir. Enjoy your dinner and your evening."

She opened the door to leave, but Nick stopped her exit.

"Excuse me, I have a quick question for you. Do all members of your room service staff wear the same kind of uniform?" he asked, eyeing her sleek black slacks and the distinctive gold jacket with buttons the size of silver dollars.

"Yes, sir. We all wear the same uniform," she said, looking down at her black soft-soled shoes. "It's required at the Grand."

She whisked out of the room before Nick could reload with another question. "Thanks," he said as the door closed and the lock clicked with a brisk snap. The reporter had hoped his soft questions would prompt the woman to talk about working at the hotel, but she hadn't volunteered information. It made Nick wonder if employees had been cautioned against open discussion with guests after the fall and death.

The ring tone of his cell phone broke the silence in the room. Earlier he had left messages with Tanya and Dave, not expecting to hear back from either of them until later in the evening. Nick answered on the second ring, not wanting to risk missing the call.

He wasn't worried about Dave, but he was fearful of losing Tanya as a result of inattention. He dreaded the thought of another man catching Tanya's eye and affections, though he was reluctant to pull her closer. Tanya had tried to take their relationship to the next level, but Nick kept hesitating. He feared it was moving too fast, and he thought he was not good enough for her. In his mind it was only a matter of time before Tanya would tire of the real Nick and move on without him.

The reporter still missed his late wife, Joanne, who had died in a car crash three years earlier. The memory made him feel guilty about developing feelings for a younger woman. Still, he missed the new woman in his life and hoped she would not give up on him.

Nick picked up the phone without looking at the number. "Hello, I'm eating a $90 steak right now, so this better be good."

"Yeah, I kind of think it's good," a distinctive, husky smoker's voice said. "This is Zeke Zimmer. I hear you're looking for me."

The sound of Zeke's voice made the reporter sit straight up. Now maybe he'd get some answers to at least some of the questions that had popped up since he first arrived on the island. "Zeke, my man. I'm so glad you're alive," Nick said, a big smile spreading across his face.

He put his fork and knife down on the table and leaned back in his soft chair to talk with the missing Bay City man. "Where in the hell have you been? You almost caused your little brother to pop a cork when we came up here to ID your body."

"Yup, that's what I hear," Zeke said. "I'm fine. Everything is good. It's kind of complicated. You want the long version or the short one?"

"Give me the details. I'm dying to know." Nick covered his food with the round silver tray lid that had come with the dinner.

Zeke cleared his throat twice and began the story behind his misidentification and long weekend disappearance. Nick could hear the tinkle of ice rattling in a glass. Some kind of whiskey, no doubt.

Zeke said he had been gambling all weekend at the Indian casino at Suttons Bay over near Traverse City. He told Nick that he'd reserved a room at the Grand Hotel in an effort to hide his gambling from Wife Number Four, who was threatening divorce in the best-case scenario or a frying pan alongside the head in the worst unless he changed his wagering ways.

As far as Number Four knew, Zeke was hanging out on Mackinac Island for a four-day International Brotherhood of Electrical Workers union convention. A career tradesman, Zeke took great pride in being a card-carrying electrician. It was one of the few stable elements of his life. But instead of going to the Grand, the skilled worker had made a beeline for the blackjack table.

"So who was in the room under your name at the hotel?" Nick asked, breaking into Zeke's explanation. "You're aware, aren't you, that the guy who fell from the balcony of your room is now among the dearly departed?"

"Yup, I got the lowdown," Zeke said. "I already told the cops, so I guess I can tell you. I let my old buddy Adam Townsend use the room. He's from Bay City, and an electrician too. He was going to the conference. Also said he planned to invite one of his old girlfriends to visit him at the Grand. I never got her name, but I had the suspicion that she was married—to somebody else."

Zeke said he'd given Adam his reservation number and credit card so he could register. "But I was never in that room," he told Nick.

"I hate to admit this, but I was really, really hung over Saturday morning," he said. "I stumbled into the bathroom and tried checking my messages while lighting a cigarette. Everything was good until I dropped the damn cell phone in the toilet. It's been sitting in a bowl of rice ever since. Just hope I don't lose my contacts."

Apparently Zeke hadn't even realized what had happened until he heard a news bulletin about a death at the Grand on a TV at the casino. The description of the deceased sounded as if the announcer had Zeke in mind as he rattled from his script. The newscast prompted Zeke to find a lobby telephone and call his brother.

"Zeke, that's pretty wild," Nick said, relaxing back into the soft cushion of his chair. The reporter held the phone in one hand and used the other to cradle the side of his head. Zeke's tale was a ton to consume, and Nick wasn't sure how much to swallow. "Are you feeling lucky to be alive? That could have been you going over that railing."

"Yeah, I'm going to find me a lottery game where I can play the numbers from the date I was supposed to have done the swan dive at the Grand," he said. "I have no idea what the hell happened. The cops told me they still think it was an accident. They notified Adam's family today. He was really a great guy and a good friend. Hope they figure out how he bit the dust."

"Yeah, me too," Nick said, quickly jotting down Zeke's line about betting the numbers of the date he was supposed to have died. It sounded just like Zeke. Readers would love that. "Cops say anything else?"

"One thing that I thought was a little strange," Zeke said. "They found a bag with a change of clothes in it that probably belonged to Adam. But they also found a bottle of champagne on a table near the balcony. I didn't order it, and I never knew Adam to drink that stuff."

As Zeke spoke, the reporter could hear another phone ringing in the background. He was afraid the conversation with the wandering electrician was about to end. Quickly he asked Zeke if the cops had found a room service slip for the champagne. The response was a hurried grunt that Nick took to mean as a no.

Now Nick could hear faint, muffled voices pulling Zeke away from him. "Hey, man, glad you're okay," Nick said. "I will be back in Bay City by the end of the week. Can we get together to talk some more?"

"Sure, Nick. Anytime you're ready," he said. "I'll call you when my phone dries out, and we'll set something up. Don't know if I'll be living at home, though. After all this, I think I may just as well go down and check into divorce court—and look for the express line. Boy, is the wife pissed at me. Guess it's time to look for Number Five . . ."

Before reengaging with his dinner, Nick thought about the odd sequence of events that he'd just learned from the electrician. He wondered how often Zeke had sneaked off to gamble. What else had he concealed from Wife Number Four? Heavy gamblers often dueled with multiple demons.

Answers to those questions would come with inquiry and time. For now, the reporter thought, it might be a good idea to find out what the locals on the island were saying about the accidental death at the Grand. He thought he might find some tongues, loosened by the influence of libations, flapping freely at a pub.

After polishing off dinner, Nick grabbed the hotel phone and called down to the front desk. He asked the clerk for the name of a good bar on the island, somewhere he could meet locals and have some fun.

"The Pink Pony is a really nice place right on Main Street, not far from the ferry docks," she said.

"I haven't been there, but the name makes me think it's kind of a tourist trap," Nick said. "I'm looking for a place that's probably a little grittier than the Pink Pony. I'm looking for a *bar* bar, like a saloon."

"Oh, well then, you'll want to go to the Mustang Lounge—no question," the young woman said with a laugh. "You will find some fun and a whole lot more at the Mustang. It's just a block off Main Street."

"Now that's a horse of a different color," he said. "I like it already."

While walking to the saloon, Nick reached Tanya and Dave by cell. One of them would drive up to Mackinaw City to pick up Nick and bring him back to Bay City Tuesday afternoon. Separately, they both asked if they could drive his gold 1972 Firebird up north.

"Sorry, nobody drives my baby," he said, trying to console his disappointed friends. The Firebird had belonged to one of Nick's best friends when he worked at *The Detroit News* early in his career. But the cruel, harsh hand of cancer took the buddy to an early grave, and Nick rescued the 'Bird, restoring it to its former glory. He treasured the rumbling vehicle almost as much as the friend he had lost. "Let her rest quietly under her blanket in the garage. You'll have to drive one of your clunkers to come get me."

Nick hung up and swung open the front door of the Mustang Lounge. His eyes lit up as he surveyed the old-fashioned watering hole. Rough-sawed lumber held all four walls together at dusty corners. An ancient wooden floor creaked under Nick's weight as he shot straight for the oak bar. Shallow indentations in the bar's top rail marked the spots where a bazillion elbows had rested. A jukebox cranked out Sugar Ray's "Every Morning." The joint stank of greasy fries and grilled onions.

A bartender with a tight top and plunging neckline asked Nick what he wanted to drink. He tried hard not to ogle her, but was still able to make out the wording on her dark-blue shirt without too much staring: "Hang at the 'Stang." Nick wondered if that was a reference to her free-swinging bosom or a general declaration about the bar. He ordered a draft of Labatt beer.

"Busy today?" he asked, surveying the barroom, which he guessed would only seat around seventy-five patrons. "I was hoping to find a little fun here tonight."

"This time of May, on a Sunday evening, things are still pretty slow," said the bartender. "But it will pick up a little later. Define your idea of fun."

"Oh, nothin' too crazy," Nick said. "I wanted to meet some folks who live here and work here, not the ferry people."

"Well, you came to the right place," she said, sticking out her hand. "My name is Chastity. What do they call you?"

"Well, I get called a lot of things, but I mostly answer to Nick," he said, grabbing her surprisingly calloused hand, which was small but gripped his hand like a set of channel locks. "I like your name—you don't hear it too often."

The Mustang Lounge was definitely the local hangout on Mackinac Island, Chastity told Nick. It was the only tavern on the island that stayed open all year long. In the winter, when snowmobiles ruled the streets, folks who lived on the island frequented the place to drink, blow off steam, or engage in raucous but dignified dancing or rowdy card games. At the end of the night, breakfast was served before the journey home.

The 'Stang had been around on the island almost forever. One of its great traditions was the annual passing of the pool table. When the table was transported out of the saloon and into storage in the spring, it marked the opening of the tourist season. When the pool table returned to its resting place in the 'Stang in the fall, it meant most island tours were done for the year.

Nick asked Chastity about the death at the Grand. He wondered what the locals were thinking about the accident.

"Is that what they're still calling it—an accident?" she said, wiping the bar down with a wet rag. "Visitors fall off horses and bikes all the time, but a balcony? Most people I talk to seem to think there's got to be more to it than that."

"Any theories floating around there?" Nick asked. Out of the corner of his eye, he saw an oval table tucked back in the shadows of the bar. It was surrounded by a bunch of older guys playing cards. Nick would try to cozy up to them next to learn what they had heard about the fall.

"You a cop?" Chastity stopped cleaning the bar and looked Nick up and down. "Never mind. You're not polished enough for that."

"I'm a reporter from Bay City."

"Figures," she said. "Now don't go quotin' me or anything. I don't know nothin' about nothin'."

"Just curious. The hotel is not saying much, and the local police are very tight-lipped about what happened," Nick said, leaning over the bar, his elbows hooked across the armrest. He took a long swig of his beer. "Thought maybe the people who lived here might have some insight. I'm not looking to stir things up."

"Yeah, well, people don't just fall out of the sky," Chastity said, rinsing her hands off and going to work with a knife on a helpless lime. "I'd put my cash on the idea that he had some help taking a high dive off that balcony. But that's just me."

Nick asked if the deceased had been in the 'Stang the evening before he died. Chastity said it was her night off, but she heard he'd been bar hopping in the downtown area with some others from the convention.

A loud thud came from the table of old guys playing cards and drinking draft beer in the corner. One of the geezers had smacked the table with his hand while playing a card. What would happen, Nick wondered, if he joined the table and asked a few questions?

Would that get them bent out of shape? He asked the bartender.

"Depends," Chastity said. "You gonna buy a pitcher or two?"

Nick smiled. The old bribery with beer trick worked pretty well in Bay City. Probably it'd go over big on the island, too.

"Now be careful with those old coots," Chastity warned him. "That's all they do is play cards. They soak up suds like sponges."

"Don't worry," Nick said, walking over to the table. "I got this."

Chapter 5

Early Monday morning

Early-morning sunshine warmed Nick's face, indicating that it was time to wake. He moaned and pushed open his eyelids. Despite the sunshine, the room was dim and shadowy, the scene blurry. The news reporter tried to ignore the sunrise alarm, but he could not disregard the hard, round end of a pitchfork handle that was pressed into his ribs and gently rocking his body. He rubbed his temples and felt soft straw on the side of his head.

"Hey, buddy. What are you doin' in here?" asked a low voice at the other end of the pitchfork handle. "Only authorized personnel in here, and you ain't authorized."

Nick's skull begged for mercy from a pounding headache. This hangover was a screamer. He tried to focus his eyes and locate the voice that he hoped would stop the hard handle from prodding his ribs.

"Take it easy, partner," Nick said. "I think I'm dying over here, and you're making my ribs hurt almost as much as my head."

"What you doin' here?" the man said, putting the pitchfork down with the tines toward the cement floor. "And how come you ain't dressed? Nearly naked man in a horse barn don't look too good."

"What? Horse barn?" Nick looked down the length of his body, confirming the absence of clothing. He was prone in his T-shirt and shamrock boxer shorts. All at once he felt stupid, embarrassed, and chilled. "I'm supposed to be staying at the Grand Hotel."

"Well, this ain't the Grand, that's for sure," the man said, a big toothless smile running the width of his face. He pushed the worn, sweat-stained Stetson back on the top of his head, revealing a shock of gray hair dangling just above his eyebrows. He tossed a horse blanket on Nick's chest. "Cover yourself and get up. We need to talk, or I'll have to call Chief Calkins."

"Oh no. No need for that," Nick said, not wanting to see the chief when he was in such disrepair. "Last thing I remember is sitting down to play a friendly game of cards at the Mustang."

"Ah, shit," the man said. "Nothin' friendly about the old bastards in this town. They probably slipped you a Mickey, the sons of bitches."

Nick stood up and wrapped the blanket around his waist. He surveyed the barn. Horses stood contentedly in their stalls, swishing away flies with their tails and munching on pale-green hay. Bales of golden straw were stacked against the far wall. An oak barrel filled with oats sat near the horses. The reporter felt as out of place as, well, a city slicker in a horse barn.

"Where am I?" Nick asked. "I mean, where am I in relation to the Grand?"

"You made it about halfway back to the Grand from the Mustang," the horse handler said. "How you feelin'? You okay to walk about another mile or so?"

Nick nodded. "What time is it?" he asked, trying to peer outside the barn door to gauge the level of activity on the street. He needed to find his wallet and cell phone and get going. It had been a hard night that had not been productive, and it had left him feeling like he'd fallen down a flight of stairs, landing on his throbbing head.

"It's about 6:30," the horse handler said. "Still pretty quiet out there." He held up Nick's possessions. "Looking for your clothes? They were on top of the oat bin when I came in here. I took a look at your driver's license to see if the wallet belonged to you. Cash is still folded up inside it."

Grateful, Nick thanked the stranger who had offered him a hand instead of taking advantage of a helpless fool. The moment was a reminder to the reporter, even in his blurry-eyed state, that he was not in the city—where his treatment would very likely have been much harsher.

"Well, I'm going to see if I can get my life back on track," Nick said, stepping into an open stall to dress. "Can I come back later?"

"Yup, on one condition."

"What's that?"

"You gotta come back and tell me what the hell happened to you," he said, the toothless grin peeking out again from behind his thin, chapped lips. "All the years I've been up here takin' care of horses, I ain't seen anything like this before."

"You bet. I'm dying to know what happened too." Nick pulled a twenty out of his wallet and offered it to the man in the sagging cowboy hat. "Here, please take this for helping me. What's your name, anyway?"

"Name's Nate," the man said, chuckling. "You keep your money. I gotta hunch you're going to need it before you leave the island. How long you here for?"

"Not sure, Nate. I'm a newspaper reporter from Bay City. Came up to see what I could find out about the man who fell to his death at the Grand," Nick said, pulling his shirt on and tucking in its tails. He brushed flakes of straw from his sports jacket. "You happen to hear anything about the guy falling?"

"People, especially old-timers, fall on the island all the time. Ever notice how many visitors use canes? Lots of accidents," Nate said, pausing to spit out the piece of straw he'd been chewing. "But not too many die up here."

"Ever any murders?" Nick checked his pockets for surprises from the night at the 'Stang. One pocket contained two bar napkins and a third had a piece of paper with a phone number on it for a late-night carriage ride service. The reporter quickly checked his pockets again for a room key card. Nothing.

"We had one murder up here way back in the 1960s," the man

said. "Woman wandered away from her hotel and was found naked and strangled with her own panties. Don't believe it was ever solved."

News of a murder on the island caught Nick off guard. He had not seen anything about a killing when he went through *The Blade*'s clip files before making the trip. Perhaps he hadn't gone back far enough to discover it.

"Never solved? Hmm. That's interesting."

"Most islanders figure the killer was a fudgy who either followed her up here or took a likin' to her while here," Nate said, shifting his weight from one foot to the other while leaning on the pitchfork. "By the time they started looking for the killer, he was most likely long gone."

"Fudgy?"

"A fudgy is like a troll, you know, somebody who lives under the bridge—a downstater—just up here for the view and some fudge."

"Okay, got it. Hey, thanks for your help, Nate," Nick said. "If you don't mind, I might swing back by to talk some more."

"Sure thing. Talkin' don't cost nothin'—stop by anytime, but wear your clothes next time."

Nick headed out into the sunlight, pulling his jacket tighter around him and measuring the steps forward until he became steady. He tried to get his bearings. Once out of the barnyard, he could see the Grand Hotel far off in the distance. His brain was still fuzzy, but he tried to focus on what to do next.

His first thought was of Drayton Clapper. What if his boss found out that he'd spent three hundred bucks on a hotel room at the Grand, but then slept the night in a horse barn? It might end up in another firing or suspension.

He particularly hoped Chief Calkins wouldn't hear about his wild night. And what about Sylvia Shane? The Grand manager would never let him live it down if she were to find out.

If the women found out about his escapade, Nick figured his credibility would be shot. Instead of working with him, he thought, they would laugh him off the island. End of story. End of Nick. He picked up his stride and hoped to make it back to the hotel without being noticed.

The slow, methodical *clip-clop, clip-clop* of horses approaching crept up on Nick from behind. He prayed that it was a team of nags pulling a work wagon and not a princely carriage full of guests headed for the Grand. The early-morning hour worked in the reporter's favor. Island workers were hauling a trash wagon to pick up garbage at the hotel.

Once at the top of the hill, Nick walked as quickly as he could to the rear of the hotel, looking for the delivery entrance. A hotel worker eyed him up and down while listening to his tale of woe. Luckily the check-in sheet was still in his wallet. He produced identification, and she helped him get into his room without a fuss.

Soon he was back on schedule. A shower, a pile of aspirin, and Nick hoped he would be as good as new. He had a big day ahead.

Chapter 6

Monday morning

At 8:55 a.m., Charlene Marx walked into the front entrance of Detroit Metropolitan Airport and headed for the bank of public telephones lining a wall just before the Northwest Airlines check-in counter. The fourth telephone rang at precisely nine o'clock. The slender but muscular woman grabbed the receiver before it finished its first squawk.

"This is Charlie," she said, eyes darting in each direction to see if anyone had seen her answer the ringing phone. "Talk to me."

"You killed the wrong son of a bitch," the male voice screeched, reaching a higher octave than the woman had heard in earlier phone conversations. "How in the hell did that happen?"

Charlie frowned and paused, hoping her employer would not have a heart attack while they talked. "Hey, take it easy. You gave me a place, a time, and a room number," she said. "Five minutes after I walked into that room, the occupant was on his way to a broken neck. I did my job."

"But you killed the wrong guy," the voice repeated in a slightly lower tone, but still almost panting. "For God's sake, do you understand that? I'm not going to give you another nickel until the job is done. And now, because of your screw-up, the death is attracting all kinds of attention. It's on the national news. How are you going to finish the job now?"

"Don't worry about it," she said. The hired killer prided herself on finishing every job she took. "This is simply a minor setback."

Again the ragged voice cautioned Charlie. He had two jobs for her to complete, and the first had gotten messy. "And what about the poor bastard who's dead?" the voice asked, trailing off.

"Just the cost of doing business," she said. "He got in the way, so he went down. Too bad, but that's tough shit. I'll reset the job and take out the target as soon as thing cool off. Don't worry. There's no record of me even being on that island, so it won't come back on me or you. Just relax and let me do my job."

Charlie hung up and walked away from the phones. The assassin felt nauseated. What she'd said about hitting the wrong victim was just macho bluster. Plus, killing the wrong target was not the mark of a professional. The mistake bothered her even more because the people she killed for money had to have abused the privilege of living. Charlie paced back and forth, cursing herself for the error.

She had set up another perfect kill. The target profile she'd put together had convinced her she could get on and off the island without being detected. It had also let her know that Zeke Zimmer was scheduled to be on Mackinac Island for a conference. She knew he fancied himself a big spender and would probably stay in one of the Grand Hotel's finest rooms. Because he liked to drink, she'd figured he would be open to a bottle of free champagne.

Once Charlie secured a uniform from the Grand's laundry near the employee back entrance, she was ready to set the trap for her prey. To get into the room, all she would have to do was unfasten the top four buttons of her jacket and offer the booze compliments of the house. When it came to most men, she had learned early in life, open blouses open doors. From there, the kill would be almost as easy as baking a pie.

The sound of a child's cry brought the hired killer back around. She surveyed her surroundings. The airport was abuzz with travelers trying to make flight connections. The smell of coffee and sticky buns filled the air. An echoing monotone from a loudspeaker announced flight cancellations and delays.

Charlie moved quickly out into the terminal entryway, heading for the short-term parking. No one noticed her. That's the way she had planned it. She was dressed in jeans, sneakers, and a green pullover jacket with the words "Wayne State" emblazoned on the back. She wore her hair in a ponytail and had not bothered with makeup. Sunglasses completed the look. The contract assassin was just one of thousands of people hustling out of the busy terminal.

As the sandy-haired beauty walked to her car, she lit a cigarette and pulled on it hard. Botched jobs were not something she was used to. Her trademark and reputation in the industry was for efficiency.

When somebody had to die and it had to look like an accident, Charlie Marx got the call. The military veteran had been plying her trade—efficiently and effectively—across the country for ten years.

Charlie knew her victims better than they knew themselves, but she rarely knew much about her employers. It was better that way. Distance worked in both their favors. The killer didn't know whom the voice on the phone belonged to. They'd never met, and she expected that they would never lay eyes on each other.

All that mattered was that the man wanted revenge and was willing to pay for the death of Zeke Zimmer and an associate. She had hoped to make arrangements to pick up the final $10,000 payment for the execution. Now, that would have to wait.

Chapter 7

Monday morning

As the first morning deadline approached at *The Bay City Blade*, reporter Dave Balz banged away at his keyboard to finish the sad and sorry story on Adam Townsend, the misidentified Bay Cityan who had died on Mackinac Island Saturday morning.

Dave had talked to Nick late in the afternoon Sunday to get the newest updates from the island. Then the veteran reporter had spent most of Sunday evening interviewing relatives and friends of the deceased.

Zeke Zimmer, the man who was originally thought to have died in the accidental fall from a balcony at the Grand Hotel, had been particularly upset and emotional during their interview, when fond memories of his friend were forced to the front of his mind.

"Adam wanted to use the room to meet a girlfriend," Zeke had told Dave in a teary conversation. "It didn't matter to me. I thought I was doing him a favor. Now he's gone. I'm going to miss the guy. He was like a brother to me."

Not only were the two brotherly, but they also shared the same occupation and were similar in appearance—close in size, shape, and age. The way Zeke framed his close relationship with Adam, it all made sense to Dave, and the reporter reflected it in his story on the deceased.

Dave believed he had filed a great piece on the Townsend misidentification. His opening paragraph, or lede, summarized the fate of the dead man by using a variation on lyrics first made famous by legendary bluesman Albert King:

"If it weren't for bad luck during his 67 years on earth, Adam Townsend would have had no luck at all. The Bay City man's final stroke of misfortune happened Saturday on Mackinac Island, when he fell to his death."

The article went on to detail Townsend's accomplishments, with glowing quotations from all who knew the man. The deceased man's life had been largely unremarkable, yet those who knew him piled on praise that seemed largely undeserved. His years on earth were as vanilla as a scoop of ice cream except for a series of unlucky events. It seemed that the Bay City electrician had a knack for being in the wrong place at the wrong time.

Adam's misfortune had begun at a young age. While at McKinley Elementary School, the lad was accidentally locked in the school overnight. When he was discovered the next day, the boy was sucking his thumb and whimpering under a pile of boxes in a janitor's closet. His mom and pop had thought Adam was safe at a friend's house for a sleepover.

But the terrible luck didn't end there. In high school, Adam recovered a fumble for the Central Wolves football team, but ran the wrong way on the field to score a touchdown for crosstown rival Bay City Handy.

He never lived it down. Throughout the rest of his days in school, he was known as "Wrong-Way Townsend." His senior high school yearbook even mentioned the blunder.

The personal disasters continued while he was at trade school. The young woman Adam had become engaged to suddenly turned up pregnant, though the couple had not had sex. Needless to say, the engagement ended quickly.

Bad luck struck again when Adam rented a small apartment for his aging parents in Bay City's historic and ancient Wenonah Hotel, which had been converted from single rooms to apartments beginning in 1970. Adam's folks were just getting used to their new digs in the winter of 1977 when a horrific fire engulfed the 70-year-old building. Some occupants leaped from the upper floors of the burning former hotel. When it was all over, ten people had perished in the fire. Adam's parents were among the fifty who were severely injured. They endured their final years together suffering from the burns and smoke inhalation inflicted by the hot flames in the Wenonah. Adam never forgave himself for insisting that they rent in the aging structure.

So it was not a shocking surprise to the people who knew Adam that the end came for him with a crashing thump at the Grand Hotel. It would be among the hottest parts of the gossipy whispers at his funeral and wake.

As Dave reviewed the article he had written, Morton Reynolds, the weak-kneed, butt-kissing editor-in-chief of *The Blade*, entered the newsroom. Reynolds was largely viewed as the mouthpiece for the publisher. He wore expensive suits, golfed at the Bay County Country Club three times a week, and played tennis at a swanky club in Midland whenever he could hide from his nagging, carping wife.

"Balz, I thought you retired," Reynolds said. "What are you still doing here?"

"Morton, you know this newsroom just can't get along without me," Dave said, bundling up his notes. "I'm helping Nick with the Mackinac Island stories. But it's already been a long day. I started working rewrites at five this morning, and I'm ready for a cold one at O'Hare's."

Reynolds waved a scrap of paper in the air. "Hey, Balz, before you go and get all shitfaced at the bar again, I've got another assignment for you. It's a feature story even you can't mess up. There's a woman out in Caseville who wants to start a new festival this summer—our first festival story of 1999."

"Oh, Caseville's a great little resort town," Dave said. "What's the festival?"

"You won't believe it," Reynolds said. "Cheeseburgers. She wants to do the first Cheeseburger in Caseville Festival this summer."

"Yeah, I heard something about that. Jimmy Buffett and Margaritaville. Cold drinks, hot food, and music at the beach."

"Yup, that's the idea," Reynolds said. "It will never catch on. This festival idea is dead before it even gets off the ground. Lyn Bezemek, the wild lady who is trying to put it together, is writing a letter to Jimmy Buffett and inviting him to come to Caseville."

"I've got news for her. Jimmy Buffett will never come to the Thumb without getting paid," Dave said, hiking his blue jeans up under his belly. His bulky plaid shirt covered the bulge nicely. "He never does anything for free. That's how he got to be Jimmy Buffett—the guy is worth millions."

"So here you go," Morton said, handing Dave the piece of paper with Lyn Bezemek's name and number on it.

Dave tried not to roll his eyes. He wanted to chase the story on Mackinac Island, not covering some crazy festival idea in Caseville. But he knew the only way he'd be able to continue working on the Townsend misidentification was to keep Reynolds off his back.

"Okay, I'm all over this piece like grease on bacon—but first, O'Hare's."

"Dave, it's not even noon yet," Reynolds said. "Don't go get all snockered up. I may need you to chase the island story some more after we hear from Nick."

"Yeah, yeah. Call me if you need me." Dave headed out the newsroom door and pointed his old pickup in the direction of Bay City's West Side, where he would enjoy a liquid lunch at O'Hare's. He would call Nick later in the afternoon for an update.

Dave wanted to stay connected to the Mackinac story because he thought it had legs. The piece was getting real interesting, and he wanted to be part of it.

Chapter 8

Late Monday morning

From his room at the Grand, Nick tried to call the Mackinac County medical examiner in St. Ignace. No luck. He got brush-off responses from the receptionists at Dodson Funeral Home and the local hospital too. The doc was busy and would return the call when he had time, which he figured would be never.

Nothing unusual about officials dodging uncomfortable questions from the media. From Nick's experience, that was par for the course. Disheartening, yes—but not disabling. The reporter knew he would have to remain persistent and keep chasing them for information.

In the meantime, Nick decided to run in another direction. He hoped he would have better luck getting an update from Chief Calkins. Certainly, he thought, the full autopsy and tox screen would have been conducted by now. The misidentification was drawing plenty of unwanted attention to Mackinac Island and the hotel. The powerful families who ran the island couldn't be happy about the kind of stink that the news about the death was generating.

When Nick located the chief in the lobby near the hotel manager's office, he could tell by the anguished look on her face that something was up. He decided to approach with caution.

"We're going to need an interview room, probably somewhere on the first floor," the chief was saying, facing the hotel manager's open office door. Nick could not see Sylvia Shane from his vantage point, but it was pretty clear whom the island's top cop was addressing.

"I've got one officer down at the ferry docks conducting interviews, another at the public docks, and a third over at the airport," Calkins said, her voice growing louder and more strident. "That leaves three of us to interview your employees. I want to get started right away—everybody on duty Friday and Saturday."

The chief turned as Nick emerged from a sea of hotel guests lugging bags around, trying to check out of the Grand.

"Look, I don't have time for you right now," the chief said in Nick's direction. "I'm busy."

The lobby area perked with activity. Children played on the floor, their parents harried and frazzled. Outside it looked like rain might be coming. Guests moved quickly, obviously eager to beat the storm.

"I can see that," Nick said. "I won't take much of your time. If you're setting up a bunch of interviews, then that means the death was not accidental. Is that what you got back from the medical examiner?"

Nick peeked over the chief's shoulder and spotted the hotel manager behind her desk, speaking on the phone. He could see at least four others in her office—assistant managers, he guessed by their appearance.

"Now, you can't write this yet, but the doc reexamined the body and found a small puncture wound," the chief said. "The tox screen has to go through the state police crime lab in Grand Rapids, but I can't wait for test results. We've got to move on this now."

"Where was the puncture wound?" Nick lowered his voice so others in the lobby would not hear his question. "And how was it missed during the first examination?"

"I'm going to trust you with this info, and how you handle it from here will tell me whether we're going to get along. So don't screw this up, and don't screw me. You got it?"

"Yeah, I got it," Nick said, making eye contact and leaning in closer to the chief. "But I've got a job to do too. I'm not here to make your job harder, but I do need to keep our readers informed—especially if this is a murder."

The chief put her hands on her hips and leaned in toward Nick, lifting her chin up to make eye contact. They stood inches apart. "Now there you go again, throwing around the murder word," she said, her voice low and even, but not loud. "We don't know yet. Don't get the horse in front of the cart."

"Okay, okay. But how about the puncture wound? That's significant, isn't it?"

"Maybe. We'll see," the chief said, looking past Nick—probably scoping out the lobby to see who was watching the two talk. "The wound is very small, located near the spine between the shoulder blades. Doc says he didn't notice it when he looked the body over the first time, thought it was some kind of blemish."

"A blemish? What the—"

"Yeah, the doc says it's like a pinprick—real tiny. But I know he feels bad about missing it."

"What else?" Nick asked. "Any fingerprints?"

"Only the victim's. But there were no fingerprints on the bottle of champagne, and no room charge, receipt, or paper bag. It's not a brand the hotel carries—somebody brought it into the room."

The chief lowered her voice to an almost whisper. "Off the record, there is a tiny hole in his shirt that corresponds to the puncture wound. And, but you absolutely cannot write this or reveal it to anyone—we found a single long, blond hair."

"Anything else?"

"If you breathe a word of this to anyone else, including your editors, I'll put you on a slab next to Adam Townsend . . ."

"Yup, I understand." Every word from the chief registered with Nick. She was feeding him inside information and he knew he was lucky to get it. Even though he could not use the details in his stories right now, it would help him frame what he did write and give it the correct context for readers. He also knew it would make great background and color later when the information was no longer confidential. Every reporter prays for this kind of candor. Nick had connected with the chief. He knew she trusted him, and that the info would keep coming as long as he didn't betray her—or get caught nearly naked in a horse barn again.

"The bar towel that was on the desk near the champagne, well, it has a hint of perfume on it. Expensive stuff. Not something an employee would wear. I figure whoever brought that bottle into the room had the towel folded and draped over an arm—real fancy-like."

"So you think it was a woman who entered the room and delivered the champagne?"

"You got it. That's why we're interviewing the staff."

The reporter asked if any video had been recovered from either the hotel or the ferry docks. The chief told him that they had reviewed everything available, but it was dim and grainy. It showed what one might expect, she said—hundreds of tourists wearing ball caps, jackets, shorts, and gym shoes, hustling about with bags and packages.

"One more thing, and I'm warning you—don't repeat a word of this," the chief said. "The balcony railing had some deep gouges in it. Probably from the victim's belt buckle, which also has some white paint ground into it."

The chief said Adam Townsend's fingerprints were found on the inside of the railing, pointing downward. His thumbprints were identified on top of the railing, pointing outward.

"Interesting," Nick said. "So he had both hands on the inside of the rail before he went over it?"

"Looks that way," the chief said. "Might have been bracing himself."

"Against a push?" Nick asked, his voice rising.

The chief sighed and rolled her eyes at Nick. He leaned back slightly, expecting another scolding, but she was not harsh.

"Maybe, or he might have been trying to steady himself. Maybe he was woozy and getting ready to hurl. Tox screen should tell us if he'd been drinking or using recreational drugs."

Nick shifted to one side to get a look back into the hotel manager's office. Sylvia Shane was still on the phone. Staff continued to shuffle in and out of her office. The stress was beginning to show. The reporter figured she was now driving through a shitstorm—with no windshield wipers.

For a moment their eyes met. She nodded, but then turned her head, probably to make sure that Nick could not read her lips while she was talking on the phone.

The chief checked her pager. Nick was afraid she was going to bolt, so he decided to engage her again. "The first word we received was that the body had a broken neck and fractured skull. Is that still the case, or did the medical examiner come to some other conclusion?"

"No, the body had the injuries you'd expect from a big fall," Calkins said. "But a puncture like the one in his back means something else might have been introduced into the body before the plunge."

"Oh, you mean he was drugged?"

The chief's eyes flashed, her voice sharp. "Now there you go again. Don't jump to conclusions. Nobody said the guy was drugged. We won't know until the tox screen comes back."

"Okay, thanks, Chief. I've got to file a story. How much can I reveal? Can I say that you're investigating a murder?'

"No. Stop that," she said, scolding the reporter. "You can say it's a possible homicide investigation. We're still gathering evidence. If you reveal any of the evidence I shared with you, then you could jeopardize our case and our chances of making an arrest. "

"I hear you. I'll low-key it," he said. "I will keep it real soft and fuzzy." Nick turned to walk away.

The chief called him back. "By the way, I heard you got a real introduction to the island last night at the 'Stang," she said. "Wasn't that horse barn a little cold?"

"Ah, yeah, I guess so," Nick said, feeling his face flush from embarrassment. "How did you find out?"

"It's a small island. Not too much goes on around here that I don't hear about. I also hear that your legs are spindly. Remember, I know more about you than you realize. I made a few calls to check you out."

Nick smiled, nodded at the chief, and walked toward the front door of the hotel. He decided not to hang around. Too much chaos. He would catch up with the hotel manager later.

Chapter 9

Monday afternoon

Nick returned to his room to call Dave Balz. The door was open, lights on. A maid was cleaning the room, humming while she worked. She carried a stack of fresh towels and toiletries into the bathroom. Nick hoped she would get chatty.

"Wow, that sure was something the other night—a guy crashing onto the front porch of the hotel," Nick said, whistling softly to emphasize his point. He waited for the maid to respond. She did not, continuing about her business without looking at the guest.

Nick gave it another shot. "Bet you don't see that every day—a guy dying right here at the hotel."

"Accidents happen all the time on the island," she said. Nick guessed that she was from Central America, perhaps Colombia, judging by her thick Latin accent and dark features. "You'd be surprised."

"Really? What kind of accidents?"

"All kinds," she said as she finished wiping down the bathroom mirror. "Horse accidents, bike crashes. Slips. Falls. People not used to walking so much, they trip. They have heart attacks, they break bones, they get sick. Sometimes they drink too much because they no drive, or sometimes they just eat too much."

"No kidding. I thought this was some kind of Wonderland, where nothing bad ever happened," Nick said, hoping to get the young woman to open up some more.

"It's all about the odds," she said.

"Odds?"

"*Si*. With thousands of people here, you bound to have accidents and sicknesses almost every day. It's all in the numbers."

Of course she was right, Nick thought. About fifteen thousand people visit Mackinac every day during the height of the summer months. The island is home to about 450 year-round residents, but that number swells to more than three thousand when you count the temporary workers who come to the island to serve its guests. With that many people coming and going all summer long, investigating a death could be a daunting task. Fortunately for Chief Calkins, this was May, and the massive horde of tourists who would invade the island like an amphibious landing by Marines were still a few weeks away.

Nick decided to push the maid a little harder to see if she would, or could, reveal more. "But what about the fall the other night?" he said. "Do your friends think that was an accident?"

"Who falls from a balcony?" she said, laughing. "You would have to be very, very drunk to fall all on your own. Most people think that poor gentleman had help."

"Did any of your friends see anything? What have you heard?"

"Nothing, just talk. When somebody dies, lots of people talk. Maybe they talk too much. Maybe I talk too much."

With that she finished making the bed, which was only slightly rumpled because it had not been slept in. Then she left the room, marking her exit by saying, "Good day."

Sighing, Nick picked up the phone and dialed O'Hare's. Sassy Sally answered it and immediately passed the receiver to Dave. Before his friend could say a word, Nick said, "Let me guess, you just polished off a small pitcher of cold beer and a giant, juicy burger with onions, olives, pickles and mustard. And—I'm not finished yet—you are about to lick your fingers and wipe your chin with your necktie."

"Wrong," Dave said. His voice was garbled, as if he was picking chunks of burger from between his teeth. "I left the tie on the front seat of my truck, so I'm wiping my chin with my sleeve because Sassy Sally won't let me use the front of her blouse."

The friends laughed, then got down to business. Nick gave the older reporter a quick update on what was happening on Mackinac

Island. Dave said he found the info about the puncture wound on Adam Townsend's body and the request for a tox screen fascinating.

Nick sat down on the corner of the big, comfy bed in his room, testing it for the first time. He moved the phone from one ear to the other. "They're not calling it a murder yet, but it's got to be," he said. "The police chief is interviewing everybody she can get her hands on while they wait for the tox screen to come back."

"Well, this is going to make our lives interesting," Dave said. "If it was murder, then the killer is long gone by now."

"Not unless the killer is an employee or full-time resident." That gave Nick an idea. "Hey, could you do me a huge favor?" he said. "Call Zeke Zimmer and tell him that there's been a turn of events up here. He needs to be careful until we figure out what's going on."

"Oh, so you want me to tell him that a killer may be looking for him," Dave said. "That should make his day."

"Yeah, try to break it to him gently," Nick said. "You know, better to be safe than sorry—that kind of thing. I will be back in Bay City soon, and I'll try to meet with him then."

Nick stretched out on the bed, crossed his feet, and stared at the white ceiling. The reporter was still tired from his restless night in the horse barn. Some sleep or even a short nap would feel great, but there was no time. He had to keep moving. No way was he going to sleep while a great story might be within reach. He asked his friend about any developments at *The Blade*.

"What's going on in the newsroom? What's the gossip?"

"Not much," Dave said. "Everybody is talking about the Mackinac story. By the way, Clapper wanted me to tell you that you've been selected to work on a building-wide committee—something to do with advertising. I figured you'd be pleased as punch about that."

Nick groaned. "I hate committees, and I hate working with the ad people," he said. "But thanks for the heads-up."

"I'm going to stay over one more night and then head back to Bay City," he added. "Could you or Tanya come and get me?"

"Tanya is already on her way up," Dave said. "I think she wanted to surprise you."

Nick hung up and decided he needed to make one more call. He dialed the number for his old buddy at the Bay City Police Department—patrolman Dan Quinn, who he figured would be getting ready for his afternoon shift.

"Hey, Quinny, how you doin'?"

"Right as rain, Nicky boy. What's up?

"Have you been following what's going on up here at the island?"

"Who hasn't? It's in all the papers and on TV," the cop said.

"Looks like Zeke Zimmer dodged the big one," Nick said, trying hard not to reveal too much. "Could you swing by his place a couple of times during your patrol, just to keep an eye on him?"

Quinn cleared his throat. "Zeke is bad news, Nick," he said. "He plays himself up to the TV cameras as Mr. Bay City, Mr. Volunteer, but he's involved in a lot of shady stuff. Gambling, numbers. Whores. They say he likes to play with matches, too."

"I'm not asking you to let him date your daughter, Quinn," Nick said. "But somebody might be hunting him. Just thought I'd give you a heads-up."

"Okay, will do. When you coming home?"

"Another day or so. This is really shaping up into a good story."

Chapter 10

Monday afternoon

As Tanya Johnson neared the Gaylord exit of I-75 and entered the last leg of her journey from Ann Arbor to Mackinac Island, she thought about her relationship with Nick.

The educator, who was working on a third master's degree at the University of Michigan, was looking forward to spending a little time with her guy in the same place where the romantic classic *Somewhere in Time* was filmed.

A little romance might be just the thing to kick Nick in the rear on their not-so-blossoming relationship. The two were still seeing each other, but things had cooled between them since last fall, when they saw each other daily.

Tanya and Nick had been inseparable while he worked on a story that rocked Bay City to its very core. It had all started when Tanya called the *Blade* newsroom to request a news obituary about her father, a noted longtime principal at Bay City Central High School, who had passed from an apparent heart attack. Nick, nursing a blistering hangover, had taken the call. Before long they were smitten with each other, even though Tanya was twelve years his junior.

Coincidentally, they also discovered a great story.

Turned out that the death of Tanya's dad had been no accident. It had followed the death of a superintendent at the school who croaked under very similar circumstances. Nick and Dave had worked on the investigation together with Tanya. They reported that the two educators had been poisoned by a parent who was seeking justice for her daughter. The teen died from suicide after having an affair with the band director at Central High.

The parent blamed the principal, superintendent, and school board president for covering up the band director's multiple affairs with young students. Though the revelations cast a shadow on the reputation of her dad, Tanya had eagerly helped Nick pursue the truth. She admired his tenacity and determination to find out what really had happened to her dad. It had blinded her to Nick's shortcomings. They remained close and dated through the winter.

Recently Tanya had been working on a surprise for Nick. She had contacted Nick's son, Joe, who had moved to California after his mother died.

The death had devastated Nick and Joe. Joe moved West to escape the pain of losing his mom. Nick stayed in Bay City, but sought solace in bottles of bourbon and barrels of beer. He only seemed to sober up when he was chasing a good story, and Tanya was tiring of his shenanigans.

Tanya had arranged for Joe to return to Bay City for a reunion with his dad. She hoped the two would help each other heal from the loss of a woman they both had loved. Tanya had come to the conclusion that her relationship with Nick could not advance until he came to grips with his wife's death and the absence of his son.

Plus, Tanya wanted to work with Nick on the Mackinac Island piece. From what she'd heard, it was shaping up to be a great story no matter what its outcome. She could hardly wait to get an update from Nick and put their minds together on the story. It would be almost as good as putting their naked bodies together, which it seemed Tanya was more eager to do than Nick.

As Tanya entered Mackinaw City, she followed the signs to the ferry docks. Arnold Transit Company, Shepler's Ferry, and Star Line Ferry transported most of the visitors to Mackinac Island through their docks in St. Ignace and Mackinaw City.

Tanya parked her car and hitched a ride to the island with Shepler's. She loved taking the twenty-minute ride to the island because of the beauty—Lake Huron's big blue waves, the Mighty

Mac reaching across and linking the two peninsulas, and the imagery of the island as it came into focus.

Every time she took the ferry, Tanya felt instant relief as it pulled away from the shore. Her shoulder muscles would relax. The island was all about escapism, and like most visitors she could not get enough of it, returning time and time again.

This ride was no different. As the ferry picked up speed, Tanya filled her lungs with cool, fresh air. Icy water from the lake splashed gently over the bow of the boat. It was exhilarating. She leaned back in her seat and soaked up the midafternoon warm sunshine as the ferry bounded across the waves to the island.

Tanya didn't open her eyes until the boat slowed for its final approach to the main landing. A smile spread across her face. There at the end of the docks stood Nick, his salt and pepper hair and open navy-blue coat flapping in the wind off the lake. She felt like she'd awakened from a dream.

"Hi, Nick," she shouted above the gentle roar of the ferry engine. Tanya stood up as the boat docked. The gangplank was all that separated her from the man she craved.

"Tanya!" Nick moved toward her and opened his arms as she stepped onto the dock. "Hey, I missed you. So glad to see you."

The couple embraced in the midst of swirling passengers eager to find their way to hot fudge and overpriced trinkets. Gentle bumping from hustling tourists did not interrupt the two. Nick looked into her eyes, held her chin up, and gave her a long kiss. He held her tightly against his chest. She wiggled even closer, savoring the moment.

Tanya was eager to go directly to Nick's room, not wanting to miss her guy's rare romantic burst. But alas, Nick begged off.

"Tanya, I've got one more set of interviews I need to complete before we relax for the night," he said as their embrace lost its urgency. "Please, let's run over to the airport. I just need to talk to the guy in charge to see if they keep track of people who fly into the island. This could be important, and it shouldn't take long at all."

"Okay, let's go," Tanya said, trying hard to conceal her disappointment as they walked down the dock arm in arm. We'll definitely pick this up later, she thought to herself.

Chapter 11

Monday evening

Charlie Marx flipped the light on in her study, a converted storage room at the back of the small condo she rented just outside Ann Arbor.

The study, which had an entry door hidden behind a rollout storage cabinet in her utility room, contained all the tools of her trade: a couple of handguns, a short-barrel shotgun, a steel cashbox, and a cabinet overflowing with target profiles.

She maintained the sparse collection of weapons mostly for her own protection, not for killing targets. By 1999 standards, Charlie was a modern contract killer. She prided herself on being an environmental eliminator, finding and using something in the subject's surroundings as the method of death.

She opened the Grand Hotel folder and looked over the notes she'd used in concocting the plan.

The balconies had been key. Hovering high above the porch deck but still covered by a roof, they made an ideal and often romantic perch for guests. They were a part of the charm of the old hotel. Charlie knew from a previous visit that guests leaned out over the hotel's balconies frequently.

Gaining entry to the room was her last obstacle. It only had cost her a hundred bucks to get it done. Then the room service uniform and a bottle of bubbly, combined with the use of her physical charms, did the rest.

She wore gloves and cradled the bottle of champagne in the crook of one arm. A white towel was folded and draped over the other arm.

Once inside, it was only minutes before the trap was set. She put down the bottle of champagne on a table by the room's overstuffed chair. Then Charlie walked directly to the balcony doors, opened them, and stepped out into the Mackinac night.

She recalled the target watching her every move. He had seemed completely captivated by the lovely woman who had entered his room. By the time Charlie turned and unbuttoned the rest of her uniform top, the victim was ready and raring to go. He nearly tripped over himself on his way to the balcony.

The two embraced, which gave Charlie the opportunity she was anticipating. A syringe filled with a triple dose of Ketamine was taped to the inside of her sleeve and within easy reach of her fingers.

Charlie plunged the needle into the meatiest part of his upper back, just below his neck. She pulled him close and whispered into his ear. He tried to pull back, but the shock from the needle froze him as he reached for his neck. He seized up and lurched forward. Charlie stepped to his side, bent him over the balcony, waited a few minutes for the animal tranquilizer to take full effect, and then hoisted his legs up and finished pushing him over the balcony rail.

The assassin had watched him hit the porch. His body twitched. Blood oozed into a widening pool. Before anyone realized what had happened, Charlie was out of the room and slowly walking down an empty back stairway.

A skeleton staff worked the overnight shift on Saturdays. Charlie had changed back into her street clothes in the laundry, hiding in a basement storage room until the hotel became still and quiet. Then she walked out of the hotel and back toward the ferry docks to await the first ride to Mackinaw City in the morning.

The assassin had counted on Mackinac Island's lust for tourists to help her cover up the kill. She had figured hotel management would want an ugly accident, such as a death from a fall onto the famed porch, to get cleaned up and pushed aside quickly—allowing her to slip away unnoticed once the job was done. Research had revealed that another killer had done the same thing several decades before.

Death made smooth and easy. That's why the target profiles were so vital; they provided the information Charlie needed to do her job, and do it well.

The hired killer shook her head and closed the folder. Charlie thought about how she might be able to improve the profiles to head off future screw-ups like the one that had happened on Mackinac Island. Zeke Zimmer is such a wild card, she thought. How do you guard against a character like him doing something so unpredictable? How many guys would make a reservation for a weekend conference at one of the world's great resorts, then sneak away to gamble while letting a friend use the room?

Charlie opened the file cabinet and flipped to the *J*s and *Z*s, grabbing two thick folders. She carried them to her desk and flicked on the lamp. The folders hit the top of the desk with a thud. The tab on the side of one folder read "Zeke Zimmer"; the other, "Hershel Jones."

The professional killer opened the first file and thumbed through its pages, looking for key information that would help her plot the final demise of her target.

The fat file was chock-full of data gleaned from public records. It contained just about everything known about the subject: copies of Zeke's birth certificate, school report cards, First Communion validation, middle school graduation, varsity sports awards, military draft card and record, trade school training record, resumes, work time sheets and history, multiple marriage certificates, district and circuit court records, and even a receipt for a cemetery plot.

Charlie expected Zeke would be using that soon, and she smiled at the thought. The guy was all ready to be planted. She just had to find a way to put him in the dirt.

In addition, the file contained a trash section, which amounted to info pulled from garbage bags placed at the curb in front of his home. Credit card bills, hardware store receipts, cashed checks, telephone records, auto service orders, home repair invoices, grocery lists, casino tickets, and rain checks—the file contained more information about Zeke Zimmer than any individual knew, including Wives One through Four.

The data that caught Charlie's eye involved police department records. Zeke had been investigated, but not convicted, in two unrelated arson cases.

One fire had occurred at property he once owned, and the other had turned a friend's home into charred toast. The records showed that both cases resulted in hefty insurance company payouts, which had been held up while the fires were thoroughly investigated. She also noted that both were electrical fires. It is very difficult to prove arson when the blaze is traced to a short in the electrical system, especially if no accelerant is found on the premises.

"Hmm," she said aloud. "This gives me a couple of options."

Charlie closed the file. She jotted down several notes to follow up on with Zeke Zimmer. A plan was already taking shape for the next hit on the electrician. This time around, there would be no mistakes. The clock was already ticking on his demise.

Hershel Jones would be much easier to dispose of—a pillow would take him out. The profile indicated Jones was a sitting duck, ready to knock off at will. Charlie had already scheduled his execution.

Chapter 12

Monday evening

While Nick tapped out his story for Tuesday's newspaper, Tanya changed into the dress that she'd brought to the island—a slim-fitting, sleeveless red just-above-the knee number with a tight turtleneck and a zipper. With her shapely figure, Tanya knew it would turn heads. Hopefully one of them would belong to Nick.

Since the two had started dating the previous fall, Tanya had been the driving force in the relationship. She wanted to advance their romance, but Nick held back. His belief seemed to be that once a couple became intimate, it was tough for either to get out of it. Better to hold back and go slow, he said, than charge in and later regret it.

But Tanya did not want to wait. Discussions about their relationship sometimes became heated. In one recent conversation, Nick urged caution until they both knew what direction they wanted to go.

"I know what direction I want this relationship to go in," Tanya said, "and that's horizontal."

The two had come close to consummation in a couple of instances, but something—Nick said it was fate—always interceded. His girlfriend, however, was determined to see that it was not going to happen again, especially while they were in what she deemed to be the perfect location to seal the deal.

Now Tanya dressed with urgency. She was convinced that this night on Mackinac Island would be a night that the two would remember forever.

* * *

As he waited for Tanya to finish getting ready, Nick roughed in the story he'd developed during the day. He planned to polish it early in the morning before sending it to *The Blade*.

He had discovered some interesting information from interviewing others on the island that afternoon. Visitors with cash in hand, he'd learned, could buy a ferry ticket, get to the island, and leave it without a trace. The use of credit cards, it turned out, was the only thing that left a trail.

Nick spiced up his story with commentary from "local residents"—meaning Nate, Chastity, and the room service maid. Their skepticism about the fall being an accident added balance to the official reports in his story. He would have quoted the old guys at the 'Stang, but he could not recall the details of their conversation. Too fuzzy to put into print.

"Let's go, Nick," Tanya said. She looked fabulous and way too fine for Nick, who was still wearing the same clothes that he'd put on at the horse barn that morning. He held his sports jacket out at arm's length and shook it like a floor rug. Dust and straw flakes fluttered in the air.

As the two walked down the stairs to the Grand's main dining room, Nick put on the necktie that Tanya had brought to the island for him. Whenever the reporter put on a tie, he always lamented that it was like donning a dog collar.

"Will you be embarrassed if I use one of my feet to scratch behind my ear?" Nick asked as they waited to be seated.

"No," Tanya said, "but I will be very pissed if you jump up on the table and start licking your balls during dinner."

The two laughed until it hurt. It was good to finally talk and catch up with one another. They'd been apart for weeks while Tanya worked on a master's paper and Nick was busy with a reporting project for *The Blade*.

Nick and Tanya held hands, even while eating. Nick could not recall a more enjoyable evening together. Even so, the reporter felt restless. Though he was having a great time, he could not completely escape the story, and deep down he felt guilty about enjoying himself instead of working the piece. It flipped around in the back of his mind. His right leg bounced up and down from nervous energy until Tanya put her hand under the table and placed it on his knee, slowly calming him down.

After dinner they decided to take a stroll on the Grand's porch. Cool May air and a light breeze coming off Lake Huron greeted the two. Soft lighting illuminated the porch without dimming the twinkle of stars. Nick took off his jacket and draped it around Tanya's shoulders.

"Nick, how come your jacket smells like a horse barn?" Tanya said, tugging the lapels of the jacket closer to her chin.

Nick was not eager for Tanya to find out about his night with the guys at the 'Stang, or Nate's nags. "Ah, uh, well, yeah, look around you. You can see evidence of horses in the street almost everywhere," he said, stopping abruptly and changing the subject. "This is it. Adam landed right here."

They both inspected the deck of the porch. An empty white rocking chair marked the spot where a final element of misfortune found Wrong-Way Townsend. The gray decking was clean, probably freshly painted.

"And that's the balcony," Nick said, pointing up to the third floor of the hotel. Iron fire escapes lined the outside walls, hanging from each of the balconies to about eight feet above the deck of the porch.

"No wonder his neck was broken," Tanya said. "Probably some other bones too, from a fall like that."

Nick walked over to the rocking chair and pushed it, making it roll back and forth. He had come to this spot on the porch several times since he arrived at the hotel, and each time he wondered how easily someone could stand on the seat of the rocker and jump up to grab the last rung of the fire escape. What he couldn't get past, he told Tanya, was the movement of the rocker. It was too tippy.

"I don't know," he said. "I just don't see it. If an intruder gained access to that room, they had to do it from inside the hotel."

Wind gusts picked up, forcing the two to retreat inside the Grand. They decided to call it an early night.

* * *

Once back in the room, Tanya made a beeline for the bathroom and washed her face, working hard to quickly remove makeup.

Then she opened her overnight bag and pulled out a light-blue negligee. It was lacy at the edges, backless, and low cut in the front. If this didn't do it, Tanya thought, nothing would. She smoothed out the slinky outfit until it hugged all her curves. She frantically combed her hair. Finally she took a deep breath, shook her head lightly to muss her hair, and gently squeezed her bosom into perky position in its lacy cups.

Tanya stepped from the bathroom into their darkened suite. She had hoped to hear soft music. Instead, the hard snoring of a prone and gone boyfriend greeted her. Nick was stretched out on the sofa in his T-shirt and slacks, sawing logs like a lumberman who'd spent a long day in the woods.

"Damn!" Tanya said, turning to go back into the bathroom to search her bag for snuggly pajamas. "Maybe next time."

As she retreated, a loud, shrill clanging noise erupted from the hallway. Fire alarm? Within a minute, a banging on the door was followed by an order to evacuate: "Everybody out—now!"

Tanya stood in the doorway of the bathroom, dazed and a little confused by the alarm and noise rising in the hallway. Nick bolted awake from the sofa, and without saying a word, bent over and scooped Tanya up onto his shoulder. He held her close with his left arm, pinning her legs to his chest, and pulled open the hotel room door.

"No, Nick, no!" Tanya screamed. She was falling out of her nightie, and her butt was up in the air for everyone to see. "Stop! Let me grab covers. I need shoes."

"No time, Tanya. We gotta go," he said, looking around—probably to see which way the flow of traffic was heading. "We're two hundred miles from home. Nobody is going to recognize you. Hold still."

As they maneuvered down the stairway, with Tanya dangling from Nick's shoulder, they were bumped and pushed by other frantic guests. The halls were filled with cries of anguish. Mothers herded their youngsters toward the exit. Old men hopscotched on their walkers. Children cried about leaving toys behind. Hotel employees tried to keep calm and direct traffic, but were struggling to maintain control.

Tanya felt Nick move to their right, but quickly she realized it was a mistake. The opening was an area where guests had fallen to the floor and were being stepped on. Before they could change course, Tanya and Nick were pushed down too.

"Oh-h-h, Nick, no!" Tanya screamed as her back hit the floor, with Nick sprawled out on top of her. She'd dreamed of this moment, but not in a hallway filled with frantic people.

Tanya felt Nick pull her up from the floor. They moved to the wall, pressing up against it and hoping the throng of people would pass.

"Well, hello, Tanya," said a man in an open bathrobe and bare feet. It was the Dean of Students at University of Michigan in Ann Arbor. He looked her up and down without even glancing at Nick. "When I told you that I hoped to see more of you in the future, I had no idea I'd see this much."

Tanya tried to cover herself with her arm, wedging herself behind Nick. "Professor, please!" she shrieked. Within an instant, the grinning, ogling scholar was whisked away by the tide of humanity funneling toward the lobby.

A room service cart had been tipped over in a corner, broken glasses and dishes piled at its edge. Tanya watched Nick grab the cart's soiled tablecloth and pull it free. He wrapped it around her. She was so pleased she hopped up and down like a schoolgirl invited to her first party.

Slowly the couple stuck close to the wall and eased their way to an open door. Soon they were outside, breathing easier than they had in the past fifteen minutes. Cool air chilled their sweaty bodies. Their matted hair stuck to their foreheads.

What had triggered the alarm? A fire truck, lights flashing, sat in the road leading to the entryway of the hotel. Though she finally felt safe, Tanya looked for signs of fire, but she could not see or smell smoke.

"False alarm, folks, remain calm," a firefighter said. "First of the season, we gotta test everything for safety. Remain calm."

Nick asked the firefighter who tripped the alarm.

"Teens smoking pot thought it would be funny to see the place empty out," he said. "We caught them down by the Esther Williams swimming pool."

Hotel employees passed out bottles of water and blankets for those who had left the hotel without grabbing enough to cover themselves.

"Well, it's a damn good thing that firefighter said this was a false alarm," Tanya told Nick. "When we were coming down that hallway I had this awful feeling that you'd somehow concocted this whole fire scheme just so you wouldn't have to sleep with me."

"What? Tanya, are you crazy?" Nick asked. "That is totally absurd. Who would ever think of such a thing?"

The two hugged. Tanya cried, emotion spilling out from the tension of the drill and their adventure in the hotel hallway. She felt a twinge of guilt for thinking that Nick might have orchestrated the emergency to avoid intimacy. But that soon passed. She was glad to be in his arms and out of harm's way. Though he had his faults, Tanya sensed that he was the kind of man who could always rise when the occasion called for it. She just wished he had done that while they were still in their room.

After an hour or so, the all clear was given and guests were encouraged to return to their rooms. Nick flopped down on the couch. Tanya dove into the bed. They were exhausted. Sleep came quickly.

Chapter 13

Tuesday morning

The lobby of the Grand Hotel bubbled with activity as Nick made his way through the mob, which seemed to have massed all at once for checkout. Youngsters played on the stairway just off the lobby while their parents wrestled their way through the line to the front desk. Luggage of all shapes and sizes, piled in small groups, littered the entryway.

Nick scooted through the stacked bags like a football running back trying to pick his way through a defense. He nearly tripped over a child's model car, but caught himself from falling just in time to see the police chief dart into the hotel manager's office.

Perfect. Nick had hoped to connect with the manager and the chief before he and Tanya headed back to Bay City. It would be a great opportunity to pick up new details from the investigation. But Nick also wanted to grease the wheels so that he could call them for updates when he was back home in the newsroom.

The final version of Nick's story for that day's newspaper had been filed by seven in the morning. *The Blade*'s first edition hit the streets at 10:30. By eleven o'clock, the manager and chief would have had a faxed copy of the newspaper's front page on their desks.

When Nick finally bulled his way through the lobby crowd and reached the manager's office, Sylvia Shane and Lucille Calkins were waiting for him. Sylvia held up her copy of the fax. The main headline blared, "Chief calls Mackinac death 'possible homicide,'" and it was plastered across the top of the front page.

Obviously the chief hailed from the school of thought that believed any publicity was good publicity—as long as her name was spelled correctly. She seemed so pleased by the story that Nick thought her eyes were actually twinkling.

Sylvia was not as complimentary. "I don't like you quoting unnamed hotel employees," she said. "All official word should come from this office. And who are the island residents you quoted? Which bar did they come out of?"

"Actually, I paraphrased the conversations I had with some very distinguished members of your community," Nick said, fondly recalling the chats he'd had with Nate and Chastity. "Most people up here believe your dead body had help going over the balcony rail."

Sylvia stiffened in her chair, clearly agitated. "You know, I could have that maid fired for talking to you," she said. "Based on your room number, I've got a pretty good idea who it is. We told all employees not to discuss the death."

"Yup, you're the boss. You could fire her because you have the power to do so. But what does canning her really accomplish? You can't stop people from speaking their minds, and you can't stop me from doing my job."

The chief piped into the discussion, clearly wanting to cool it down before it boiled over and someone got burned. "Of course we're checking all leads and continuing our investigation," she said, "but my gut tells me the killer is already off the island."

"That's what I think too." Sylvia said. "We've talked to every employee and gone through all of their records. Nothing out of the ordinary. I'd be shocked if it ended up being somebody who works here or lives on the island."

Still, the chief said, tourists who had already left the island were being called and interviewed. Mackinac County sheriff's deputies were urging visitors to tell them about anything suspicious or out of the ordinary that they might have witnessed during visits to the island the previous weekend.

Tips were piling up like bricks of fudge at downtown confection outlets. Turns out that plenty of people saw all kinds of odd and weird happenings during their visits to the island—sightings of everything from suspected drag queens to celebrities to aliens.

Needless to say, Nick could see that this rankled the hotel manager. All of the resorts on the island counted on repeat business and word-of-mouth referrals. They wanted visitors recalling fond memories of their trip, not images of falling bodies and an island full of walking weirdos. The sooner this case was solved, the sooner business could return to normal in never-never land.

Nick moved closer to the women so he could lower his voice and still be heard. "Well, here's the $64,000 question—did the killer get the right person? Who was supposed to die—Adam Townsend or Zeke Zimmer?"

"We're still focused on the body we found," the chief said. "Only one dead person here, so we've got to chase this lead until we've exhausted all possibilities." She looked at Nick. "Even so, I put in a call to the Bay City Police Department late yesterday—just to give them a heads-up about Zimmer. They said you'd already called."

Nick wanted the women to know that Adam and Zeke were as different as the sun and moon. "Adam Townsend is a choirboy compared to Zeke Zimmer," he said. "Everyone we talked to said he was even more mild mannered than Clark Kent. He's what you'd call Mr. Plain Jane—especially when compared to a rogue like Zeke."

A radio squawked as the trio chatted. Lou Bega's "Mambo No. 5" played gently in the background, filling the office with a humming buzz.

"When will you know something on the tox screen?" Nick asked, turning away from the women and moving toward the office door. "That's your best lead, isn't it?"

The chief indicated that the state police lab was putting a rush on the tox screen request. Now that the authorities were focused on solving a homicide, the toxicology evaluation had become paramount. She'd let Nick know as soon as she heard something.

"The test will let us know if he was drinking and drugging—all the basic stuff like sleeping pills, sedatives, barbiturates, pain-killers, and many of the illegals like coke, pot, heroine, crack, and meth," the chief said. "The more advanced screen, which would look for foreign substances, takes a lot longer."

The hotel manager and reporter listened without interrupting, Nick trying to soak up the technical info. Then Nick indicated he was getting ready to leave.

Calkins stopped him. She had one more question for the reporter. "Hey, I noticed that you used Red, my nickname, in your story today. Where'd you get that?"

"I made some calls on you too," Nick said, a smile lighting up his face. "I know more about you than you realize. Catch you later."

Nick met Tanya at the front desk. A receptionist printed out his tab and handed it to him. He let out a low groan. $1,100, including room charges, dinner, and taxes, for two nights at the Grand—and he never slept a night in a bed at the legendary inn.

Nick thought to himself, Drayton Clapper, get ready for cardiac arrest.

Chapter 14

Tuesday afternoon

The three-hour drive back to Bay City gave Nick and Tanya more time to talk. Tanya directed the conversation, loving every minute of it—it was not often that she had Nick in a captive position. They had lots to discuss. She started with the fast-approaching ceremony at Bay City Central on Friday.

"I don't want to go, Nick," she said. "I hope that's okay. I know it's important for you to be there because your story last fall brought all this out. But for me, it's too close to home. With my dad's involvement in the scandal and his ties to Charlie Joselyn, I don't want to be there when they rename the field house."

"I get that, Tanya," Nick said. "I'm actually expecting the whole ceremony to be pretty low-key. I have the sense that people don't want to dwell on what happened at the school. I think everyone wants to move on."

Nick fidgeted in his seat. Tanya glanced at him out of the corner of her eye. She had been hoping to talk about what happened, or didn't happen, between the two on Mackinac Island. But she decided not to push it unless Nick brought it up. Tanya waited, lightly tapping her fingers on the steering wheel, eager for Nick to express his feelings about their relationship.

But no such luck. Nick pulled out an envelope containing faxed material that he said had been left for him at the front desk. He told Tanya that Annie, the longtime and largely unappreciated librarian at *The Blade*, had researched and sent him info that he'd requested.

Tanya was curious about the multiple-page package Nick was sorting through on his lap. Was it something important?

"Turns out the tip I got was right," Nick said, holding up a page. "The island did have a murder awhile back."

Tanya focused on the road as Nick read the details aloud. Apparently Mrs. Frances Lacey, a wealthy forty-nine-year-old Dearborn widow, was found strangled with her own panties in a wooded area just north of Devil's Kitchen in July 1960. She had been robbed and sexually assaulted.

"Says here the murder was never solved," Nick said. "Mrs. Lacey was staying at the Murray Hotel and decided to walk to visit friends at British Landing. She never made it."

Tanya was surprised. She'd lived in Michigan her whole life and had never heard of the murder. She briefly took her eyes off the road to ask how long it had taken to find her body.

"Once they figured out she was missing, the local cops called in the sheriff's department and the state police. Bloodhounds, search teams, the whole shebang. Took four days, then they found her under heavy brush off of a pathway."

"Any suspects?" Tanya asked.

"Not really. Says police arrested a man with a history of mental illness, but he had an airtight alibi and they let him go. I'll bet the cops needed to make an arrest, so they merely looked around for the local nut-job and took him into custody just for show."

"Interesting," Tanya said. "Even though it was a long time ago, it fits with what might be going on now. "

"You got it," Nick said, packing the faxed pages back into the envelope. "Interesting in that the local cops figure the killer got off the island before they even knew they had a murder on their hands. True back in 1960, and probably true forty years later."

Nick jotted down some notes on the back of the envelope. The two traveled south on I-75 for about an hour without speaking. The only noise in the car was the low murmur of the *Johnny Burke Morning Show* on the radio, broadcasting from Saginaw. Johnny and Blondie, his sidekick whose real name was Bonnie, were talking trivia.

The two listened to the radio banter until Tanya had all she could take. The chatter gave her the courage to turn the conversation to Nick's son and his possible return home.

"I contacted Joe," she said, dodging in and out of I-75 traffic. Tanya tried to gauge the expression on his face by glancing at him as she drove. She wasn't quite sure how he would feel about it.

"He's coming back to visit," she added, forcing a smile as large as she could spread it. "Isn't that great?"

"Well, of course I'd love to see him," Nick said, looking down at his hands. Tanya could see that his face lightened at the news.

Nick paused for a moment, then spoke slowly. "But I guess the real question is whether or not he wants to come back. How did he react?"

"I told him that you and I were friends—that I'd helped you with a story you were working on," she said, staring straight ahead at the rushing pavement as their vehicle picked up speed. "I told him I was calling because you and I had talked and I knew that you wanted to see him. He acted surprised."

"He was surprised?"

"I could hear it in his voice," she said. "Then he got quiet—kind of like you do when you're searching your thoughts looking for the right words. So I nudged him along."

She paused, letting her words take effect.

"Joe said he missed you, he missed Bay City, and his old friends. Nick, he wants to come home. I think he wants to hear it from you."

She continued to track his facial expressions, trying to measure the impact of what she'd told him. She watched Nick turn away from her. He looked out his window into the passing scenery of northern Michigan woods along the freeway.

The late spring had kept the maples from budding, but the evergreens looked lush. Tanya loved the symbolism of spring, when everything felt fresh and new. She hoped Nick would grab at the chance to reconnect with Joe and take another step toward getting his life back together.

"I would love that, Tanya," Nick said, his voice breaking as he spoke her name. He reached over with his left hand and touched her right hand as it rested on her leg.

Tanya handled the steering wheel with her left hand and looked out at the traffic. She sensed that saying less was really saying more right now.

"Thank you for reaching out to Joe. I need my boy in my life. He's all I got left."

"You got me too, Nick. That is, if you want me."

"I do, Tanya. I do."

Tanya beamed at the familiar words. A grin spread across her face. Nick had just made her day.

Chapter 15

Tuesday afternoon

The telephone behind the bar at the Paddock Lounge on Bay City's West Side rang without relief. The bartender, a balding, burly guy with an apron wrapped around his waist, poured four fingers of bourbon into a rock glass and pushed the drink in front of his lone customer, a barfly known as Ginny.

The barkeeper pushed away the notebooks and calendars burying the screaming telephone. Ginny asked for a separate glass of ice. The bartender held up his hand in her direction, motioning for her to hold on, while he pawed at the telephone receiver.

"Paddock, whaddya want?"

"This Ralph? I'm looking for Ralph," a woman's voice said.

"Yup, you got him."

"Ralph, I'm told you're the guy I talk to if I need a bug."

"Oh yeah, where'd you hear that?"

"A friend of yours, Tommie—the numbers guy."

"Hmm. What kinda bug?"

"Commercial, not residential. Needs to be electrical."

"I'll put out the word."

"I need the best around, Ralph. I will pay double. See what you can find."

"Okay, got it. Call me back Thursday afternoon."

* * *

Charlie Marx hung up and stepped away from the bank of public telephones at Metro Airport. An older woman had approached to use a nearby telephone. Charlie looked her over from top to bottom. She listened to the woman. It sounded like she was asking her daughter to pick her up at the airport for a ride home.

Innocent enough, Charlie thought. But she had learned a long time ago that you could never be too careful. Dangerous to trust anyone. She had come to believe that there were only two types of people in this world: those who wanted to use you or those who wanted to take advantage of you.

She moved into an area where she could see jets taxiing to take-off locations. The engines of the big, majestic planes whined as they readied for sprints down the runway before hurtling into the sky.

Charlie sat on a cushioned bench seat and watched the jets launch one by one into the bright blue sky. Sun through the large windows warmed her face and relaxed her. Blending into the hubbub at the airport allowed her to loosen up a little.

While she waited and gazed out the windows, her mind drifted back to her youth, a not-so-happy time. Charlie's parents had died in a head-on car crash when she was a tot. Their deaths had tossed her into Michigan's foster care system like a toy doll thrown onto a scrap heap.

The abuse of children by foster parents in Michigan was documented vividly in a series of articles by *The Flint Journal*'s lifestyle department during the late 1980s. The series showed that the state was so desperate to find foster parents that officials ended up giving children to criminals who would use them to make money—often in illegal enterprises. Felons, including rapists, murderers, child molesters, kidnappers, and armed robbers, got their hands on foster kids of all ages.

That's the system that had shaped little Charlene's life. She needed love and attention. She needed someone to give a damn. Instead she was passed around like an orphaned refugee who had dollar signs tattooed on her forehead. She soon figured out that most of her new parents had taken her in for the monthly check sent by the state.

When Charlene turned thirteen, the state put her in a home where the young girl was rented out. After home schooling in the morning, she would be driven to work afternoons and evenings in the back room of a dry-cleaning shop. At the end of her shift, her foster mom would pick her up and receive payment from the laundry owner. Charlene never saw a nickel of the money, not even the small change that fell from pockets during cleaning and pressing.

At another temporary home when Charlene was sixteen, her unspoken chores included a visit to her room twice a week from the dad of the house. Charlene soon dreaded the sound of his footsteps coming up the stairs to the attic where she slept. During his first visits, he stopped after fondling her. But each session progressed. After he started raping her, Charlene could not take any more.

She decided the creaking attic steps that had given her chills would serve as the killing device. The steps were steep and narrow, connecting the third floor of the home to the storage area where Charlene slept and kept her things. A thin handrail ran up the right side of the passage.

Week after week, the dad would use the handrail to make his way up the stairs. Once at the top, he would pause to stand up straight, let go of the rail, and reach to turn the doorknob. Charlene had timed his ascent up the stairs and knew every movement he'd make on his way to the attic.

On her final day in the home, the house was empty except for the dad. Charlene waited for the stairs to start creaking. She sat behind the attic door and counted his steps to the top. Her heart beat so loudly she was sure he could hear it pounding. When the dad neared the top step and paused, Charlene opened the door and lunged at the dad's chest, pushing him back down the stairs. He crashed hard, hitting and breaking the railing with his head. Charlene saw him somersault and land hard at the bottom of the stairs.

Charlene watched the throw rug under him soak up the blood that dribbled from the back of his head. He moaned, looked up at her, and let his final words spill out: "You bitch!" The dad then blinked repeatedly before allowing a final croak to seep from his body.

His last breath sent exhilaration shimmering through her body. She felt more alive than ever before. Later she would recall the rush of feelings and emotion and wonder if it was her first orgasm. If it wasn't, she thought now, the thrill had to be damn close.

Before walking downstairs to call 9-1-1, Charlene had waited several minutes for the body to quit jerking. She calmly told investigators how the dad had fallen from the top of the stairs while trying to retrieve a book that had been stored in the attic near where she slept. Somehow she mustered up tears to well in her eyes and trickle down her cheeks. Because of the accidental death in the home, she was removed that night.

From the house with the attic of horrors, Charlene was juggled from one juvenile holding facility to another until she won independence at age seventeen. From there she joined the military, where she signed up for every martial arts class available. Weapons became one of her specialties. Survival training was a hobby for her. She had transformed from Charlene to Charlie, a snot-nosed tough who had learned the art and technique of killing from hardened Vietnam veterans.

The high-pitched whining of jet airliner engines brought Charlie out of her daydream. Her head swiveled from left to right, surveying her surroundings. Still no one around.

She pushed the thoughts of her youth out of her mind. Charlie would only let herself recall them when she felt as though she were getting soft. The recollections stiffened her resolve, renewed her mental toughness, and hardened her for her work.

She jumped up and headed out of the airport. The phone call she'd placed earlier had started the death clock ticking on Zeke Zimmer again. In a matter of a few days, she would have him in her sights for a second kill.

This time there would be no slipups, no mistakes. Zeke would go down just like the other man targeted for execution by the man with the raspy voice. Charlie would get paid for both kills and blow town. Already she had jobs lined up in Toledo and Buffalo. No shortage in the demand for hired death.

Charlie was delighted to accommodate those who wanted people killed, as long as she believed the targets deserved to die—just like the foster dad, who had forfeited his right to live because of his monstrous behavior. In her mind the world became a better place whenever their bodies fell at her skilled hands.

Chapter 16

Late Tuesday afternoon

When Nick arrived back at the *Blade* newsroom, he discovered his desk piled high with mail and sticky notes. As the reporter leafed through the mess, Drayton Clapper approached. Nick felt a sense of dread creep across his body, kind of like a dark cloud passing the sun in a clear sky.

"Hey, good stories from Mackinac, Nick," Drayton said. "The misidentification thing really made that piece fly. I think every wire service in the country carried your stories. Glad you're done with it. I've got lots of other stories for you to develop."

"Thanks, but this story isn't finished yet."

"What do you mean?" Drayton sat on the corner of Nick's desk. "I know the island police are saying that it's a possible homicide, but what have they really got? In two weeks everyone will have forgotten about it and moved on. Let's let the cops do their jobs. If they turn up something, we can jump back on the story."

"Drayton, not only is this a murder, but I also believe the killer got the wrong guy," Nick said, his voice rising to make his point. "That means we may have a psycho on the loose and the intended victim still walking around breathing."

Nick, fearing that his boss was ready to pull him off the Mackinac piece, decided to go on the offensive to make a case for continuing to work the story. He laid out a laundry list of ways to chase the story as it developed and the official investigation continued. The biggest question, Nick said, was who wanted Zeke Zimmer dead.

"We're way ahead of the police on this, Drayton," Nick continued, gesturing wildly with both hands up by his ears. "Give me and Dave some elbow room on this, and we'll produce."

"Wait a minute, wait a minute," Drayton said, standing up, stepping back from the animated reporter, and crossing his arms.

The two had been down this road many times. Nick's time management, drinking, and unconventional methods had long been a major source of conflict between the two. More than once the clashes had resulted in Nick's suspension or dismissal from *The Blade*.

"Nick, you really need to be more of a team player," Drayton said. "The needs of the paper come first—your needs come second. I think you're going off the deep end here on this. We've got other stories to chase down. Plus, you're on a committee."

"A committee? What kind of committee?"

Drayton explained that the publisher of *The Blade*, D. McGovern Givens, had appointed a building-wide committee to study advertising revenue and come up with ideas to generate more cash for the newspaper. Committee members were to meet once a week for as long as it took to develop a plan. Every department, including marketing, circulation, advertising, and human resources, would have representatives on the panel.

"Nick, the publisher picked you for this prestigious committee because of the great work you did on the Bay City Central scandal last fall," Drayton said. "So you went from being fired during the height of the developing story to full reinstatement, to appointment to a top-level committee. You went full circle!"

"Yeah, but I've got a great story to work on right now," Nick said. The last thing he wanted was to be on some stinking committee, especially an advertising committee. "The ad people don't care what we think. Most of them don't even read the paper. They're afraid their lips will get tired if they get past the comic pages."

"Now, that's not fair, Nick," Drayton said, speaking calmly and slowly. "I know for a fact that the director of advertising is a very good reader. Why, nobody can read a golf scorecard faster or better than he can."

Nick rolled his eyes. He knew his boss had to take the role of the diplomat. That's what good managers and good company people do. That's how they play the game. But Nick had no interest in cozying up to management or playing footsie with advertising. His only desire was to gnaw at the Mackinac story like a dog chewing an old leather shoe.

"Please don't put me on that committee," he said. "It will drive me crazy."

"Well, sorry, Nick. The first meeting is at 10:30 a.m.," Drayton said, turning to leave. "Be there, don't be late, and don't come to it all hung over after a hard night at O'Hare's. Got it?"

"Yeah, yeah. I got it, but I'm still going to chase this Mackinac story, even if I have to do it on my own time," Nick said. "In fact, I'm going to try and meet with Zeke Zimmer tonight."

Drayton said nothing in response, walking away. Nick took that as tacit approval of his plans to pursue the island murder story. The reporter smiled at what he believed was a victory. He would work nights, weekends, even holidays—whatever it would take to put this piece together.

Chapter 17

Tuesday evening

Zeke Zimmer's three-bedroom bungalow was located on Bay City's West Side, just two blocks east of Euclid Avenue and not far from the old Handy High School. His place was just across the Saginaw River from the *Blade* offices.

Nick was to meet with Zeke at his home at 7:30. But the reporter decided to stop at O'Hare's Bar & Grill on Midland Street for a fast beer before going to see the electrician. Nick parked his Firebird in a restricted area behind the pub, picked up an abandoned McDonald's burger sack, and put it over the Restricted Parking sign. Frequent visitors to the area were used to seeing Nick's beloved ride resting safely in the zone. When the 'Bird wasn't parked there after normal work hours, everybody figured Nick was at home sick, on an assignment out of town, or on vacation.

As he whisked into the bar, Nick waved at Michael Davidson, the newly appointed Bay County prosecutor. The lawman had his arm around a dark-haired woman in a short skirt. Nick also spotted his old friend Dave Balz sitting alone in his usual spot at the back of the long, narrow watering hole. Just above Dave hung O'Hare's upside-down Christmas tree, which was attached to the tin ceiling year around.

"Hiya, Dave," Nick said, sliding up next to his friend. "Are you all set to go to the Townsend funeral tomorrow?"

"Yup, all ready," Dave said, motioning for Sassy Sally to refill his beer mug and get one for his pal. "I connected with what's left of his family—an ex-wife who had fallen out of touch, and two adult children—through the funeral home. They still think this was just some sort of unfortunate accident. The kids seemed very anxious to move on and settle his affairs. They've already talked to a Realtor about selling his house."

"No kidding. Even after I quoted the island police chief saying this was a possible homicide, they still think that it was an accident?"

The two talked about where they were with the story. Nick told Dave about making a connection with the island chief and the wealth of background information he had picked up. Unfortunately, he said, most of the best info was off the record for now.

Both reporters knew that time was working against them. They agreed that the longer the story lingered in the "possible homicide" category, the more likely it would get pushed into the "just another unfortunate incident" category and fade into the background.

"I know Clapper wants me to drop it and move on," Nick said. "As you know, he's got me serving on a committee—advertising, of all things."

As the two friends talked, the front door of O'Hare's swung open. It brought in a cold May breeze and Zeke Zimmer, who apparently was stopping to have one more drink before meeting Nick at his home.

Nick said hello to Zeke and introduced him to Dave, whom he had spoken with on the telephone earlier in the week. The trio decided to take a table near the center of the bar. It put them squarely under the heavenly but frozen gaze of Mona, the nearly nude woman in the painting that hung proudly behind the bar at O'Hare's.

For midweek, the tavern was relatively busy. Besides the prosecutor nuzzling the brunette, a half-dozen stools at the bar were full. Regulars filled the seats around five tables, including Nick's. Bob Seger's "Ramblin' Gamblin' Man" poured from the jukebox at half volume.

Zeke wobbled and almost fell out of his chair. He confessed to Nick and Dave that he'd made the Midland Street bar rounds, meaning he'd stopped at Lucky's, Hooters, the Sawmill, and the Rathskeller before stumbling into O'Hare's.

"Don't worry, I ain't drivin' tonight. Caught a cab down here and I can walk home. Handy's not that far away. I can make it. In fact, a little walk would probably do me good."

The electrician reached to swat Nick on the back and nearly fell out of his chair. Sassy Sally saw what happened and put Zeke on notice by pointing at her eyes, then pointing at Zeke and holding up one finger.

"Better watch it, Zeke, two more fingers means the door hits your ass on the way out," Dave said—obviously speaking from his experience with Sally.

Zeke said he was feeling low because of his good friend's impending funeral. He was also bothered by the idea that his buddy might have had help going over the balcony rail.

"Ya know, that's been keeping me up at night," Zeke said. "I have not slept worth a shit since this whole thing blew up.

"I saw your story, Nick—possible homicide? That scared the hell out of me. Adam was a damn great guy. Nobody would want to hurt him—not even his ex-wife. My ex-wives, on the other hand, would love to see me go down."

"Well, Zeke, that's what I wanted to talk with you about tonight," Nick said, leaning closer to the two at his table to keep his voice low. He figured that there was no point in trying to meet at Zeke's home later, given his condition. The reporter decided to plunge ahead, and simply pop the question. "In addition to the ex-wives, who would want to see you taking up permanent residence in the dirt?"

"Hold it, hold on. What are you saying?" Zeke asked, poking himself in the chest with his thumb. "Does that mean somebody could still be out there looking for me?"

"Well, that's a damn good question that nobody seems to have an answer to right now," Nick said. "The cops are still chasing around after Adam Townsend's possible killer, but I think we should be more worried about you. So again, besides Wives One through Four, who else would like to take you down?"

Zeke sat ogling Mona as Nick asked about the ex-wives. The electrician shifted in his chair, causing it to creak and groan. He stared down at his shoes. The lines in his forehead looked like furrows in a farmer's freshly plowed field. His cheeks were hollow, his jaw slack. He rubbed the fingers on each of his hands—first the left, then the right.

Nick prodded him along. "We all know you like to gamble—that's what you were doing instead of going to that conference on the island. Do you owe a lot of people big dough?"

"Well, I wouldn't say that I owe a lot, but I must admit that Lady Luck has not been smiling at me much lately," Zeke said, finally looking up at Nick and then at Dave. "I mean, I suppose there are a couple of guys I owe a few bucks to—they might be a little pissed."

"How much is a few bucks?" Dave asked.

"Oh, maybe $75K."

"$75,000? Hell, I know a lot of people who would shoot you for $75,000 without blinkin' an eye," Nick said. "That's a ton of gambling debt for a guy on a pension."

"It's $75K spread out over four or five guys," Zeke said. "Sure, they want their dough, but they don't get nothin' if I'm dead. I don't think it's them."

"Okay, who else? Did you ever cheat anybody in a card game? Does somebody want to get back at you for a bad bet?"

"Well, I gotta think about that for a bit," Zeke said. "I've been playin' cards and bettin' the ponies for a long time. Then of course I like to bet the numbers a couple times a week. And pro and college sports. The betting slips—I probably get in on three or four slips every weekend. Maybe a pool or two."

That was a pretty wide net, Nick thought. He asked the electrician to put together a list of people he owed money to or people he may have cheated.

"Including the wives?" Zeke asked. "A couple of the wives I still owe, and they may be under the mistaken perception that I somehow cheated them."

"Yes, include everybody. And one more thing. One of the Bay City cops I talked with said you like to play with matches," Nick said. "Is that true? Are you covering your gambling debts with arson?"

"Nick, I'm surprised that you would even dare say that out loud," Zeke said, getting indignant and straightening himself in his chair. "First off, those were just allegations from many years ago. I have never been charged with arson. Nothing has ever been proven in a court of law.

"And secondly, and this is important, Nick, I would never play with matches. I am a card-carrying electrician. If I were to ever engage in such an activity, matches would definitely not be my style."

Nick and Dave looked at each other and rolled their eyes. Somebody out there might be hunting the guy at their table over an arson job, and Zeke was splitting hairs about his possible style and method of operation.

As the three men talked, Sassy Sally interrupted. She said Zeke had a call from behind the bar. Zeke stood up, weaved and wobbled to the end of the bar, and took the receiver from Sally's outstretched hand.

"You got Zeke. What's up?" the electrician said into the phone, loud enough for the reporters to hear. After a couple minutes of mumbling into the receiver, Zeke concluded the conversation with an audible "That will work. See you later."

Zeke told Nick and Dave that he wanted to get home to rest before the Townsend funeral. He also mentioned that he had a lot of thinking to do regarding their discussion.

The three guys shook hands and Zeke headed toward the front door, bumping into a barstool as he lurched and reeled his way out. Nick and Dave looked at each other. It was an odd phone call and sudden exit, especially after Zeke's surprising revelations about his gambling and debts. It made Nick wonder what Zeke was up to. They sat down to absorb all that they had just learned.

"Wow, if he's not the target of the killer, he should be," Dave said. "Can you believe all that? And he probably only told us a fraction of the shit he is really involved in."

Nick agreed. "We didn't even get around to asking him about girlfriends and whores," he said. "Wives One through Four would probably take him out just for playing around all the time."

Zeke certainly wasn't making their investigation any easier. This was a guy whose lifestyle meant that he was in constant need of money to feed his bad habits. Any number of men and women could want him dead. Nick really did not know where to begin.

"Start with the ex-wives," Dave said. "I'll bet they know a whole lot more than Zeke is letting on. I'll do some scratching around and get some names and phone numbers tomorrow morning. We got a lot of digging to do."

Chapter 18

Wednesday morning

A large conference room separated the publisher's and editor-in-chief's offices on the fourth floor of *The Bay City Blade*. A twenty-foot wooden table with fourteen cushioned chairs dominated the room.

Framed award-winning photos from the paper's crack photographers consumed one wall. Windows on the opposite wall flooded the space with natural light.

Nick approached the conference room with trepidation. It was foreign, enemy territory—the lair of corporate management. He could only imagine the amount of butt-kissing that went on among assorted editors, managers, department heads, the publisher, and the big mucky-mucks from Grand Rapids.

As he reached the doorway, Nick picked up a whiff of a putrid smell that he couldn't quite make out. He sniffed the air gently. Rotting cheese? The editor-in-chief's gooey hair mousse? Old, wet cigars wrapped in dirty socks? Bird poop?

Nick sniffed again and walked in. The sight in the far corner of the room shocked him. It couldn't be true. Sadly, it was. There before him, fifteen minutes before the advertising meeting was to begin, was Morton Reynolds, editor-in-chief of *The Blade*, on his hands and knees, wearing rubber gloves and working with a small bucket, paper towels, and a bottle of spray carpet cleaner.

Morton was picking up steaming, wet dog poop and scrubbing the carpet. The turds were compliments of the publisher's two Shih Tzu dogs, hairy little creatures with colored bows on their heads.

The frisky shitting machines rarely left the side of publisher Diane Givens. Nick figured the pooches must have done their business in the conference room and retired to her office.

Before the reporter could say anything, the publisher's voice could be heard through the open door to her office.

"Morton, you don't have to do that," she said. "They're my little darlings. I'll take care of it."

Without looking up from his task, the editor said, "You always say that, Diane, but then you never take care of it. It always falls to me because I use this room for meetings more than anyone else."

Nick decided to slip away and pretend he hadn't heard or seen anything. He was mortified for Morton. But before he could escape, the publisher came out of her office and greeted him.

"Why, hello, Nick. You're a little early for the meeting, but I'm glad you're here," she said, motioning for the reporter to come into her office. Her words prompted Morton to stand and take off his gloves. Nick could see a look of despair on the editor's face, his humiliation now complete.

"Want me to call down to maintenance?" Nick asked. "I saw Mick down there when I came in this morning."

"No, that's okay," the editor said. "The janitor won't do it—says it's not in his job description, and then he cusses and hangs up on me. Easier and faster just to take care of it."

Silence filled the room. Morton opened a window and turned on a fan. The publisher walked over and took Nick by the arm.

"Nick, why don't you come into my office," she said, surveying the room. "Morton, I think you might have missed a spot right over in the far corner. Let's kick it up a notch, okay? Committee members will be here in a few minutes."

As the publisher and reporter walked toward her office, Nick could hear Morton grumbling quietly. He wasn't sure, but he thought he heard him end a sentence with the word "bitch" for emphasis.

Nick knew that Morton had become a total submissive, but he was surprised how low the editor had stooped. Others in the building snickered and whispered about Morton. They also talked about the publisher and her controlling and cruel nature.

Building politics were usually outside Nick's purview; he didn't want to be involved. Even so, the publisher's domineering ways were legendary. Diane was the person in charge, and she wanted everyone to know it. Employees of *The Blade* saw how she treated Morton and other members of management. It's one of the reasons she was nicknamed the Castrator.

The meeting was scheduled to start at 10:30—right after the newspaper's first morning deadline. It was supposed to last one hour. Committee members arrived via the stairway and elevator.

"My golf meeting is noon today," said Tom Stevens, the advertising manager, who was also known as Tee-Time Tom. He entered the conference room crowing about his workday. "I'm going toe-to-toe out on the golf course with a rep from Meijer Thrifty Acres, Hagen Ford, and my old friend Al Singer. Can't be late."

Others followed Stevens into the room. Circulation manager Joe "Tiny" Kowalski slid sideways through the door because his large circumference would not squeeze through in a frontal assault. Roberta Michaels, the marketing manager—and publisher wannabe—marched in next and scurried to take a seat next to the Castrator's chair at the head of the table. Michele LaPorte, the publisher's personal assistant, followed. She hustled to sit across from Michaels at the other end of the table. Bob Queen, the pressroom foreman, entered and sat across from Nick, who used the arrival of the managers to slip away from the Castrator. Queen may have been the only person at the meeting who hated being there as much as Nick. The last one to arrive was Morton, who had gone to the restroom to wash his hands and joined the meeting late.

Each member of the committee reported a tale of woe. Falling numbers from the display and classified advertising departments quieted the room. Declining statistics from the circulation department—both in home delivery and single-copy sales—made it even more depressing.

Less cash coming in the door and rising expenses meant change had to happen. For people as entrenched in their routines as this bunch, change was difficult to think about. Resistance popped up at every level.

Finally Nick held up his hand, two fingers outstretched.

"Yes, Nick," the publisher said, her voice filled with enthusiasm. She was clearly pleased that Nick wanted to participate. She even wiggled in her seat. "You don't have to hold up your hand to speak in a meeting like this."

"I know, but what I wanted to indicate is that I have two numbers for you that could change the fortunes of the paper—and you've not heard them from anyone at this table."

"Continue," she said, smiling.

But others at the table were not as enthused to hear what Nick had to say. Two rolled their eyes. Two others crossed their arms. And Tiny muttered quietly, "Here we go. Just what we need, another lecture from editorial."

"The first number is two," Nick said, ignoring them. "We have a Bay City man who is dead up on Mackinac Island and another one right here in town who is probably being hunted by a killer. And the second number is one. If you add them together, you get . . ."

"Three," shouted Tee-Time, breaking into Nick's presentation. The ad man could barely contain himself. "Three, the answer is three. I got it, I got that one right."

Nick sighed and looked down at the floor. He did not want to offend Tee-Time or anyone else in the room, but that was going to be difficult. He had learned in journalism school that it was best to write or communicate at an eighth-grade level to reach most readers. As he surveyed the managers in the room, he thought eighth grade might be aiming pretty high.

"Well, yes, Tom. Your math skills are impeccable," he said in an even tone. "One plus two does make three, but that's not the point I was trying to make."

The reporter explained that the events taking place on Mackinac Island added up to make one great story, and that's what the paper needed more of to improve all of its numbers. Nick said he believed the newspaper needed to do more to connect with readers. The worst thing that could happen to newspapers, he said, was to become irrelevant.

Nick told the group about a conversation he'd recently had with one of his apartment building neighbors, who happened to be the manager of Bay City's largest recycling center. The neighbor had warned Nick about a disturbing trend he had noticed.

"My neighbor says half the newspapers that come into the recycling center are still rolled up with the rubber bands around them," Nick said. "That means a lot of people are still getting the paper delivered, but not many are actually reading it. Now to me, that's scary. How long before they realize they're not reading us, decide to save a few bucks every week, and just quit taking the paper?

"If you want to sell more papers, and more advertising," he said, "then it's my belief that we need more great stories like the Mackinac piece I've got in the works. Publishing great stories and meeting the needs and desires of our readers will improve all our fortunes."

Tiny Kowalski apparently begged to differ. The circulation manager tried mightily to rise to make a point, but failed because his behind had become lodged in between the arms of his chair.

"Come on, Nick," he said, pausing until the noise from his crashing chair stopped echoing across the room. "We all know what you were doing up at the island—getting drunk every night and sleeping with your girlfriend at a swanky hotel on the company dime."

Nick tried to conceal volcanic rage. He looked at Diane, then at Morton. "See, this is why I hate these kinds of meetings. How can you honestly expect to improve the future of the newspaper when we are surrounded by morons?"

Nick turned to face Tiny, who had rolled his chair back as far away from Nick as he possibly could while still staying in the conference room.

"Who I sleep with is none of your concern," Nick said, his eyes narrowing to razor-sharp slits and the veins in his neck popping out like electrical cords. "If you even mention my girlfriend again, I will kick your fat ass all over this building."

A low murmur rumbled across the room. Diane grinned from ear to ear. She seemed to be enjoying the discourse even though it had turned ugly.

"What we all need to be concerned with is our falling numbers," Nick continued, looking away from Tiny and addressing the others at the table. "As a newspaper, we have to care about those two Bay City men and find out what happened to them for our readers. And it's my duty as a journalist to find justice for them and their families. That's why I got into this business."

Roberta Michaels, the marketing manager, offered the group her view. She agreed with Nick about the importance of giving readers strong, compelling content. But she also suggested that the newspaper should consider other sources of revenue.

"The Internet is rising," she said. "More people are using it, and everyone can deliver their own message using email or through individual websites. As more people get connected, the less relevant newspapers become."

"The Internet is crap," said the ad manager. "It's just a fad. Nobody likes to read on the computer. For crying out loud, you can't even take it to the bathroom when you've got to take a dump."

The marketing manager would not back down. She suggested looking into a new service that was just beginning on the West Coast.

"It's called Craigslist," Roberta said. "I've been doing some research. It's a brand-new Internet-based service that's catching on in the San Francisco area. It's a new classified ad service. People love it because it's cheap and it works."

"Craig's what? What the hell is that?" the ad manager said, looking at his watch again. "Hey, listen, I gotta go. This is an important golf meeting with some of our key advertisers. But before I do, let me just make it clear that nothing on the Internet will ever replace our classifieds—they're here to stay."

With that, the meeting deteriorated quickly. The publisher asked for more information from each department for the next meeting. She also wanted hear more about Craigslist. The marketing manager beamed.

Nick and the pressroom foreman were elated that the meeting had ended. They headed for the door. Nick wanted to make some calls on the island piece before the Townsend funeral later in the day.

As committee members funneled toward the door, the Castrator called out Nick's name and asked if he could stay behind a moment.

"Sure," Nick said, wondering what was up.

When the room cleared, she motioned for Nick to move to a chair at the table next to her seat.

"Nick, I want you to know how much I appreciate you sitting on this committee," she said. "If we're going to fix our problems, it's going to take a big view, a broad vision, to clearly see the path ahead."

"This really isn't my thing," Nick said. "But I did find it kind of interesting. I also heard a lot of people not interested in doing anything differently."

"That's why I want a lot of different voices on this committee," she said, shifting in her seat and rolling her chair closer to Nick's. "Just keep adding your voice to the discussion. It will make a difference."

The publisher also complimented Nick on his Mackinac stories. She leaned toward the reporter and put her hand on his knee.

"I've been reading your stuff with great interest," she said. "Don't worry about what Tiny said. Sometimes jealousy gets in the way of people being able to focus on a clear vision."

The Castrator leaned back in her chair, but did not remove her hand. After a moment she patted his knee and then gave it a firm grip before releasing Nick.

"Well, thanks," Nick said, quickly rising from his chair. It was the second time in one day that Diane had physically touched him—something that had never happened once in all the time that the two had worked in the same building. Nick decided not to say anything. He wanted to get out of the conference room as quickly as he could. "I gotta go. Talk to you later."

"You bet, Nick," she said, a smile on her face. "We'll be talking a lot more."

Chapter 19

Wednesday morning

Charlie Marx pulled into the driveway of a big country home on Three Mile Road in Monitor Township. She scanned the property as she waited for the Realtor from Starlight Realty of Bay City to meet her. The Monitor home was one of four that Charlie was scheduled to view with the real estate agent.

While she killed time, Charlie decided to walk around the home. It was big and pricey enough to meet the killer's criteria. It needed to have a decent-sized value to make it worth burning down. The property also had to be in a remote area, and unoccupied.

The other three properties on the Realtor's show list for Charlie were very similar: country homes in secluded areas, with a ballpark price range of $200,000. One was located in Bangor Township and two others were standing empty in Frankenlust Township.

The Realtor pulled up in her yellow Volkswagen Beetle. She was late. Charlie thought she looked a little frantic.

"Hello, I'm Barbara Fowler," Charlie said, reaching to shake her hand. "Thanks for putting this together and meeting me."

The agent was as slender as a swizzle stick, with dark, bushy hair at one end and big floppy feet at the other. But her dominant features were big, round blue eyes and an easy, captivating smile.

"Hi, I'm Mary Rose Hayden," she said, gripping Charlie's outstretched hand. "I'll be tickled pink to help you find a home that suits your needs and budget."

Charlie smiled and nodded, allowing Mary Rose to make her standard real estate pitch: "Purchasing a home is a major investment, and finding just the right place takes time. Very few people see one place and actually make a decision. This is part of a process, and you're taking the first step."

The killer followed the Realtor to the front door of the house and positioned herself so she could look over the agent's shoulder. Mary Rose opened the storm door and punched a four-digit number into the lockbox, which was attached to the doorknob. Inside the lockbox were keys to the house and a nearby outbuilding. One-nine-five-two. Charlie took note, writing it on the inside of her wrist while the agent wrestled with the door key.

The home had a slightly musty smell because it had been closed up. Mary Rose lit a scented candle on the kitchen counter and showed Charlie around the house, commenting on the property's many attributes as they viewed each room. Charlie opened a notebook. She asked questions that any prospective homebuyer would, but along with her notes on the house she jotted down one-nine-five-two, transferring the info from her wrist to a corner of the page.

Charlie liked this place because the utilities were all still connected to the house, and the property had a gas fireplace. She also noted that a gas grill with an attached propane tank had been dragged into the rear entryway. While the agent watched, she opened the top of the grill and then jiggled the propane tank. She was delighted that it was not empty. "Does this nice grill come with the property?" Charlie asked.

"It's not included in the items on the listing fact sheet, so it does not come with the home," the agent said. "But everything is negotiable. If you want it, then let's make it part of your offer."

"Okay, we'll see how this all works out."

Within twenty minutes, they were on their way to the next property on the show list. Two hours later, their tour was complete. Each of the four homes had the same lockbox number, which Charlie guessed was the Realtor's birth year.

When the two women parted, Charlie gave the agent a card with Barbara Fowler's name and a cell phone number. She asked the agent to call and leave a message if any similar properties came on the market. "We probably won't be ready to buy until the end of the summer," she said, "but I thought I would start looking now—just to see what's available."

As Charlie drove away from the last property, she thought to herself that any of the houses would work for her purposes, but the first home she had viewed with the agent would be the perfect kill site. Now all she had to do was get Zeke Zimmer inside the place with her for about ten minutes and finish the job she'd started.

CHAPTER 20

Wednesday afternoon

The family of Adam Townsend had given Nick and Dave permission to attend and cover the deceased's funeral at St. Boniface Catholic Church on Lincoln Avenue. Family members appreciated the work the two had done on the story. They also believed the two *Blade* reporters had been respectful since the tragedy had struck.

But Dennis Townsend, Adam's oldest son, refused to allow TV cameras and news reporters from other cities into the funeral home or into the church for the funeral Mass. Since the story had broken about the death and case of mistaken identity on Mackinac Island, media from across the country had inquired about covering the story.

The family did not want to feed what appeared to be an emerging frenzy. The Townsends did not care to be part of the limelight; they were private people who did not covet notoriety.

However, the family's desires didn't stop the media from setting up on public sidewalks outside the funeral home and church. A TV crew from the Tri-Cities area and one from Detroit tried to find mourners who would speak with them. They yelled questions from their perches on public property.

"How does it feel to hear about a death and then find out later it's somebody you know?" was one of the questions shouted out to a weeping relative.

Then came this profound question: "Is your friend in a better place now?"

The short response from one of Adam's former coworkers: "No, my friend is dead. He's not in a better place. Go away, you asshole."

The TV crew from Detroit, desperate to find subjects to interview, even tried to line up Nick and Dave to speak on camera. They declined to be interviewed because they didn't think the family would approve. So far the two had the trust and cooperation of the family, and they did not want to do anything to lose it. Besides, they did not want to help media competitors in any way.

As usual, the TV crews and reporters outside were having their best luck interviewing politicians from the Bay City Commission and Bay County Board of Commissioners. Men and women running for public office will do just about anything to get their mugs on camera. This was no exception. They preened, straightened their apparel, and used handkerchiefs to blow their honkers as they waited for camera lights to switch on.

Zeke Zimmer had made a brief appearance at the funeral home and was attending the Mass with Wife Number Four, who told Nick that Adam Townsend was probably the most decent human being her husband had ever associated with.

Zeke pulled Nick aside for a moment. "Hey, Nick, sorry I was so screwed up when we talked last night," he said. "It's been a very rough few days. I guess I'm not handling it well."

"I understand, Zeke. You lost a good friend. But I would like to talk with you some more about what's happened. I'm expecting to get word from the island on the tox screen for Adam. Thought it might come today. Should be any time."

"Yeah, let's try to do tomorrow. Sounds good."

The church filled with friends and family members, who marched in somberly. The St. Boniface parish had a long and proud history. Established in 1874 by German Catholics overflowing from nearby St. Joseph's Church, St. Boniface was the center of activity on North Lincoln Avenue in the modest middle-class East Side Bay City neighborhood.

Bay City is a community of small, centralized neighborhoods. Most have their own ethnic flavor. Neighbors are protective of their schools, shopping districts, corner bars, and churches. Families know each other and mind each other's children.

The folks attending the funeral Mass for Adam Townsend knew the deceased and his family very well, but they also regarded each other as extended family. They had lost one of their own, and they gathered at the church to pay their final respects.

By 1:30 p.m., the body had been transported from the funeral home to the front entryway of the church. The casket was set up on a large pedestal with a prayer kneeler in front of it. Fresh flowers, plants, tall candlesticks, a crucifix, and photographs of the deceased with his sons surrounded the body box. Finally, the casket was opened for the last viewing and farewell at two o'clock.

A deliveryman from Keit's Nursery was struggling to lug a huge peace lily into the church. He bumped into Nick as he tried to get the large green and white plant close to the casket. Nick noticed the plant's handwritten card, which said, "So very, very sorry. RIP—Charlie."

As more mourners approached, Dennis Townsend pulled Nick to the side. "I want to thank you for your articles about Dad. I thought they were very sensitive. We've heard a lot of nice comments from folks about Dad, and most people mention reading about him in *The Blade*."

"Thanks," Nick said. "Glad you're happy with the way we handled the story—all very tricky the way this came out."

"I was especially pleased that you called us to let us know about the mistaken identity before you published the first story about Dad," Dennis said. "It would have been a horrible shock to learn of Dad's passing on your front page. Giving us a heads-up softened the blow. I won't forget that."

The two men shook hands and watched family and friends gather near the casket.

Nick noticed a mother letting go of her five-year-old son's hand to hug a member of the Townsend family. When she did, the youngster stepped on the kneeler and jumped up, grabbing the edge of the casket with both hands. The added weight on one corner was just enough to upset its balance on the pedestal. The casket tipped down on its side, allowing the top half of Adam Townsend to flop out onto the floor of St. Boniface.

Women gasped and covered their mouths. Men scrambled to help church ushers get Adam back in his box. Family members wept openly. The priest stepped forward and blessed the body and casket repeatedly, dousing both with holy water.

As the casket was lifted back up on the pedestal, an usher on one end of the box fell. The heavy box dropped and tipped again. This time, Wrong-Way came all the way out and lay facedown on the floor.

To the family's horror, the bottom half of the body was not clothed. Even more shocking is what else rolled out onto the floor with Adam. A nude blond female blowup doll, a bottle of Johnnie Walker Black still in its box, a carton of Marlboros, and a set of ivory dice landed outside the casket not far from Adam's naked white butt.

Later Nick found out that Adam had made the bizarre burial request several years earlier during a formal pre-planning arrangement with the funeral home, which prided itself in honoring family requests.

Word soon spread on the street outside the church that an accident had occurred with the casket. Within minutes, one of the huge wooden front doors of the church burst open and a TV cameraman came into the entrance area. Tagging behind the cameraman was an assistant with a microphone in one hand and a spotlight in the other. The camera crew tried to get footage of the chaos, no doubt thinking it would make a lively and interesting segment on the nightly news.

"Get those sons of bitches out of here," the head usher shouted as some of the men attending the funeral rushed toward the intruders. "Kick them down the front steps—the bastards!"

The priest who was supposed to conduct the funeral Mass gasped for air and clutched his chest. "We're all God's children," he said desperately as he tried to separate the usher from the cameraman. "Just let them go back outside."

"Not this heathen, Father," the usher said, swinging wildly at the cameraman, who retreated to the door. "Once I get him outside, I'm going to give him a lesson or two about proper conduct in the house of the Lord."

Once order was restored in the church, the funeral Mass for Adam finally started. It was a very nice, normal ceremony—many glowing remarks and lots of wailing and nose blowing. Still, Nick breathed a sigh of relief when Adam was buried without incident at Green Ridge Cemetery on South Tuscola Road.

After the funeral, Nick and Dave headed back to the newsroom.

"You were right about Adam not having much luck," Nick said. "Today was one hell of an exit for Wrong-Way Townsend."

Chapter 21

Wednesday evening

Nick pulled into the Johnson family driveway to pick up Tanya. They had planned to meet Dave at Mulligan's Pub for an evening of food and fun.

After the excitement of the Townsend funeral, an evening of libation was definitely in order. Plus, it would give the three of them a chance to talk about the Mackinac Island story. Nick had some interesting news to share with Tanya and Dave.

Tanya opened the passenger's side door of Nick's Firebird and slid into the leather bucket seat. She leaned across the center console and gave Nick a kiss on the cheek, leaving a trace of ruby-red lipstick on his mug. "How was your day, big boy?"

"Wild. First time I ever attended a funeral where the deceased got rolled out of the casket—not once, but twice," Nick said. He filled Tanya in on the unusual events at the church as he backed out of the driveway and headed for Mulligan's. He had decided to save the big news of the day until the twosome connected with Dave.

As they rumbled down Center Avenue, Tanya reached over and rested her hand on top of Nick's without saying a word. Her soft touch felt good and right to Nick, who breathed deeply and settled back into his seat. The silence in the Firebird was comfortable and fulfilling for both.

But there was nothing silent about Mulligan's. The pub was nearly packed when Nick and Tanya found Dave in a booth near the back of the bar. The aroma of spilled beer and burned burger permeated the air. Shania Twain's country hit "That Don't Impress Me Much" blared from the jukebox.

They slid into Dave's booth and exchanged greetings. Dave asked if Nick had filled Tanya in on the funeral. She nodded, indicating she'd heard the story.

"I've got to admit I've never witnessed anything quite like that," Dave said.

As they settled in and ordered, Nick told Tanya and Dave he'd been in touch with a friend at the state police crime lab.

"The preliminary tox screen on Adam Townsend came back clean," Nick said. "My lab buddy gave me a heads-up on it. He's going to release it to Chief Calkins in the morning. No drugs or sedatives. I think that means they're going to call it accidental."

Dave shrugged. "You surprised by that? You have to figure that the chief is getting lots of pressure to close the case," he said, "Besides, the Townsend family wants to move on."

Nick shook his head and swirled the foam from his beer in the glass.

Dave was probably right. The island was likely back to normal by now—and full of visitors who were not there on Saturday, when Adam hit the deck. Even so, Nick had nagging doubts about it being an accident. He reminded the others of the puncture wound on the body, the hole in Adam's shirt, the foreign champagne bottle, and the blond hair in the room.

Dave shrugged again. "So what does that prove?"

"I suppose you could rationalize that Adam brought the champagne into the room," Nick said, "but there were no fingerprints on it. And I suppose you could say that the hair came from a previous guest and was missed during cleaning. But how do you explain away the holes in his back and shirt?"

Silence fell over the table for the first time that evening. Tanya took a sip from her drink and asked if Nick had heard anything else from the island. Weren't the cops interviewing employees?

"Nothing new that I'm aware of," Nick said. "But I kind of expected that. Many of the employees are young temporaries from other countries. Even if they did see something out of the ordinary, why get involved, why get dragged into something messy?"

"Okay, I guess that means we're back to square one," Dave said. "If this was not simply an accident involving Adam Townsend, then what are we looking at? Someone out to get Adam Townsend? Or did the killer hit the wrong victim?"

Nick sat back in the booth to think about the Townsend angle. Sure, the man had liked to drink and smoke and gamble a little. But aside from the blowup doll in the casket being a little kinky, was Adam really such a bad guy? Who would want to take him out?

He posed the question to his friends. If you were to hold up a summary of the lives of Zeke and Adam, Nick asked, who would be more likely to have made the kind of enemies who'd commit murder? The three sat quietly for a moment, mulling the question.

"This was a very clean, smooth operation," Dave said. "Killer swoops in undetected, hits the target, and then quickly and quietly vanishes. That's the work of a professional. Only problem for the pro is that Wrong-Way Townsend is in the wrong place at the wrong time."

"Hard to imagine a smooth professional killing the wrong person," Tanya said. "That's a pretty major screw-up for a pro."

"True, but I'm still kind of leaning toward Dave's thinking," Nick said. "I think you have to be a professional to do an injection that doesn't show up on a standard tox screen, then complete the kill. Getting on and off the island undetected, that's the mark of a pretty cool customer."

"Here's another thing," Tanya said. "If it was a professional hit, then I'm betting it was a woman. That's the only way a stranger gets into that room with him. That's womanhood 101."

"Wow, that would mean we got us a hit lady," Dave said. "Don't see too many of them around."

Even if it was a professional, figuring out who had hired the assassin wouldn't be easy. The trio agreed that the list of people who would like to see Zeke Zimmer in a grave was very likely a long one.

Another disconcerting note was that the kind of people on that long and growing list would have the means to hire a contract killer.

The electrician was connected to so many seedy operators that they did not know where to begin looking for people who would want him dead.

Chapter 22

Wednesday evening

Zeke Zimmer walked to the far end of the bar in the Paddock Lounge and took a seat. Most of the tables in the lounge were filled with diners. Soft yellow light cast deep shadows into the corners of the joint. Both the fake leather seats and the carpet were red. The tables and bar top were black. The place gave off the feel that sticking to a seat was definitely a possibility if a patron had the courage to sit down anywhere.

Zeke sat alone, his elbows resting on the bar's edge. A young couple groped each other and giggled at the other end of the bar. Ralph waited on them, pouring out two fruity drinks and taking their money. As he finished making change, he nodded at Zeke.

"Zeke, glad you made it in tonight," Ralph said. He handed the electrician a short scotch and water on the rocks. "Rough day, huh? Saying so long to Adam must have been tough."

"Yeah, it was tough all right. Lots of crying and hugging. I hate going to those things."

"Me too. Heard there was a little dustup at the funeral today. Is it true what they're sayin'? Did Wrong-Way fall out of the casket?"

"Oh, God, it was horrible," Zeke said, taking a big swig of whiskey. "Poor son of a bitch. Really hated to see that. Adam was such a good guy—that was a damn dirty shame."

The two didn't say much for several minutes. Ralph walked away to fill a drink order for one of the waitresses standing at the bar.

When he returned, he had another scotch for Zeke—this time a double, easy on the water, no ice.

Zeke got down to business. "You mentioned you might have something for me."

"Yup. You still doing a few side jobs?"

"Got to. I'm a little low on cash right now," Zeke said, scanning the bar. "What you got?

"Took a call from a woman who knows Tommie," Ralph said, wiping down the bar near Zeke with a stained white towel. The bartender inched in closer and lowered his voice to a whisper. "Said she needed a bug, had to be electrical, and it had to look like an accident. No amateurs. Insurance job."

"Did you get a name?"

"No name. She wants to talk to the torch directly."

"Like I said, I need the money," Zeke said. "The bastards at the casino want some serious dough, and they want it now."

"Standard fee?" Ralph looked around the bar.

"You bet. If the job pans out, I'll give you $500."

"I'll give you a buzz if I hear back from her, so you're ready for the call."

"Thanks, buddy." Zeke pounded down the rest of his drink, left a twenty on the bar for Ralph, and headed out into the cool night.

Chapter 23

Thursday morning

When Nick left his apartment for work at 7:30 a.m., he discovered Jenni, his landlord's panting, slobbering Labrador retriever sitting outside his door. She jumped to her feet and greeted Nick by sticking her nose in his groin.

"Jenni, stop that. Bad dog," Nick said, protesting the overly familiar salutation probably for the hundredth time. "I can't go to work with wet pants again. Down, girl."

Nick patted the dog on the head. She immediately flopped down and rolled over so he could rub her belly. It was a daily ritual.

The commotion brought Nick's landlord, Mrs. Babcock, out of her lower-level apartment. "Nick, is that you? Didn't hear you come in last night. That's a good thing. It means you're not drinking as much these days. Is it the girlfriend, what's her name, Donna? Am I going to hear wedding bells one day soon?"

"No, her name is Tanya, and she's a good influence on me, Mrs. Babcock, but no wedding bells, please. My life is too complicated. But I've also been really busy the last couple weeks. I don't have time to feel like crap in the morning."

Nick gave Jenni a final scratch under her chin. The dog whined because she knew that signaled the end of her morning rub. The reporter bounded down the stairs and stopped in front of Mrs. Babcock's door, with Jenni right behind. The sweet older woman was standing in her doorway, wearing one of her more colorful red and gold neck-to-floor flannel bathrobes and sipping coffee. Jenni sat down at her feet.

"I saw in the paper where you were up at Mackinac Island. Pretty weird things happening up there, if you ask me."

"You're right, Mrs. Babcock," Nick said. "The story is not over yet. I just hope I can convince my bosses to let me keep writing about it. I've got to do a big-time sales job when I get into the office this morning."

He reached for the apartment building front door. "I'll see you later. If I get a chance to clean my place, maybe I'll bring Tanya by to say hello." The door closed behind Nick as Mrs. Babcock issued her standard farewell: "Have a blessed day!"

Nick drove to the newsroom, rehearsing his pitch to devote more time and energy to the Mackinac Island story. He would spill everything he knew about the events surrounding the death of Adam Townsend. He felt confident that once Drayton knew about the champagne bottle, the fancy perfume on the towel, and the stray hair, the editor would authorize more resources to pull the final story together.

Nick pulled into the parking lot and put his Firebird to rest in the spot reserved for Morton Reynolds. The reporter knew that the editor-in-chief would not be in the office before two o'clock.

This early, Morton would be at the Bay Area Chamber of Commerce Eye Opener Breakfast. The early-morning meetings were great opportunities to make connections and rub elbows with all the region's head honchos. It was one of the things that Morton was really quite good at.

From there the editor would make his usual stops, including a two-hour lunch at the Bay County Country Club and at least one round of golf. He was great at sifting through a crowd of business people, finding the top ass-kissers, and melding with them. He adhered to the idea that sycophants of a feather flock together. At some point in the afternoon, Morton would eventually make it into the newsroom. By then all the important decisions for *The Blade*'s editorial department would be made.

Nick whisked into the newsroom, looking to corner Drayton Clapper to make his pitch. No such luck. The local news editor was in a meeting in the pressroom, trying to work out a solution to the configuration of that day's newspaper. The publisher had decided to reduce the number of pages for the weekday papers—a result of the dismal Wednesday meeting that had been designed to find new sources of revenue, but only found more golfing opportunities for Tee-Time Tom.

Instead of finding Drayton, Nick found a note on his desk from the newsroom editor: "Nick, go to federal court this morning. Attorney for Denny McLain is appealing the latest ruling in the Peet Packing pension scandal."

"Hmm," Nick thought aloud. "Denny McLain, baseball great gone bad, is back in court. Well, okay, that should be pretty interesting."

Along with the note, Nick found a fat clip file chock-full of articles about McLain. The early clips trumpeted the athlete's baseball triumphs, including his two Cy Young awards and his thirty-one wins while leading the Detroit Tigers to the World Series in 1968.

But the file also showed the troubled athlete's connections to organized crime, gambling, and bookmaking schemes, his suspensions from major league baseball, and finally the scandal at Peet Packing.

It made Nick wonder if Zeke Zimmer had ever crossed paths with the Tigers legend.

The articles revealed that McLain and Roger Smigiel, co-owners of the Chesaning Peet Packing Co., were convicted in 1996 of stealing more than $2.5 million from the company's pension fund and laundering the money. The company had collapsed in 1995. More than two hundred workers lost their jobs and had no pensions to ease their fall. McLain maintained that he knew nothing of the shady financial deals at Peet, but the evidence proved otherwise. The conviction sent McLain to prison for six years, and the federal government garnisheed McLain's baseball pension and gave it to the former employees of Peet Packing. The hearing in federal court would deal with the possibility of appealing the judge's ruling.

Nick figured the hearing would take a couple of hours. McLain would probably not attend the meeting, but the reporter thought he might be able to corner the former pitcher's attorney and request an interview. Besides delivering a potent high hard one to right-handed hitters, McLain was famous for his outspokenness, outrageous commentary, and love of the limelight.

Even if he couldn't arrange an interview with the pitcher widely known as "Dennis the Menace," Nick thought the trip to federal court would be worthwhile. He would come back to the office, bang out a story for Friday's newspaper, make Drayton happy, and then try to connect with Zeke in the afternoon.

The reporter also hoped to get in touch with Chief Calkins again later that day. Nick wanted to use the chief as a sounding board for some of the theories that he'd discussed with Dave and Tanya the night before.

As he jotted down follow-up notes, Nick overheard a commotion on the copy desk. The debate focused on how much casket disaster information should be used in Dave's story about the Townsend funeral.

Dave had summarized the event, referring only to an "incident with the casket tipping from its pedestal at St. Boniface." He had not revealed the details.

"I heard that among his personal effects were a blowup doll, a small but sweet selection of porn, and booze and cigarettes," said one young male editor. "If that's true, then it should be in the story. People are talking about it all over town. If we don't include it, then it looks like either we didn't attend the funeral or we're covering up something."

The opposing argument urged discretion. "That's simply salacious detail that does nothing to inform or enlighten readers about the funeral," said an older woman on the desk. "Including more information only embarrasses the family and close friends of the deceased. We're not the *National Enquirer* or *People* magazine."

After several minutes of raised voices, mild swearing and name-calling, and the throwing of soft erasers and jumbo paper clips, Nick decided to offer his two cents.

"I attended the whole service—everything from the funeral home to the graveside prayers," Nick said. "The casket tipping was really just a small part of what happened—very incidental. And there was no porn collection. Overall, it was a very nice sendoff for Adam Townsend. I'd hate to see too much emphasis placed on an unfortunate accident that lasted five, maybe ten minutes. If you wanted to add a little more detail, I guess that would be okay. But I think Dave handled it right."

With that, Nick grabbed his notebook and headed for federal court. He hoped to find McLain's attorney before the TV cameras showed up.

Chapter 24

Thursday afternoon

Zeke sat in his living room watching soap operas. The melodramatic TV shows served as background noise while the electrician flipped through that day's edition of *The Bay City Blade* and waited for his phone call. Earlier, Ralph had buzzed him and indicated that he could expect a call from his potential new customer sometime midafternoon.

Zeke zipped through an article about new repairs ordered for Bay City's Liberty Bridge. He was curious about updates to the Liberty because his dad had been injured when the old Third Street Bridge, the span that preceded the Liberty, collapsed and fell into the Saginaw River back in the summer of 1976.

As Zeke flipped through the newspaper, his phone rang.

"Got this number from Ralph because I need an electrician for a job," a female voice said. "Am I calling the right guy?"

"Maybe. Ralph told me you needed a professional," Zeke said.

As he paused, Zeke could hear a voice over a loudspeaker in the background behind the woman's voice: "Final boarding call for Flight 7029." Wonder if it's Tri City Airport, he thought to himself.

"What kind of a job you got?" he said. "More important—how much you willing to spend?"

"The job is a house I own outside of Bay City. It's empty and for sale, but it ain't selling, so I got to unload it. Can you help me dispose of it?"

"What's the fee?"

"$3,000 up front, and $7,000 when the job is finished."

"How do you want it to go down? How much leeway do I have in getting rid of it?"

"The job has to look accidental—no flammables. No fuss, no muss. I need a quick turnaround on the insurance claim. Can you handle it?"

"No problem. I got a couple of ideas on how to do it. Would be good to get inside the place before I do the job. That possible?"

"You'll get a chance to check out the job before I need it done. I have to make sure nobody is in the house when you work on it."

"Thought you said it was empty." Zeke fidgeted, drumming his fingers on a table while he talked. He needed dough, but he didn't want a big job with possible complications.

"It is, but real estate agents are showing the place. The house has got a Realtor's lockbox on the front door. I'll give you the combination when you need it for a walk-through before the job—then all you have to do is go back and get it done when I give you the signal."

"Yeah, that should work." Zeke paused again to see if he could pick up any more background noise. This time, muffled garble over a loudspeaker was all that came through. "Can you give me a number to call you?"

"Nobody has my number. I'll call you when I'm ready to put the plan into place."

"Okay, sounds good."

After a slight pause, the woman lowered her voice, urging discretion and caution. "Now, not a word of this to anyone, including Ralphie Boy—before or after the job. If you run your mouth, this will blow back on you."

"Got it. I never talk about my work. Been doing this a long time."

Zeke clicked off the phone and leaned back in his soft, cushy chair. The job sounded easy. Empty house out in the sticks. No witnesses, nobody gets hurt. Easy as pie. Quick cash to keep the bookies off his back.

Chapter 25

Thursday afternoon

When Nick returned to the *Blade* newsroom from the courthouse, he found Drayton Clapper waiting by his desk. A young woman stood at his side. A tall and slender brunette, she was dressed in a modest sweater and skirt and sensible shoes. Long locks fell across both shoulders. Nick guessed it was Drayton's granddaughter or a great-niece.

"How'd the McLain hearing go?" the news editor asked, sitting on the corner of Nick's desk as the reporter plopped down in his chair.

"It didn't. Postponed," Nick said. He tossed his notebook on top of his desk. "But I did get a chance to talk with McLain's attorney. Said he thought we could arrange a jailhouse interview with Denny after the final hearing on his case. McLain doesn't want to say something controversial—stir the pot—before the judge rules."

"Let me know how that goes. Denny McLain is always good copy. People want to read about him no matter what he says."

"Is this your granddaughter, Drayton?"

"No, Nick. This is Greta Norris," Drayton said, standing and stepping sideways to complete the introduction. "Greta, this is Nick Steele."

The two shook hands and smiled politely.

"Nick, say hello to your new partner."

The smile on Nick's face turned upside down as he eyeballed the young woman from head to toe. "Drayton, Drayton. No, no. You know I don't do partners," Nick said, turning his full attention to his boss.

Nick complained that he did not like the idea of training a young person who might one day replace him. It was a growing trend across the newspaper industry. Get rid of the old coots with experience and replace them with recent college grads who would work for half the pay and benefits. Deep down, the reporter also worried that one of his future escapades outside the newsroom might result in a firing—without reinstatement. He would be permanently dumped and a youngster would get his desk and work.

"Nick, nobody has said anything about dumping you," the news editor said. "I expect you to be a team player and work with anyone that I assign to you."

"Okay, then. Where's the diaper bag and baby bottle?"

Now it was time for Greta's smile to flip upside down. She responded to the slight before Drayton, his mouth gaping, could say a word. "Diapers? Gosh, I would think an old-timer like you would be much more comfortable in Depends. And from the look of the bags under your eyes and the deep crevices in your face, the only bottle you're referring to is probably Jim Beam."

"Hold it, hold it, you two," Drayton said, hiking his arms up to waist height as if to separate the dueling reporters. "I'm not asking you two to get along and work together, I'm telling you to. It's an order."

Drayton's words brought a sudden cease-fire to the verbal sniping. Nick and Greta took deep breaths and folded their arms. Nick looked at the floor, trying to find a comfort zone.

"Nick, Greta is new to the staff, but she's a good reporter. All she needs is a boost and she'll be off and flying in this newsroom and across Bay City."

"Boost? As in booster seat?" Nick said, his voice flaring.

"That's it, gramps. I'm not taking any more shit from you," Greta said, again beating Drayton to the punch.

"Okay, hey, that's enough there," Drayton said, trying to halt the warfare. "Now, I want you to stop that crap. We have to work as a team. You two do not have to like each other, but you do have to work together and get along. Nick, I need you to show Greta the ropes."

"If I show her my ropes, you'll fire me for sexual harassment," Nick said, a big smile spreading across his face. "Dave's got a set of ropes in his apartment that I could show her."

"In your dreams," Greta said.

Nick liked her spunk—young, but feisty and a fairly quick wit. The veteran reporter decided to give her the benefit of the doubt. He took a deep breath and extended his right hand for a second shake. A truce was struck.

"Welcome to *The Blade*, Greta. You're going to love Bay City. It's a great town."

"Thanks, Nick. I hear it's a great place to live and a great place to party."

"You heard right."

Drayton smiled. "All right, then. That's more like it. Nick, walk her through the routine. Show her the cop shop, the courts, the county building. Take her on a tour of the business districts on each side of the river, and then run her through the neighborhoods. After that, take her to City Hall and introduce her to the mayor. We'll probably start her out covering city government. Greta, soak up everything you can. Nick's the best. That's why I'm connecting you two."

Drayton walked away from the reporters and Nick pulled out a chair and offered a seat to Greta. She took it without speaking.

"I've got an important phone call to make before we head out into the city," Nick said. "But first I might as well fill you in on how things work inside the newsroom."

The younger reporter took out her notebook, flipped it open, and jotted down the date and time. She also wrote Nick's name at the top of the sheet and circled it. "I'm ready."

"I don't know that you have to take notes about the newsroom stuff," he said. "But let's start at the top. The publisher is nicknamed the Castrator because she loves kicking around men whenever possible."

"I love her already."

"Not so fast. She also loves to kick around women. Anybody, really. She's tough and wants things done her way. Stay on her good side.

"The editor, Morton Reynolds, he's a spineless worm—only interested in keeping his job or getting himself lined up for a promotion at one of our sister papers. The Castrator walks all over him—nobody pays much attention to him."

Nick shuffled the files in his desk drawer. Mentioning Morton's name made him recall the editor picking up dog poop. He shook his head, then continued the rundown for Greta.

"The power in the newsroom is Drayton. Obviously you already know him. He hired you, so he likes you. Make him your closest ally. The copy desk is a mix of old dogs and young pups. Personally, I don't think the editors on the copy desk are as good now as they used to be, but they're okay.

"The newsroom reporters are mostly young, like yourself, some maybe a little older. Management is getting rid of us old farts."

"Look," Greta said. "I understand how you might be feeling a little uncomfortable with younger people moving into what's always been your space. But that's what's happening everywhere. I can't help it. I'm here to get my start in the business. I'll live lean and do what I have to do to get my career started."

"That's smart," Nick said. "Lots to learn in this newsroom and in this town. Bay City is a really good news town. Members of the city commission and county government are very contentious—they fight all the time. We've even had real fistfights break out.

"This newsroom is like a lot of others," he continued. "Remember to always feed the gaping maw—the news hole. It takes a lot of local stories to fill up our paper every day, so you've got to take care of that first so the editors will stay off your back."

Greta looked surprised. "I thought all stories were important, or there wouldn't be a reason to write them."

"That's what they teach you in J-School. Wrong. You gotta do a bunch of junk to make time for the gems. Once you've been around here for a while, you'll figure it out. But the quicker you do, the better stories you'll be working on, and the faster you'll be on your way to work at the *Detroit Free Press* or the *Trib* in Chicago or one of the really good papers."

"Well, okay, thanks for the advice," she said. "But if the *Free Press* and the *Trib* are the really good papers, what are you still doing in this newsroom? Drayton says you're hot shit, so why haven't you moved on?"

"Good question," Nick said, shifting in his seat uncomfortably. "It's complicated. I put my roots down in Bay City for my family, so now this is my home. Problem is, my family is gone now—wife is dead and my son is out West—but that's another story."

He suggested that Greta take some time to wander around the newsroom and introduce herself to anyone who did not look like they were pulling-their-hair-out busy. As she thanked him, pushed her chair back, and looked around the newsroom, Nick dialed the Mackinac Island cop shop and asked to speak with Chief Calkins.

Chapter 26

Thursday afternoon

The front desk officer put Nick on hold, explaining that the chief was finishing the processing for a shoplifter who was nabbed just outside one of the trinket shops on the main drag. Seemed that some poor fool had tried to walk off with a small replica of the Mackinac Bridge—made from toothpicks.

While on hold, Nick took an incoming call. It was Zeke Zimmer.

"Zeke, thanks for calling. When can we get together?"

"You still want to talk to me, ask more questions?"

"Yes, as soon as we can," Nick said. The reporter wanted to press Zeke some more to find out who might be hunting him.

"Well, how about a half hour from now. I'll meet you at O'Hare's. We can have a couple of pops and wrap this up."

"Sure, see you there."

Nick hung up with Zeke and went back to the Mackinac Island line, where a Billy Joel tune filled dead time with pop-rock noise.

The reporter leaned back in his chair and watched Greta work the newsroom. The rookie was definitely not shy. She moved from desk to desk, saying hello with a smile and shaking hands. Very confident, very friendly. She moved with ease and purpose, Nick thought. Drayton might have struck gold by hiring her. Working with her might work just fine—and he could definitely use some help sorting out the mess surrounding Zeke's life.

The chief's sudden voice on the line brought him around.

"Hey, Chief, it's Steele. Thought I'd check in with you for an update. "Have you gotten the tox screen back yet?"

"Yes, it came in this morning. I was going to give you a call. Nick, it came back negative. The general screen showed no foreign human substances."

Thanks to the heads-up he had received from his friend at the crime lab, Nick already knew the results of the screen, but he wanted the chief to explain her thinking about the status of the investigation. "Hmm. That's interesting. So where does that leave your probe?"

"I talked to the medical examiner briefly. I think he's going to stick with his original assessment—death resulting from an accidental fall."

"What about the puncture wound and the hole in the shirt?"

"He didn't want to discuss that. I think he's getting pressure to put this thing to bed and move on," the chief said. "He's saying he thinks they are purely coincidental, probably caused by a pin left from the wrapping paper and cardboard in his new shirt."

"What do you think of that theory?"

"I think it's bullshit," the chief said, "but it's not my call."

Nick loved the chief's candor. It was one of the things he admired about her. He hoped she would say that she was going to continue investigating Adam's death as a homicide, but he also realized that continuing on her own without the support of the medical examiner might result in her getting flak from the rich and powerful on the island.

Silence momentarily filled both ends of the phone. Nick thought for a moment and decided to unload on the cop.

"Well, here's what I'm thinking. Tell me if I'm crazy. I believe someone, probably a professional, mistakenly killed Adam Townsend. Zeke Zimmer was the real target and Adam just happened to get in the way."

"Good luck proving that, my friend," the chief said, her voice filled with skepticism. "Not enough evidence to support your theory."

"What about the blond hair in the room," Nick said, "and the bottle of booze that didn't belong there?"

"Not sure—maybe Adam's girlfriend did make it to the room but left early, or maybe it didn't get vacuumed from an earlier guest. And the champagne? Adam could have brought that with him to impress his girlfriend, who we have never been able to find, by the way.

"This is all circumstantial stuff," the chief said. "No witnesses. If this was a contract killing, don't you think somebody would have seen someone or something out of the ordinary?"

"Does this mean you're shelving the case?"

"So far we got nothing. Until I find some real evidence, I've got other concerns that need attention."

"But if this was a case of mistaken identity, then Zeke Zimmer is still walking around with a price on his head." Nick told the chief that he planned to continue chasing the story as if Zeke was the target. He said he hoped that combing through Zeke's past would turn up something helpful. The reporter added that he was supposed to meet with Zeke in twenty minutes for another interview.

"What should I tell Zeke? What advice would you give him?" Nick asked.

"I'd tell him to be careful—just in case."

"Any advice for me as I chase the story?" Nick asked.

"Follow the money, Nick. Ask him if anybody had a big insurance policy on his head. Start with the ex-wives. Also find out whom he owes money to. And keep revenge in mind when you're asking questions. Revenge is always ripe as a motive in any kind of killing."

The reporter thanked the chief for her advice and said he would keep her posted on developments in Bay City.

"Please do. Oh, and Nick, remember that all that background info I gave you—the puncture wound, the hole in the shirt, the blond hair, the strange bottle in the room—that was all off the record. You can't print that, and I'm going to hold you to it."

"I figured you would. Don't worry. I always honor my commitments."

Nick hung up the phone and spotted Greta talking to a photographer near the back of the newsroom. He waved at her to get her attention.

"Greta, come on. We gotta go."

Chapter 27

Thursday evening

Nick pulled open the Midland Street entrance to O'Hare's. While driving from the *Blade* newsroom to the West Side pub, he had updated Greta, informing the young reporter that he was going to delay her tour of Bay City because he needed to meet with Zeke Zimmer right away. "City Hall will still be there tomorrow, and so will Mayor Newsham."

Greta was fascinated by what Nick told her about the Mackinac Island story. She said she'd read his news reports about the death on the island, but the added background he gave her confidentially put the story in a different light. She was eager to meet Zeke, and Nick wanted to hear Greta's take on the electrician.

When Greta got inside the bar, she stood frozen, surveying the whole pub. The look on her face suggested she thought she'd walked into a den of iniquity. Her gaze focused on the upside-down Christmas tree that hung from the ceiling and the huge painting of Mona behind the bar.

"Why is there a Christmas tree hanging upside down? This is May. And why is that woman in the painting almost naked, with a 'You want it, you can have it' smile on her face? And spittoons, there are spittoons on the floor."

"Well, the spittoons are mostly filled with busted lottery tickets. And that's Mona," Nick said. "She's been here for as long as I can remember. Everybody loves her."

"Nice rack," Greta said. "What about the tree?"

"Just another tradition, like the Birthday Midget."

"The birthday what?"

"They bring in a midget on special nights. He's dressed in a big white diaper with brown stains on the back. He sings a lewd version of 'Happy Birthday' to women and sits on their laps."

"At worst, I think that may be illegal," Greta said. "At best, it's way over the line and crosses the boundaries of common decency."

"This is O'Hare's—more fun than a barrel of monkeys."

Sassy Sally approached their table and asked Nick if he wanted the usual.

"Got to see a photo ID, sweetie," Sally told Greta. "I don't know you yet, and you're definitely on the edge."

"I'll just have a Coke, light ice," Greta said.

Nick could not let the moment pass.

"It's the end of the day," he said. "You can have a drink if you want to. That is, if you're old enough to drink. Please tell me that you're twenty-one. You graduated from college. Wouldn't that make you at least twenty-two?"

"Okay, I'm twenty—if you must know," Greta said. "I skipped the fifth grade and the seventh. My school pushed me ahead. I didn't have much say in it. My parents thought it would be good."

"Oh my God. You really are a child."

Greta bit her lip and looked Nick dead in the eye. "Let's not go there again. It wasn't pretty the last time, and you're not going to like a return trip. But what does it really matter?" She shifted in her seat. "I had a fake ID in college. I partied," she continued. "The real question is why we are meeting a news source in a bar to begin with. Shouldn't we be in a conference room at *The Blade*?"

"You make a good point, but the source of information suggested the location for the interview," Nick said. "Sometimes it's better to meet people in friendly locations where they'll feel comfortable talking about uncomfortable subjects. Standing right up there at the bar is the Bay County prosecutor. Now doesn't he look comfortable?"

"You mean that guy slouched over that dark-haired tramp? Looks like he's turning her ear into finger food."

"That, my dear, is a supervisor at the women's shelter in Bay City. She runs the place—it's where abused women and children go for refuge."

"Looks like she could use a little refuge herself. That guy is an animal. Look, his hands are all over her."

Greta's statement was so loud that half the men and women in O'Hare's turned to see what was happening. As they did, the dark-haired woman gave the prosecutor a shove in the chest with her left hand and a swat across the face with her right. She grabbed her purse from the bar and headed for the pub's back door, where she ran into Zeke Zimmer, who was just coming into the establishment.

"What's the rush, sweetie?" the electrician asked. "Can I get you a drink—wanna sit on my lap for a while?"

"Zeke, you bastard," she said, stopping to slap his face with her quick right hand, which must have been hurting by now. "What about your wife? Did you forget about her?"

"Well, she's a little pissed at me these days because I took a little gambling side trip last weekend," Zeke said. "We had a funeral to go to, and then she took off for her mother's—and I don't think she's coming back."

"You guys. I just can't believe the men in this town."

Zeke was still holding the right side of his jaw when he came upon the prosecutor, whose face was red and slightly swollen. The two didn't speak, though they knew each other by reputation. They simply looked each other up and down and then let their gazes drift away.

"Hiya, Nick," Zeke said as he pulled out a chair at the table. "You beat me here. And who's this lovely little filly—she your granddaughter, Nick?"

"Oh my God," Greta said. "Not you, too. No, I'm not related to him. My name is Greta Norris. I'm a new reporter at *The Blade*, and Nick is showing me around. I never envisioned that I'd end up in the bowels of Bay City my first day on the job."

"Well, she's got spit, Nick. I'll give her that." A grin the width of a football field wedged on Zeke's face as he looked Greta up and down, stopping to admire her ample bosom and lean, shapely legs.

"Hey, up here, buster. My eyes are up here. If you want to talk to me, you have to look me in the eye, not rake my body like I'm a slab of beef ready for the grill."

Nick interceded to get the interview on track. He asked Zeke if he'd had a chance to think about their last discussion.

"Jeez, I thought of a few names, but I really don't think they hate me enough to kill me," the electrician said, sipping the rum and Coke Sally had brought to the table. "I owe the Indian casinos the most dough, but lots of people owe them big-time. They do all their scalping at the craps tables these days."

"Listen, I talked to the cop up at Mackinac Island today," Nick said. "It sounds like they are closing the case, or at least letting it sit for a while. Right now they are going to call Adam's death the result of an accidental fall.

"But I told her you and I were meeting tonight," Nick added. "She said you need to be careful. She also suggested we find out who you owe, or who wants revenge against you. Or anybody got a big insurance policy on you?"

Zeke sat for a moment, swigging his drink in short, quick gulps. The glass was already about half-gone. Greta watched closely—clearly trying to read body language, not study his body.

"Wife Number Three used to have a policy on me," Zeke said. "If I recall, it was good for $500K, but I haven't talked to her in a while, and she's in no hurry to talk to me."

"Wow, that's a pretty big insurance policy. Would you mind if I talked to her?" Nick said. "Just a casual interview."

"Go for it, but wear a hard hat. She likes to throw shit."

"My buddy, Dave Balz, has got her address and telephone number," Nick said. "I'll probably try to connect with her this weekend."

Greta touched Nick's outstretched arm on the table. "May I ask a question?"

"Fire away," Nick said. Zeke nodded in agreement.

"Nick mentioned on the way here that you earned high praise and recognition for union activity—I believe it was in Flint. What did you do to win an award?"

Nick and Zeke looked at each other. Good question.

"I was a UAW member working in one of the General Motors shops," Zeke said. "One of the big assembly plants. I was stuck on third shift and running routine maintenance. One night I discovered an electrical box in one of the supervisor shacks. Real simple. Set of buttons that let them speed up the assembly line or slow it down any time they wanted."

Nick jotted notes as fast as his pen would fly.

"Why is that significant?" Greta asked.

"Well, the speed of the line and the number of people working the line, in addition to the number of parts produced, are all negotiated in the local contract," Zeke said. "If you change the speed and the output without changing the number of people working, then that's a big-time contract violation. So I got an award for pointing it out."

The three sat at the table in silence. By now O'Hare's was filling with the after-work crowd. Voices rose and the jukebox had been turned up to fuel the hum and electricity in the bar. To make himself heard, Nick leaned in toward Zeke so that Greta could not hear the sound of his voice.

"Okay, Zeke. My buddy Dave and I are still going to nose around some and see what we can find out. In the meantime, be careful where you go and what you do."

"Thanks, Nick, but I'm not going to start acting all paranoid. If this really was some kind of a contract killing, I'd already be dead. The pros don't mess around. Checking under my car before I start it or dodging shadows in the alley—that's not my style."

With that, Zeke jumped up and shook Nick's hand. Then he reached for Greta's, pulled her hand to his lips, and kissed it. "A real pleasure meeting you, Greta."

"Likewise," the young reporter said. When the electrician turned and walked away, Greta rubbed the back of her hand instinctively. "I really, really do not like that man," she said. "He makes my skin crawl. I think most of what he said was just crap. You can tell when someone is lying. Did you notice the lack of eye contact when he was talking about his gambling? His facial expressions and his gestures didn't match what was coming out of his mouth."

"He's not a choirboy, that's for certain," Nick said, wondering what Greta's assessment would be if she knew about Zeke's multiple affairs and penchant for hookers. "We can talk more about this tomorrow. We'll also do your tour. But I've got a dedication that I have to go to over at Central High School, so I'll connect with you after that."

Chapter 28

Friday morning

As Nick and Dave pulled into the parking lot next to the field house at Central High School, they noticed a small group of people gathered near the entrance to the facility. Early-morning rain had made the parking lot sloppy. The smell of earthworms filled the air. The reporters pulled their jackets tight as they walked toward the group, dodging puddles.

Before today's ten o'clock ceremony, the impressive high school sports facility had been named Joselyn Field House in honor of long-time school board president Charles Joselyn.

But that was about to change, largely because of the series of articles that Nick and Dave had done about the scandal at the school.

A large purple and gold drape—the school colors—covered the sign above the entrance to the building. It hid the new name: "Central Field House—Home of the Wolves."

A podium stood on the top step in front of the entrance. A handful of administrators and front office personnel milled around, waiting for the ceremony. There were no TV cameras, but two reporters from local radio stations were on hand. A *Bay City Blade* photographer arrived to capture an image of the event for the newspaper.

Two women in their mid-twenties approached Nick and Dave as they moved toward the front steps of the field house. One asked if the two were reporters from *The Blade.*

The inquiry surprised Nick. He braced himself, figuring the upcoming conversation would go one of two ways. Either the women were relatives or friends of Charlie Joselyn and wanted to rip into the two, or they were victims of the scandal and wanted to thank the reporters. Nick was relieved to learn it was the latter.

"My name is Lilly, and this is Justine," the taller of the two said. They shook hands with the reporters, smiling politely but avoiding direct eye contact. "We just wanted you to know how much we appreciate what you did. We never told anyone at the time—we were too afraid, or too stupid, to speak up."

"No, you weren't stupid at all," Nick said. "You were just young and in a very awkward situation. Darrin Appleton violated his trust as an educator. He hurt a lot of young girls while he was in charge of the marching band here."

Appleton had been band director at Central for eight years. While in that position of authority and power over students, he seduced more than a dozen young women—some as young as thirteen. He had sex with them in the band room, in his office, and at his home.

Bay City school officials—the school board president, the Central superintendent, and the principal—could no longer ignore the abuse and confronted Appleton. They insisted that he resign his position and leave the school immediately. When he did, one of the young women he had been seeing took her life. Later it was learned that she had been pregnant.

The parents of the young woman complained to authorities and school officials about the abuse, but she had reached the age of consent. At the time, Michigan law did not make such contact illegal. Several parents of the band director's victims became outraged—and one parent, who had access to the medical prescription records of the school officials, plotted revenge. Over time, the parent altered the prescriptions of the superintendent and principal. The changes in prescriptions made it look like the school officials died from heart attacks—but they hadn't. They'd been slowly poisoned and killed by the parent.

That's what happened to Tanya's dad. But while the parent bent on revenge was in the process of changing Charlie Joselyn's prescriptions, Nick had picked up on the story. After their investigation, Nick and Dave wrote a series of articles about how school officials had turned a blind eye to the abuse because they were in the middle of a millage campaign to raise money to build Joselyn Field House.

Needless to say, public outrage over the episode caused many changes within the school district. Joselyn survived the attempt on his life, but the scandal and resulting public shame took their toll on the aging educator. A few months later he died from natural causes. That's when the school district decided to change the name of the field house.

What school officials could not do, however, was extend any punishment to Darrin Appleton. The charismatic teacher had simply moved on to become band director at other schools in other states. When Nick and Dave tracked him down in other communities, he pulled up his stakes and left town.

But the women who approached Nick and Dave on this morning outside the field house had information that excited the two newsmen.

Lilly nudged Justine with her elbow. "Show him the letters."

The slender young woman opened her purse and pulled out a dozen missives from the band director. Justine, it turned out, had stayed in touch with Appleton. Though they had not seen each other in years, they had continued to correspond. The band director sent her notes and cards each year on her birthday and at Christmastime, the young woman said. The latest birthday card for Justine had come in April. The return address on the envelope indicated that it had been sent from Knoxville, Tennessee.

"You were always my favorite," he wrote. "My heart longs for the day when we can be together again." Each note, Justine said, was signed the same way: "Soon we will once again be united. Love always, Darrin."

Nick and Dave were stunned.

Nick spoke first. "Justine, could we take these back to the office to make copies?"

She nodded.

"Have you had any verbal contact with Appleton?" Dave asked.

"Not since he left town," Justine said. "I really don't know why I responded to them at all, probably foolish. But he just had that way about him—guess I wanted to believe what he was saying. I saved the notes. Lilly and I, well, we were hoping you would know what to do with them."

"You bet we do," Nick said. "Thanks. We'll make copies, and Dave will return them to you today. We've been trying to track him down since last fall. This is a really big help. Thank you so much. We will take it from here."

The loudspeaker crackled as D.L. Chambers, the new superintendent at Central, addressed the small gathering. The school leader did not mention the scandal or Charlie Joselyn. He kept his remarks short and to the point. Chambers said he was honored to give the field house new life and purpose. With that, he pulled the drape and revealed the new name.

A smattering of applause marked the occasion. Coffee and doughnuts were waiting inside the Central Field House cafeteria.

After his speech, Chambers sought out Nick and Dave and shook their hands.

"Look, I want you to know that this was a very painful time in the school's history," he said. "It caused Central plenty of embarrassment and unwanted attention. Many of our alumni wanted to condemn you and your work for hurting the school.

"But I offer my thanks," the superintendent continued. "This caused a lot of self examination—not only within our school district, but across all the districts in the county. I think our students have benefited from it. So again, thank you very much. Now please go away and leave us alone."

The reporters laughed. Nick thanked the school leader for his kind words and the invitation to the ceremony, and returned to the newspaper office to write the story about the renaming of the field house for Saturday's newspaper. But he did not plan to reveal what he had learned about the whereabouts of Appleton from talking with Lilly and Justine. That would have to wait. The Mackinac Island story now sat atop Nick's priority list. Adam Townsend needed justice, and a professional killer might have Zeke Zimmer in a set of cross hairs.

Dave had set up interviews with Zeke's ex-wives. Hopefully they would provide key information that might reveal who wanted the electrician dead.

Chapter 29

Friday afternoon

Connie Bilarski peeked out her front window, waved, and then opened the door to let Nick and Dave into her small but comfortable South End Bay City home.

"Hi, I'm Nick Steele and this is Dave Balz. We're from *The Blade*."

"Yes. From your appearance, I didn't think you were selling Bibles," Connie said, holding the door open. "Come in. Please leave your shoes at the door. I just had the carpet cleaned."

The short, stocky woman led Nick and Dave through the house to the kitchen, where she said she was cooking. Her graying brown hair was cut short. If she had makeup on, it was faint. But her nails were polished and she wore delicate, tasteful jewelry. She escorted them to a small wooden table in a large nook just off to the side of the stove.

Nick sniffed the air. "Hmm. Let me guess. Chicken noodle soup?"

"With dumplings, Polish style," Connie said. "It's called *rosul.* The secret to the recipe is fresh dill. It needs to simmer for at least two hours more, or I would offer you some."

Instead Connie placed a plate of *kolaczki* in the center of the table, where a pot of black coffee steamed. "Please try these Polish cookies. I made them this morning. Raspberry filling."

Nick and Dave dug in, pouring themselves cups of coffee and snagging enough pastry to fill their round bellies. Nick nudged Dave to slow down. His buddy sounded like a hound wolfing down a bowl of Purina.

When Dave first called Connie to request a meeting, she had been hesitant to let two reporters into her life. Nick figured she wasn't keen to open up about a man and a part of her life that she would really rather forget.

After she'd spent time thinking about it, however, curiosity seemed to have gotten the best of her. Now Connie told the reporters she had read Nick's stories in *The Blade* about the misidentification on Mackinac Island. She wondered why two reporters would ask her for an interview. What had Zeke gotten himself into now?

Dave started the conversation, mostly because Nick was still stuffing his face.

"As I mentioned on the phone, we want to talk with you about Zeke and Adam Townsend," he said. "Zeke was a lifelong friend of Adam's, and we're doing a follow-up. Just making some inquiries. Nick has interviewed Zeke, and he said it would be okay for us to contact you."

Connie nodded. She seemed willing to help. "Zeke and Adam were almost like brothers—very close. Adam was the calming influence on Zeke. I only wish they'd spent more time together.

"Like everybody else in town, I was flabbergasted when it turned out that Adam was dead and Zeke was still alive. But I was not surprised that Zeke was off somewhere gambling. If he's breathing, he's betting on something."

Nick paused between bites of cookie. "Can you tell us a little about your life together?"

Connie hesitated at first, as though she did not want to reveal too much to the reporters. She finally began by telling Nick and Dave that she would help them with information, but she did not want to be quoted in the newspaper in any way, shape, or form. She said that her friends and neighbors would take any comments she made the wrong way.

Connie had been Wife Number Three, succeeding women who, like her, thought Zeke's flair for wild and risky living could be tamed. She had seen Zeke as a handsome, funny, smart guy who could lead her in a walk through life that would be full of energy, adventure, and romance. Instead she found a life of mystery filled with shady characters, boozing, gambling, womanizing, and danger. She discovered that Zeke was not the man she thought he was—always walking a tightrope that had him one step on either side of the law. When she finally caught Zeke in bed with one of her so-called friends, she said, it was the last straw.

"If you talked with Zeke about our life together and our separation, then he probably told you about the insurance policy," Connie said. Their divorce had been relatively quick and mostly painless, but the one thing that she had insisted on in the final divorce decree was that Zeke maintain a life insurance policy worth half a million bucks. Because of Zeke's wild, unpredictable ways, she told the reporters, she was certain the policy was as good as gold. Sooner or later his dangerous life would catch up to him, and she would receive a final kiss good-bye from Zeke in the form of greenbacks.

"When I saw in the paper that Zeke had fallen at the hotel, I was shocked," Connie said. "But let me tell you, I've got my insurance agent on speed dial, and I called him right away."

"The policy is good for a half-mil, right?" Nick said. "That's kind of unusual."

"Maybe, but I knew Zeke had extra money," she said. "One day I found two shoe boxes full of hundred-dollar bills in his workshop. I asked him about it. He said he got lucky with the ponies, but there's no telling where that money came from. He was involved in so much.

"I wanted the big policy because I thought that was the only way I would ever get compensated for seven very difficult years of marriage to him. I would never wish death upon anyone, but when the Grim Reaper found him I wanted what was coming to me."

Nick and Dave looked at each other. Clearly neither wanted to ask this sweet, hospitable woman the big question. Nick knew it would be incredibly indelicate to suggest that their host had hired an assassin. Nevertheless, Dave plunged ahead. Subtlety had never been his strong suit.

"When you say you would never wish death upon anyone, does that mean you would not hire someone to kill Zeke for the insurance loot?"

The awkward silence lasted what seemed like an hour, but was only a moment. The three checked each other's facial expressions. Connie broke the tension with a belly laugh, which made Nick and Dave join in the merriment.

"Ha ha ha, for a minute there I thought you were serious," Connie said, taking her glasses off to wipe the tears from her eyes. "That's a good one. Ha ha ha."

When the three stopped laughing, Dave plunged ahead again.

"But I was serious. Have you ever thought about having him killed to collect the insurance?"

Nick kicked Dave in the leg under the table. His buddy had gone too far.

Connie straightened up in her chair and lashed back at the reporter. "I don't like where this is going," she said. "Zeke and I have had our differences, and there certainly is no love lost between us. But I am absolutely insulted that you would suggest I would want him killed—for money."

Nick stepped in, hoping to keep the two reporters from being booted out of the house. "Actually, what my friend meant is that this is a very big and unusual insurance policy, and when we asked Zeke about who might want to see him dead, your name came up."

"Oh, now that breaks my heart," Connie said, sadness returning to her face. "Did Zeke really say that?"

Nick dodged the question and asked one of his own. "Did Zeke have a lot of enemies—I mean real serious enemies, people who would like to see him hurt or even taken out?"

"Zeke has lived the kind of life that can make people very, very angry," Connie said. "You can't drink and gamble and carry on like he did without stepping on some pretty big toes."

Connie's mood took a downturn. Nick could see the emptiness in her face. She started to weep softly. Dave reached for a handkerchief in his pocket, but Nick stopped him. "Keep that filthy snot rag in your pocket," he whispered to his friend while pulling a clean, monogrammed linen from his jacket pocket. He held it up for Connie and she took it, dabbing her eyes.

"Sorry, guys," she said, clearly trying to regain her composure by taking deep breaths and swallowing hard. "Your visit and these questions are bringing a lot of old hard feelings to the surface. I guess I don't understand why you want to know if someone hates Zeke enough to hurt him."

Nick looked at Dave before responding. "We're working on a hunch here, but we think there may be a possibility that the Mackinac Island death was not an accident.

"If that turns out to be the situation," Nick continued, "then the case of mistaken identity might mean the killer took out Adam Townsend instead of the intended target, Zeke. We think there may be a hit man out there looking to complete some unfinished business, namely taking out your ex."

"Oh my God! That's a pretty wild story with a lot of ifs built into it," Connie said. "Wow. Wow. Wow. I'm trying to wrap my head around that idea."

Connie poured Nick and Dave some more coffee and filled a cup for herself. Nick could see that she was quickly pulling herself back together. He took out his notebook and pen and asked about Zeke's gambling enemies.

"I think it would be easier to list the people he doesn't owe money to. Why sugarcoat it—he's an addict. Very compulsive," Connie said, settling back into her seat. "Zeke would bet on the sun rising if he could get the right odds."

But as far as she knew, she told the reporters, most of the bets were relatively small-time. She said he played cards, bet at the racetrack, and gambled on sports—both college and pro.

"They used to have a secret card game out at the Bay County Country Club—high stakes, all the big rollers in town. Zeke finally got banned from the tables there. Same thing on Columbus Avenue.

A bar on Columbus used to run card games, dice, and craps after hours. Players would park their cars on neighborhood side streets and walk to the bar. After two in the morning, they covered the windows, bolted the doors, and broke out the games. You had to have a password to get into the place."

Dave acknowledged that he'd been to the Columbus Avenue games, but thought the Bay County Country Club game was folklore. "But do you know if any of the players at those games would want him dead?" he asked.

"Don't think so, but you should probably talk to some of the guys he played with. Call Nick LePaige. I think he's still living over in the Banks area on the West Side. French Catholic, I think."

Nick noticed Connie had been glancing up at the clock on the wall more frequently. He looked at his watch and decided they should wrap up the conversation, but ask to call back later.

Another soft kick to Dave's leg indicated that Nick was taking the interview into its final lap.

"Connie, we really appreciate you spending this time with us," Nick said. "I have just one more set of questions, and then we'll get out of your hair."

"Okay, shoot," she said. "How did you know I had a hair appointment this afternoon? Boy, you reporters are good."

Nick wanted to know more about Zeke's days working at the GM plant in Flint. He asked Connie what those days were like for them.

"Oh, you'd have to ask Wife Number Two," she said, sipping from her cup again. "I came into the picture right at the end of his days in Flint. He was trying to transfer to the Chevy plant here in Bay City when we met.

"Do you want to hear that story—how we met?" Connie added, her eyebrows dancing on her forehead as she put down her cup.

Nick knew this was going to be good by the way she reacted to her own suggestion. He and Dave smiled at the woman and nodded.

"Well, I was bowling in a league at Monitor Lanes—over on

South Euclid," she said, revving up to deliver the story. "I was hot that night, rolling way above my average. I didn't know Zeke then, but I had seen him playing at Monitor before. I always thought he looked like Gregory Peck—so suave, so sophisticated. I could tell he had his eyes on me. I could just feel it. After his game was finished, he strolled over to watch us finish our game.

"First thing he did was pull five twenties out of his wallet and holler, 'I got a hundred bucks right here that says this blue-eyed beauty with the great legs finishes the game with strikes on every roll. Who wants the action?' "

Connie said Zeke's proclamation caused gasps in the small crowd because a hundred bucks was a lot of dough. She said one man stood up to take the bet. His wife was on the team playing against Connie.

"It energized me," she continued, grabbing the edge of the table with both hands. "I caught on fire right then and there. With Zeke and everybody in the place watching my every move, I went to work. Every time I got up to get my ball, Zeke led the cheers. I finished with all strikes. Zeke gave me a big hug and asked if I wanted to celebrate. We partied all night, and three months later, we heard wedding bells. The rest is, as they say, history."

Nick and Dave were smiling like they'd just grabbed the last piece of pie in a pastry shop. They both applauded lightly, and Connie stood up, took a bow, and curtsied. The telling of the story, which seemed very well rehearsed from at least a thousand tellings, illuminated Connie's face. Nick and Dave could see what Zeke saw in this delightful woman.

When she took her seat, Nick tried taking her back to the final set of questions. "Let me ask you the Flint question this way. When Zeke pulled out of Flint, did you get the sense that he was running from something? Did he get in serious trouble down there? Why did he come back to Bay City?"

"The auto plants are a tough place to work," Connie said, picking up her coffee cup again. "Zeke used to talk about everything that went on in the Flint plants. He always said you could get anything you wanted inside the plants that was outside on the streets. Drugs, booze, gambling, and the car parts that got stolen—Zeke said it was unbelievable."

"But do you think he was in trouble down there?" Nick asked again.

"Something happened in Flint that spooked him," she said, speaking slowly and staring at her coffee cup. "I know he was big in the union—got an award for his activity. But I'm not sure exactly what it was. All I knew was that he was in a big hurry to move back to Bay City. I was happy because we were trying to start a life together. But he always woke up with nightmares. I don't know what it was. Wife Number Two might be able to help more."

When they got back to the newsroom, they found Drayton Clapper standing at Nick's desk, his arms folded and resting atop his round, bucket-shaped belly. "Steele, where the hell have you been?"

Instantly Nick realized he'd forgotten all about Greta and her tour. "Ah, ah, sorry, Drayton. I got tied up and didn't get back here as early as I'd hoped to this afternoon. Where's Greta?"

The news editor stepped in close to Nick and Dave—obviously invading their space to sniff for a hint of booze. "You two been out drinking? Tell me the truth, no bullshit now."

Dave took the offensive with the newsroom boss, something he could do because he was retired and working on assignment. "Why, Drayton, I am offended. How could you possibly accuse us of such despicable behavior?"

"Because I know you two, that's how," the editor said, lightening up. "And I know that's what I would do if I had the run of the town like you do."

Nick scanned the newsroom. He didn't see Greta at any of the desks or in any of the side offices. Just as he was about to ask Clapper about her again, Greta walked into the newsroom with another reporter, Beth McKenna. When the women spotted Nick, they both gave him the finger simultaneously.

"Uh oh, you had Beth take Greta on the tour?" Nick said, turning away from the agitated women.

"Somebody had to get her out there, and you were nowhere to be found," Drayton said. "From now on, check in and let me know where you're at and what you're doing, okay? Where were you, by the way?"

Dave stepped in and rescued Nick. "We had some more follow-up to do on the Bay City Central ceremony from this morning. Boy, that turned out to be something. Nick's going to have a great story for you for tomorrow's paper. The radio guys were there, but they didn't get the interviews that we got."

Drayton looked at Nick for assurance. The reporter nodded at his boss. He would use some of the comments from school officials, but not the information he had picked up on the band director. He had plans for that. In fact, he'd been thinking about ways he and Dave might be able to use Greta's youth and attractive appearance to chase the band director later.

"I'm going to get going on it right away," Nick said. "But let me apologize to Greta and Beth first—then I'll start writing. You'll have something to read shortly."

After Nick finished kissing butt and mending fences with Greta and Beth, he returned to his desk to finish writing the story about the ceremony at Central and the renaming of the field house. It would be fast work, and then he could turn his attention back to the island story—but it would be on his own time.

Nick and Dave had made plans to meet at O'Hare's later. Nick planned to invite Tanya to the skull session because he wanted her input. She had a great analytical mind. He needed help trying to figure out which way to chase down Zeke Zimmer's very complex and very dark background.

Chapter 30

Friday afternoon

Each of the public telephone stations near the entrance of Detroit Metropolitan Airport was occupied with travelers trying to make connections.

While Charlie Marx waited for at least two phones side by side to open up, she watched the flight deck from an adjacent window wall. She loved watching the giant birds land and take off.

But when a stranger approached and stood a few feet away to watch the same thing, Charlie turned and walked away. Once she'd walked a safe distance, she looked over at the man. Was he watching her? Did he get a good look at her face? Could he identify her if asked to by police?

After a few moments the stranger, dressed in tan slacks and a dark jacket, moved in the opposite direction. He walked away, heading toward an exit. He did not even glance her way. The paid assassin breathed deeply and relaxed. People in her profession could never be too careful with strangers. The next one who came along could lead to her downfall.

Three phone stations in a row were now open. Charlie walked to the center one and dialed a number.

"Zeke here. What's up?"

"Hi. You still looking for side jobs?"

She could hear Zeke open and fumble through a desk drawer. The sound of a paper tearing from a tablet followed. Then silence before Zeke finally responded to her question.

"You bet. I was wondering when you were going to call back. Ready to move ahead on that job?"

Charlie described the empty house in the country and gave Zeke the address. She suggested he go there midafternoon the next day, park in the driveway, and walk around the house, examining it as if he were a prospective buyer.

"As I mentioned earlier, the place is for sale," she said. "If anyone sees you, they'll just think you're looking at it to buy. The lockbox is on the front door. The combination is one-nine-five-two. Once you're inside, you can size up the job."

"Now, you're sure no one is using the place, right?" Zeke asked.

"That's correct. I own it and I've got to get rid of it," she said, getting impatient with Zeke. The killer did not like repeating herself, but Zeke seemed to need reassurance. "The Realtors haven't been able to unload it for me, so that's why I'm calling you. But it's got to look accidental, or the insurance company won't pay. Got it?"

"I know all about insurance companies. Those bastards are tough."

"Once you've got a plan of disposal all worked out, we'll fine-tune the final details," she said. "I'll call you at the bar Monday afternoon. For your planning purposes, our target date will be Tuesday."

Zeke asked about payment.

"Go outside and check your mailbox," she said. "You'll find an unmarked envelope. Open it. Wrapped inside two sheets of blank paper you'll find a thousand bucks—all twenties and fifties. That's good-faith money."

"Oh, okay."

Charlie could hear relief in his voice. The idea of cash in small bills would put his mind at ease—that's why she had put it there.

"Hmm. Twenties and fifties. I'm going to have some fun tonight."

Charlie was overcome by a feeling of disgust. Plus, she was afraid he might use the cash to go on a drinking, gambling bender and then fall out of her cross hairs again. She let him have it, ordering him to keep it together.

"Try not spending it all in a card game or on whores, okay? I need you to stay cool and under the radar until you've finished this job for me. Then you can do anything you want. Got it?"

"Oh, you bet. I'm all business."

"Be at the bar Monday afternoon, and we'll take the next step."

Charlie backed away from the bank of phones and scanned her surroundings again. Nothing unusual. The airport hummed with its typical activity. She felt confident that no one was watching, monitoring her activity or movements.

The professional killer checked her watch. The call she was expecting would not come for another ten minutes. She spotted a sandwich and drink café off to the side, not far from the entrance of the terminal, and walked to the self-serve drink bar to get a small coffee. After paying, she walked back to the phones and waited for the fourth phone to ring. She hoped it would come when no one was nearby, but knew that could change in an instant. Conducting her business in an airport terminal gave her cover, but anybody—including a plainclothes cop or a federal agent—could approach and use the phones at any time.

Finally the call came. It was three minutes late. She let it ring a second time before picking up. "Yes?"

"This Charlie?"

"You got her."

"Please tell me that you're ready to finish the job," a raspy male voice said, stopping as if to take in a gulp of air. "I want this done as soon as possible."

"A new plan is set." Charlie glanced around again to see if anyone was trying to eavesdrop on the conversation. "The job will be finished Tuesday night. It's already in motion."

"Wonderful. You know how long I've waited for this," the voice said. "I saved money for nearly twenty years so I could hire you."

"I know we had a setback on the island, but that's all died down now," the killer said, trying to reassure her client. "I watched the news on four different stations last night and there wasn't a word about it. People have already forgotten what happened up there."

"Have you been reading *The Blade*?" the voice asked. "A *Blade* reporter has been dogging the death up there pretty hard. Friends of mine say he's asking a lot of questions—getting nosy about Zeke's past. We don't want him to get too close."

"Don't worry about him," she said. "I've dealt with the nosy types before. All he needs is a little scare, and he'll go back to the puff stuff. I've got something in mind for him."

"Well, be careful," the voice said. "You've already bungled the job once—don't make another mistake."

Charlie hated being criticized about her work. She was a professional. The word "bungled" made her stomach tighten and churn.

There was a momentary pause and silence while she searched for the next words, but the raspy voice spoke first. "After reflection, I'm glad Zeke didn't go down on the island. That death would have been too quick for him. Promise me this—please make Zeke suffer. I want this to be very painful for him, and I want him to know that he's going to die before it happens. Make this right by me, and I'll make sure you get a bonus."

"A bonus is always good," Charlie said. "Thanks, and I'll get this done right. He will get what he so richly deserves."

"I would like to talk to you again Tuesday before you do the job. Will that work?"

"Yes, but it will have to be early in the afternoon," she said. "I don't want to be late for my appointment with Mr. Zeke Zimmer."

"Lovely, simply lovely. And will you tell me how it's going to happen and an approximate time, so that I can get ready to celebrate?"

"Up to you. I will expect final payment on Wednesday morning," she said. "The misfire on this job screwed up my schedule."

"You will find your money Wednesday morning in the same place and in the same manner in which you found the advance payment. Believe me, it will be the most joyful money I ever spent."

"Talk to you Tuesday."

* * *

Both hung up at the same time. The man with the raspy voice leaned back in his wheelchair and smiled. Judgment day was near for Zeke, and that made the elderly man happy.

Chapter 31

Friday evening

After Nick finished writing, he headed home to shower and change before meeting Tanya and Dave at O'Hare's. The threesome had much to discuss. It would be a good opportunity to decide how they were going to continue chasing the Zeke Zimmer story.

The reporter ran up the stairs to his apartment. He thought it was odd that Mrs. Babcock's door was closed. Jenni, the slobbering, drooling lab, was nowhere to be seen or heard. It wasn't like Mrs. Babcock to be out on a Friday night. Nick wondered if she and Jenni were visiting a relative.

As he turned the key in his door, Nick could hear music coming from inside. The reporter was sure that he had turned off the stereo when he left that morning. Perhaps he'd left the TV on and forgotten about it.

Nick opened the door. All the lights were off. The apartment was dark except for a soft light shining in his bedroom. That's where the music was coming from, too. He stepped inside, one foot at a time, scanning the darkened living room and kitchen as he walked through his place. He sniffed the air quietly. Something was burning. His place didn't usually smell this good.

"Hello, who's here?" he asked, stopping near the dining room table to pick up an empty flowerpot just in case he needed it. It was the only thing he could see that was heavy and that he could swing.

No answer.

Nick, armed with the ceramic club, inched forward toward his open bedroom door. "I'm warning you. I've got a weapon and I know how to use it. Reveal yourself, and you won't be harmed."

Silence, except for the soft music. Nick's heart pounded. He was afraid the intruder could hear his labored breathing and the sound of his heart jumping out of his chest. He moved closer and stood just outside the door. "This is your last warning. My weapon is loaded and ready. Step out now."

As he stepped into the doorway of his bedroom, Nick lifted the pot above his head, ready to deal a crippling blow to the invader—whoever it might be.

"Hi, Nick. What took you so long?" Tanya said, sitting up in his bed. When she did, the sheet that had been tucked under her neck fell to her lap, revealing her naked body. She stretched and yawned, then ran her fingers through her long blond hair.

Nick's jaw dropped to his chest and the pot fell to his side. "Tanya, what the hell are you doing here?"

"Waiting for you. You've been on the run so much we've had no time together since Mackinac Island. Mrs. Babcock let me in. I told her I wanted to clean the place. I wanted to surprise you."

"That you did," Nick said. His eyes darted around the room. A bottle of white wine chilled in a bucket. Four candles, each a different size, gave the room a soft haze. The air smelled like warm spring flowers. Tanya looked like she had walked off a movie set. Sexy, alluring, hot.

"Come here, big boy. I want to play for a while."

"Tanya, you know how much I would love to, but we really must get going. I told Dave that we would meet him at O'Hare's. I just shot home here to get a quick shower."

Tanya smiled and moaned softly, almost purring like a kitten. "So hop in the shower and then come here. Quit wasting time."

Nick knew he was losing the battle. He took off his jacket and sat on the edge of the bed. It was time to take the next step. "Tanya, I'm . . ."

As Nick turned to embrace her, Jenni bounded into the bedroom and jumped onto the bed. Obviously Nick had not pulled his apartment door hard enough for it to latch.

And of course right behind Jenni came Mrs. Babcock. Nick and Tanya could hear her voice as she entered the apartment, which gave the blonde just enough time to pull the bedsheet up under her chin. The lab swabbed Nick's chin and cheeks with her long, wet tongue.

"Jenni, you bad dog," the elderly landlord said as she entered the bedroom. "Oops. I thought you said you were going to clean the place, Tanya. I guess you decided to start between the sheets. Jenni, come now, we're interrupting—Nick and Tanya want some privacy."

Mrs. Babcock approached the bed and grabbed Jenni's collar. Tanya sat stunned under the sheet, which was now tucked around her neck and up under her ears. Nick felt terrible for her. Minutes ago his girlfriend had been alone in the apartment, but now she was hosting a convention in Nick's bedroom. He imagined her romantic notions had evaporated quickly.

Nick walked Mrs. Babcock and Jenni to his front door. His landlord apologized for the untimely intrusion and left with "Have a blessed day!"

When Nick returned to the bedroom, Tanya had already pulled on her jeans and was buttoning her blouse.

"Let's go meet Dave," Tanya said. "I guess this wasn't such a good idea."

"Sorry, Tanya."

"No, you're not. Just like up at Mackinac Island, you're actually glad when these distractions come up. You're more interested in work than you are in me. That's okay. I can take a hint."

Nick thought Tanya was about to get teary. It made his heart ache. The last thing he wanted to do was hurt the woman who had given him so much in the relatively short time they had known each other.

"Tanya, that's not it at all. I can hardly wait to make love to you." Nick tried to comfort her. He searched for the correct words. "I just want to make sure it's right for both of us. I don't want passion—or lust—to make this decision for us. Is it wrong for me to want to wait until we're both absolutely sure of what we're doing?"

"I'm sure of what I'm doing, but I'm beginning to have doubts about whether you're convinced that I am the one for you. I already know your job is your love. I'm beginning to think it's your mistress as well."

Tanya grabbed her purse as she headed for the apartment door. Nick scooted in front of her, turning to face her and block the exit.

"You're right," Nick said, pausing to think how he was going to explain this to Tanya. "I love what I do. No question about it. But that's only one part of my life. Until I met you, the other parts were empty. You're changing my life in a good way, and I want that to continue. But it's been so long since I let anyone get close—so long since I opened my heart to anyone—that I've just got to go slow. Does that make sense, or am I just old and crazy?"

"Crazy? I think you're close to being nuts, but maybe I should be thankful that you're not simply interested in using me and then tossing me away like old tissue paper," she said, sighing and looking down at the living room floor. "Well, let's talk some more. I'll lighten up, and we'll give this some more time. But do not, I repeat, do not, string me along. Agreed?"

"Agreed." Nick pulled Tanya into his arms. They embraced and he held her to his chest. Nick could feel her heart beating. He liked the feel of her warm breath on his neck. Nick pulled back slightly and lifted her chin, and they kissed. Tanya turned her head and rested it on his right shoulder. They both closed their eyes. He held her tightly, and together they swayed gently.

"Okay," she said, stepping back and breaking free. "That's enough. Let's go find Dave and figure out what's happening with this story."

"That's exactly what I was thinking."

Chapter 32

Saturday morning

When Nick arrived at the *Blade* offices, he and the rookie reporter, Greta Norris, were the only two souls in the newsroom. Nick waved at Greta, who was wearing a headset and making out-county phone checks with police and sheriffs' departments. She smiled and waved back, never slowing in her effort to dial for news updates.

Otherwise the office was quiet. A soft glow illuminating the work areas of the two solitary reporters gave the newsroom a library-like feel.

But when the office was in full swing, it hummed with the activity of forty reporters and copy editors. They sat at individual desks which were grouped by category. The sports grouping sat way in the back next to the lifestyle quad. City and county reporters were in the center of the room. The suburban reporters were assigned to another corner. The copy desk occupied the other corner and ran almost the length of the room. Heavy-duty tan carpet, accented with dark, circular coffee spills, softened the floor. The use of computers in the newsroom demanded dim lighting.

Nick sat at his computer and typed in all the notes he'd taken the previous two days. He lingered over what he'd jotted down from interviewing Wife Number Three, whom he liked and had enjoyed talking to. The reporter thought Connie Bilarski had been honest with him and Dave, though she really didn't have to talk to them at all.

Something the woman had said stuck with Nick. Nightmares. Insomnia. Headaches. Excessive drinking. She said a dark cloud hung over Zeke, something horrible from his days in Flint. She said it was one of many things that he kept from her, dooming their long-term relationship. Nick hoped that the trip he and Dave were going to take to Flint would open up the electrician's past.

The publisher's sudden appearance caught Nick off guard. The last time he had spotted her in the *Blade* building on a Saturday, he had ended up getting fired for stepping over the line during an interview, among a litany of minor infractions.

The Castrator strode into the office like she owned it and all its contents. Nick kept his head down, tucked behind his computer terminal—but he followed the publisher's movements in his peripheral vision. First she stopped by Drayton Clapper's newsroom desk and dropped off some papers. The publisher said hello to the new reporter, whom she had met, but only briefly. Greta pretended to talk into her headset.

The woman seemed to hesitate for a moment before marching toward Nick's desk. Saturday had put her in casual attire with light makeup and no jewelry. The tall, leggy brunette was wearing black slacks, which Nick had noticed fit her snugly when she bent over Drayton's desk. Her white blouse accented her long dark hair. At forty-five, she looked fit and healthy.

She smiled and greeted Nick. "Well, what are you doing here on a Saturday morning?"

"Just finishing a few things. Got an interview, actually two interviews, this afternoon. Thought I'd catch up a little. When it's quiet in here and the phones aren't ringing like crazy, I get more done."

"Will you be here long?" the publisher asked, planting her impressive, firm rump on the corner of Nick's desk. The reporter got a whiff of perfume. It was distinctive and feminine, but not overpowering. Her scent reminded Nick of violets.

"No, just a few more minutes," he said. "Almost done."

"Would you mind stopping by my office before you go? There's something I'd like to go over with you. That is, if you have time."

"Sure, I can swing by. I'll be up in a few minutes."

"Thanks, Nick."

The Castrator walked away from Nick's desk. He noticed two things immediately. First, he had been right about the snug fit of the publisher's slacks; and second, Greta had stopped dialing for news. She was watching them.

Nick checked his watch to see how much time he had. It would take nearly an hour to pick up Dave and drive to Flint. He finished his interview notes, packed his tape recorder and notebooks in a satchel, and headed up to the publisher's office on the fourth floor.

Diane's large corner office hearkened back to the days when newspaper publishers were the kingmakers of the community. Mahogany paneling, soft leather chairs, and lush carpeting gave the room a rich, powerful feel. The Castrator's wooden desk was the size of a Fiat. It dwarfed her. But once again it reminded Nick how much she loved being in control, being the most powerful person in the building.

"Come in, Nick," she said, motioning to a chair in front of her desk. "Relax. I'll be right with you."

Nick smiled and nodded. He could smell freshly brewed java, some kind of dark roast. He looked around Diane's office. No family photos on her desk. Nick knew that she had never married, but he wondered why she didn't display pictures of her folks or her brothers or sisters, or her nieces or nephews.

On one wall, however, Nick spotted a large photo of her two Shih Tzus, the hairy fur balls that were always running around the fourth-floor offices. If they had been here this morning, they would have been all over Nick, mostly because he often carried the smell of Jenni, the black lab, on his pant legs.

The other photos on her walls were of the Bay City Fireworks Festival and the big Great Lakes freighters that plied the Saginaw River and Lake Huron.

The publisher closed the notebook she had been writing in and walked to her office door, pulling it shut behind her. Nick thought he heard the lock click, but was sure he must have been mistaken.

She asked Nick if he would like some coffee.

"No, thanks," he said.

"Is there anything I can get you?" she asked, her voice lilting up an octave. "Anything at all?" The woman walked over to the chair next to Nick and sat in it. She leaned in closer to Nick, which made him uneasy.

"No, I'm good," he said, pulling back away from her. He noticed that her blouse was now open to the third button. She was wearing a light-cream-colored bra, one of those push-up jobbies that women wear with low-cut evening gowns.

"You know, Nick, I'm a woman who gets what she wants," she said. "I've always been interested in you. That's why I asked for you to be on the ad hoc committee. You're not afraid of anything, including me."

"Well, I appreciate it, Diane," he said. The reporter felt awkward. He wondered if her windows were locked—in case he had to dive out one to escape her. "I didn't think I would like being on your committee, but I find it interesting."

"What else do you find interesting?" the publisher asked, shifting forward in her seat and leaning toward Nick even more. The movement pushed her bosom out in front of Nick's face. The fourth button on her blouse was now under immense pressure. The reporter hoped it would not burst and pop him in the eye.

"Diane, I don't know where you are going with this, but it is making me feel very uncomfortable," he said. "You said you wanted to go over something with me. Do you have something you want to show me other than what's in your shirt?"

Nick could see that she was miffed. He braced for a storm, but instead she unexpectedly mellowed. Diane stood, walked behind the two chairs, and stopped directly behind Nick. She put her hands on his shoulders and gently massaged them. Then she reached down and pulled Nick's shirt up, revealing his hairy belly and chest.

"Gorilla man! I love it," she said, raking the fingers of both hands up through Nick's jungle of curly hair. Her fingertips stopped at his nipples, which she squeezed until Nick grunted. "I knew that deep down you were an animal, you beast, you."

"Diane, please." The reporter tried to maintain his composure, but was nearly frantic. He hoped her phone would ring. He wanted the furry little shitting machines to come bouncing into the office. Any distraction to get the Castrator off of him would help.

"Nick, don't say anything. We don't have to take this further today, but I want you to think about a few things. You're a smart guy. You know that I can make things very difficult around here for you. It's your choice."

The publisher walked away from behind Nick's chair and went to her office door. She unlocked it and opened it slightly. "But remember that I always get what I want."

Nick was dumbfounded. He didn't know quite what to say. "Okay, Diane," he said, standing up and poking his shirt into his pants as he moved toward the door in three quick strides. He thought of Tanya and paused. "You are aware that I'm seeing someone, aren't you?"

"Oh? The chatter in the newsroom is that your thing with Sonya really isn't going anywhere."

"It's Tanya, and we're still seeing each other," Nick said, surprised that she would be tuned into the newsroom gossip.

"Nick, she's too young for you and you know it." The publisher smiled and put her right hand atop her hip. Her legs were spread apart. "That's what's holding you back with her. That's why it's not working."

The fourth button on her blouse had given way to the strain she'd placed upon it. The push-up bra and two half moons were clearly in view. Her hair was tousled slightly. It was a power pose, Nick thought, and it was definitely very sexy.

Nick focused on the door. As he grabbed the doorknob, she stepped closer and put her hand on top of his. The two were now standing inches apart.

"I will be in the office tomorrow at 4:30 p.m. No one will be here that late on Sunday, but I expect you to be here, Nick."

"I have an obligation on Sunday," Nick said. It was a lie, but that was the only thing he could think of on the spur of the moment.

"Be here, Nick, if you know what's good for you."

Chapter 33

Saturday afternoon

Nick gunned the Firebird's V-8 as he waited for Dave outside his friend's apartment. Then he did it again and again.

The encounter with the Castrator had made the reporter nervous. No way would he show up at the office on Sunday. He had no interest in having an intimate encounter with the publisher. But Nick was angry that she thought she could force him into a physical relationship by threatening him.

And what about Tanya? Suddenly Nick wanted her more than ever. It bothered him that the Castrator had dismissed their relationship. If Tanya knew what had happened, Nick was certain that his girlfriend would confront and flatten the publisher without hesitation. She would go ballistic if he told her about it.

Nick also feared the publisher's wrath if he did not go along with her demands. The last thing he needed was another reason to get fired. And he certainly did not want Diane making his life any more difficult or complicated than it already was. The publisher's harassment bothered him so much that he could not chase it from his mind. Hopefully Dave would have a sympathetic ear.

"Hey, buddy. Ready to roll to Flint?" Dave said as he opened the door and slid into the 'Bird's passenger seat. "This should be fun. Wife Number Two is waiting for us, and we've got a union official ready to talk."

"Yup, all set," Nick said, pulling out of Dave's driveway and pointing his vehicle south. "But I've got something I have to tell you first, and you have to promise not to tell anyone about it."

"Sure thing. Shoot," Dave said.

The dour expression on Nick's face should have been a clue. He felt like he was ready to throw up. Still Nick hesitated, trying to think of the right way to frame what he was about to tell Dave. Finally he just blurted it out: "The Castrator cornered me in her office and wants me to have sex with her."

Dave did not respond, as if waiting for his buddy to deliver the punch line to the joke. But Nick's eyes were riveted to the road. He did not grin or chuckle. He did nothing to indicate that there was anything funny about what he'd said.

"You got to be shitting me," Dave said, breaking the dead silence. "You're kidding, right?"

"No, and I have no idea what to do."

Nick laid out the whole story for Dave, including how the unbuttoning of Diane's blouse went from being a conservative two-holer to an eye-popping four-holer in the space of about twenty minutes.

"Well, hot diggity dog, then you've got to go where no man has gone before," Dave said. "Give her the high hard one, my friend. Give her a go right there in her office on top of that megadesk and in full view of all that shiny mahogany."

"Dave, that is absolutely not going to happen," Nick said. "I am not going to be blackmailed into having sex with someone I have no interest in. Forget it."

But just saying no to a woman as powerful and controlling as D. McGovern Givens would not be easy. If Nick was going to get fired again, it had to be for standing his ground as a journalist—not for refusing to lie down with the publisher.

"I've got to find a way to get out of this horrible situation without getting canned or demoted, or put on the copy desk—a fate worse than death," Nick said. "Help me. I'm in trouble here."

The two friends talked about the predicament as they drove down I-75 toward Flint.

Dave's next idea was to have Nick play along with the publisher and get her to go to Nick's apartment, where they would have a video recorder all set up to capture the two coupling. But Nick shot down that idea because he didn't want her in his place at any time, for any reason. Mrs. Babcock would not approve, and Jenni would be unforgiving.

Should he call Drayton Clapper and have his boss come up with a phony Sunday assignment? No, that might result in both of them getting canned. Plus, he felt too ashamed to tell Drayton, or anyone, about getting blackmailed for sex.

Nick even briefly considered running off the road on their way back from Flint, faking a car accident. But the Castrator would just say, "I have no interest in screwing the car—get your ass up here in my office. Now!"

By now they were nearing their destination, and the two friends decided to continue their discussion after their interviews. Right now they had to focus on the island story as their top priority for the afternoon.

Wife Number Two was waiting for Nick and Dave when they pulled into her driveway on Bradley Avenue on Flint's West Side. The home was a tidy little bungalow, not far from Ballenger Highway and the huge mansions just south of Miller Road.

Sandy Messner sat bundled in a chocolate-colored sleeveless down coat, a white scarf, and knit hat on her front porch. Her arms, thick and toned from twenty-seven years of using her hands and upper body to put together parts on a moving assembly line, were covered with a tight nylon long-sleeved shirt. She huddled herself against the cool breeze of May in Michigan.

The woman stood up as the reporters got out of Nick's machine. She was short and stocky too, big enough to look like she'd make a good pulling guard on an offensive line.

"You Sandy?" Nick asked.

"You found her," the woman said. The smile on her face revealed a full set of straight white teeth. Long dark hair fell on her shoulders from under a gold beanie. The smile also revealed dimples and sparkling blue eyes that would melt most men's hearts. "You guys from Bay City?"

Dave nodded. “I talked to you on the phone the other day. This is my buddy, Nick. Thanks for meeting with us.”

“Come on up—let’s get out of this wind,” Sandy said.

They followed her into the front room of her home. Nick and Dave took off their jackets, tossing them on top of one another on a corner chair, and sat down on a blue corduroy sofa with big fluffy yellow pillows at each arm. A coffee table the size of a pirate’s treasure chest stood sturdily in front of them. Worn tan carpet covered the floor and extended into what looked like a dining room. The focal point of the room was the TV set, which was housed in a bulky wooden entertainment center.

“Coffee? Can I get you some coffee? I’m all out of beer,” Sandy said, pointing toward a small corner table that was all set up with a steaming pot and cups and saucers.

“Yes, that would be terrific,” Nick said, studying the family pictures on the living room wall. Lots of smiling faces in front of the Christmas tree, or at the beach, or around a picnic table—there was plenty of joy among young and old in those family scenes. But Nick did not see Zeke in a single photo.

“Love the family shots,” Nick said, moving to another part of the room, where more pictures were displayed. Dave helped Sandy with the coffee. “I don’t see Zeke in any of them.”

“Well, that’s on purpose,” she said. The three sat down around the coffee table and sipped the steaming liquid. “Wasn’t much to be happy about when Zeke was around, and most of these pictures were taken when he was literally out of the picture.”

Sandy seemed to have decided to take the offensive. She said she was puzzled by why two reporters from Bay City wanted to know about Zeke’s past in Flint. Couldn’t they get that information from Zeke?

Nick explained that Zeke had talked about his years in Flint in general terms, but they were trying to help him by delving deeper and looking for information that he had not considered.

Sandy shrugged her big shoulders. She said she would help if she could, but didn't know what she could provide.

Nick asked her to talk about their early days together. "Zeke, well, he was very handsome and charming," she said. She told the reporters they had met while working together at the same assembly plant—she was on the final assembly line for Chevy half-ton pickup trucks, and Zeke serviced the same line as a skilled tradesman. They were on the graveyard shift together. "He used to tease me unmercifully. Zeke knew just about everybody in that plant, and he had his fingers in everything.

"I should have known better, but I was just young and ignorant. I fell for him and his bullshit like a load of slag hitting the cement. First thing you know, we got married, and it was all downhill from there. Didn't last three years."

"We know Zeke liked to gamble and party," Nick said. "But we keep hearing stories about him being involved in something more serious, something dark during his days there."

"Personally, I always thought he was somehow connected to the mob," Sandy said, taking another sip of coffee. "Of course he would never discuss his connections, but he always hung out at the Shorthorn, a bar and steakhouse over on Dort, near Court."

Sandy walked over to a bureau in the dining room.

"Take a gander at this," she said, pulling out a photo album and flipping through the pages. "Here it is. I knew this damn picture was in here someplace. Zeke and Denny McLain sitting at his organ, singing in the Shorthorn. Has to be from the late sixties, early seventies."

The reporters jumped from their seats and joined her as she pulled a photograph from its plastic binder, holding it up to the light for a better look.

Nick studied the photo. He figured Sandy was probably correct about the era, judging by the moppish hair and the powder-blue and light-orange leisure suits. A lit cigarette dangled from the two fingers of Zeke's right hand. The other held a rock glass half-filled with what looked like whiskey. The Tigers pitcher was banging away at his keyboard. Busty women with beehive hair ogled them from the opposite side of the organ.

"Denny and Zeke were all buddy-buddy back in those days," Sandy said. "In my humble opinion, that's how he got pulled into the wrong crowd—drinking, gambling, whoring, hanging with bad guys, thugs, really. Denny was connected to a lot of bad guys, no doubt about it. He introduced Zeke to too many bad dudes.

"Zeke always had wads of cash, big wads," she continued. "The kind of dough you can't make from the shop—even if you're in the trades and getting tons of OT."

"OT? What's that?" Dave asked.

"Overtime, doofus," Nick said, frowning at his partner.

"Oh, well, I'm a newspaper guy," Dave said. "No wonder I've never heard of it."

Sandy put the photo back where she'd found it, and shook her head. "I could never figure out if all the money came from gambling or torching."

"Torching?" Nick asked. "Then you were aware that he was burning down buildings for money?"

Sandy said she had discovered his firebug activities by chance. The house they shared had a landline with the main phone in the living room and an extension in the bedroom. One day when he was talking on the phone in the bedroom, she accidentally had picked up the living room phone and overheard Zeke finalizing details to burn down a house in one of Flint's run-down neighborhoods.

After that, she said, she started paying more attention to his comings and goings. It became obvious that he was involved in something very shady. But the only thing she caught him red-handed at was cheating with a redhead named Renni.

"Eventually I tossed him out of the house when I caught him in one of the supply rooms at the shop with a woman who used to hang dashboards on the line," she said. "Zeke got his own place, and the divorce was final in about three months. Heard he was involved in some real nasty stuff with a total lowlife at the shop, and then the next thing I knew he up and transferred to the Chevy plant in Bay City. Haven't seen him since."

"What about the union?" Dave asked. "One of the things that keeps coming up is his union activity. We're going to meet with the former president of his local union this afternoon—right after we leave here."

"The president? Why, he's just a figurehead at the union," Sandy said. "If you want to find out what was going on in the plant, then you need to talk to whoever was shop committee chairman at the time. Those are the guys who pull the strings on the shop floor. Just a minute."

Sandy reached over to a rolltop desk, opened a drawer, shuffled through some papers, and held up a card, examining it under a lamp.

"Here's the guy you want to talk to," she said, presenting it to Dave. "Big Bill Basswood. He was the union big shot on the factory floor. He was really tight with Zeke. Give him a call. He's retired now, but I know he's still around because I saw him in the Factory Lounge last week, over on Van Slyke. He still hangs out there."

Nick and Dave thanked Sandy for her time and hospitality and headed for Van Slyke Road, the heart of Chevy truck building and the UAW in Flint.

Chapter 34

Saturday afternoon

Zeke took his time driving by the property on Three Mile Road in Bay County's Monitor Township. As his client had indicated, it looked secluded and vacant—an easy target for a man of his skill.

Still, the veteran torch did not like checking out his next burn in broad daylight. Zeke always felt more comfortable working in the dark. Most of his life—professional and private—had been lived in the shadows. That's where he felt most comfortable, where he could move easily and freely.

This stretch of Three Mile Road was very remote, very quiet. Zeke had not encountered any vehicles moving in either direction—nor did he see any people out walking, jogging, or biking in the area. No prying eyes anywhere.

Finally he pulled into the drive and parked just past the Starlight Realty For Sale sign. An attachment to the sign encouraged those who saw it to "Call Mary Rose today for your personal showing."

Zeke had no plans to call the agent or anyone else. The instructions from his client were simple: check out the place, size it up for an easy burn, get out, and wait for final instructions.

The two-story frame-construction house was sided with rough-sawed cedar. Zeke smiled. Once ignited, the thing would burst into flames. He stepped onto the porch and reached for the lockbox on the front door. Zeke pulled a small slip of paper from his shirt pocket and punched in the code. One-nine-five-two.

Once inside, he spotted the electrical panel in the utility room. He unlatched its front door. Another smile. The house's electrical system had not been updated with breaker switches. Modern appliances would overload the wiring. It was an antique, waiting to spark and burn.

Zeke walked around the rest of the first floor. When he saw a gas grill sitting inside the rear entryway, he walked over and lifted the propane tank. Nearly full. What luck, he thought—it was like having a small bomb inside the house.

In the living room, Zeke checked the fireplace. A flexible metal natural gas line ran up through the floor to the pilot light and the ignition switch. Not up to code. Somebody had cut some corners to convert the fireplace from wood burning to gas fired. It would be easy for that flexible line to spring a leak, which would flood the whole house with natural gas. A spark would cause an explosion that would turn the place into a charred pile of debris. It doesn't get any better than this, Zeke concluded, chuckling to himself.

A corner staircase ascended to the second story of the house. Zeke bounded up the stairs to make sure squatters were not using the place as a crash pad. He did not want to repeat that mistake.

On his way back through the kitchen, he noticed a scented candle on the counter. Instantly a plan to turn the house into rubble began to form in Zeke's mind. The experienced torch thought he could break the flexible tube in the fireplace and light the candle as he went out the door. That would give him plenty of time to drive away from the scene before the explosion and fire.

Within twenty minutes, Zeke had closed the house back up and returned the key to the front-door lockbox.

As soon as he got the final go from his client, this place would burn to the ground before the Monitor Township fire trucks rounded the corner a half mile up the road. Firefighters would not be able to save this house. Their only job would be to hose down hot coals. Best of all, there would be no trace that Zeke had even stepped onto the premises.

Easy pickings. Fast money. Just what he liked.

Chapter 35

Saturday afternoon

Nick and Dave walked into the Factory Lounge. Instantly a graveyard silence fell over the place. Strangers had entered the domain of the locals. All eyes in the bar turned to the entryway, where a flood of light cast a backlight against the two reporters.

"Shut the damn door," a voice called from among the men lined up at the bar. "You're creatin' a draft and you're makin' my beer go flat."

Nick followed orders, pulling the steel windowless door shut. The Factory Lounge was as dark as a dungeon. Neon illuminated a jukebox at the end of the bar. A single bulb dangling from an orange extension cord threw light across the pool table. Two yellow lamps, most likely stained from cigarette smoke, shed enough light for the barmaid to keep track of the liquor bottles lined up on a back-wall rack behind the bar.

The two reporters waited a moment for their eyes to adjust. They studied the men who had just been studying them. Guys in jeans and sweatshirts—some wearing ball caps, a couple sporting cowboy hats. All had steel-toed work boots. The men leaned against the bar, nursing their drinks and shooting the breeze. Nick and Dave walked slowly to a table near a support beam at the center of the establishment.

A young waitress barely old enough to serve hooch came out of the shadows and pulled up at Nick and Dave's table. "Whatchya need?"

"Two coffees," Nick said. Again the bar went silent, and all eyes turned to their table.

"Only got coffee in the morning," the waitress said. "I'd have to make a fresh pot, and I'm busy making sandwiches for the second shifters."

The young woman was dressed in faded blue jeans, tennis shoes, and a green and white sweatshirt that blared, "I love Sparty." She looked at the watch on her wrist. Her ponytail bobbed up and down as she said, "About thirty guys will be piling through that door in about fifteen minutes. If you want something to drink, you better order it now, 'cause you ain't gonna see me again for about an hour."

"Okay, two drafts—PBR," Nick said.

"We got Stroh's on tap for fifty cents."

"Two Stroh's would be great," Nick said. He noticed that the small talk had resumed at the bar. Ordering beer instead of coffee must have meant that he and Dave were okay.

Dave leaned in toward Nick to guard his words. "When she brings our drafts, I'll ask for Big Bill. I don't see anybody at the bar who fits that description, but who knows."

"Good idea," Nick said. "Ask loud enough for the guys to hear. If he's not here, maybe one of them will know where to find him."

The waitress returned, carrying two draft beers and a paper cup of peanuts and pretzels. She placed them on the table with two napkins. "That will be a buck."

Nick gave her two dollars, figuring that he would not see her again because she would be tied up serving the second shifters.

Dave cleared his throat. "Say, you know Bill Basswood? He around?"

Nick and Dave could feel the stares from the rest of the men. The young woman looked up at the guys standing at the bar before responding to Dave. "Who wants to know? You guys cops?" she asked.

"No, not hardly," Dave said. "We heard this is his hangout and we know a friend of his from the shop. Thought we'd just say hello and chew the fat with him a little."

"Yeah, he hangs out here, but he's usually gone when the shifters come in," she said. "Gets too noisy for him."

"Okay, I got his number. I'll give him a call later."

The Stroh's was warm and stale. It did not pass the two-sip test. Nick and Dave were just about to abandon the remainder of their drinks and head for the door when one of the guys from the bar approached.

"Heard you lookin' for Big Bill," he said. "He's a friend of mine. Whatchya want him for?"

"We've got a common friend, just wanted to say hello and talk for a few minutes," Nick said.

"You ain't from around here, are you?"

"Nope. We're from Bay City."

"He should be back later. If you're still around, swing back by."

"Okay, thanks."

"Hey, you gonna leave them there beers?"

"Yup."

The man grabbed both glasses of brew, smiling broadly. "Lettin' good beer go to waste is kinda against our religion around here. Thanks," he said, raising the glass in his left hand in a half salute, half toast.

"By all means, be my guest," Nick said.

The beer hoarder gulped down the contents of one glass in three chugs. As foam drizzled down his chin, he smiled and let a low growl of a belch climb slowly from his gut to a high-pitched noise coming through his nostrils. It echoed across the cavernous watering hole, to the chuckles and high fives of the other guys languishing against the bar. He then swung the other mug up to a half-filled pitcher sitting atop the bar in front of his stool. The gold liquid splashed into the container, but it was so flat that it did not make a discernible head.

"Heh heh heh," he said, turning to the crowd at the bar. "Can you believe those two guys—walking away from live beer? Why, that's downright criminal."

The door closed behind Nick and Dave. "I think we're getting out of there at just about the right time," Dave said.

"You're right, my friend," Nick said as they walked to his car to map out a plan. "I had a feeling that it was about to get ugly in there. We can try again later."

The two decided to meet with the president of the local union while they waited for Bill Basswood to slither out from under his rock and reappear at the Factory Lounge.

It was not hard to find the UAW Local 588 union hall among the booze joints, strip clubs, tattoo parlors, pawnshops, and used-car lots that dotted Van Slyke Road. Those places had a fair amount of success sucking cash out of the hands of factory workers before it could be safely deposited in family bank accounts.

The union hall stood out from the gaudy crowd of businesses because of its matter-of-fact drabness. Gray cement block. Two stories with a basement. Small windows. Concrete steps leading to a glass-door entry. The only ornament on the front of the building was the iconic UAW emblem of workers holding hands in a circle—solidarity.

A receptionist who was typing a report at a desk behind the front counter greeted Nick and Dave without looking up from her task. The tip of her pointy nose was the only thing that kept her glasses from sliding down across her heavily glossed lips. About forty, with long sandy hair, she sat in a chair on rollers and was obviously losing a poorly fought battle to keep her short skirt from revealing her scant undergarments. A UAW nametag identified her as Becky.

"Do you want something, or are you just going to stand there trying to look at my undies?"

The reception caught the two reporters off guard. "Ah, ah, yes, we want something," Nick said. "We have an appointment to meet Sam Dooley this afternoon."

"Go on back to his office, last door on the right," she said, pointing the way with her chin. "He said somethin' about visitors this afternoon."

"Thanks, Becky," Dave said. "Hey, and nice panties. But you really should think about changing them every couple weeks."

The receptionist gave Dave the finger as the two reporters walked toward Sam's office.

"You know, if you're going to flirt with a receptionist, it's usually a good idea to do it with a compliment," Nick said.

"That was a compliment," Dave said. "You have your technique, and I have mine. Let's see who has better luck—me with Becky, or you with the Castrator."

"Not funny," Nick said, as he punched Dave in the shoulder. The last thing he wanted to be reminded of us was his meeting with the publisher.

Once in the hallway, they could hear the soulful wailing of Wilson Pickett's "Mustang Sally" rolling out of the last office on the right.

A phone rang, signaling an abrupt end to the Pickett recording. Sam Dooley, the president of UAW Local 588 for twenty-five years, stepped out into the hallway. A smile spread across his face as he welcomed Nick and Dave to the union hall and the home for workers who spit out Chevy Silverados as fast as Colonel Sanders pumps out deep-fried chicken.

Immediately Nick recognized the union leader from regional TV news reports and photos pushed across the Associated Press news wire by *The Flint Journal*. Tall and slender, with an unkempt, graying Afro and sparse mustache, the leader looked more like an insurance salesman than the leader of factory workers. A brown-checked sports jacket drooped from his narrow shoulders. Cream-colored slacks hung above brown cowhide platform shoes.

"How you Bay City boys doin'?" he said, sticking out his right hand. "Last time I was in Bay City, probably 'bout ten years ago, I didn't see one black man in the whole damn town. Still like that?"

"Well, this is 1999," Nick said. "Bay City's a great place, with all kinds of people from all types of backgrounds."

"Aw, bullshit," Sam said, kicking Nick's attempt at diplomacy to the curb. Flint and Bay City were polar opposites regarding black and white issues. In Flint, race is a factor in all aspects of life. It permeates politics, religion, education, work, and social life. Not so in Bay City, and it's something Sam had tried to assess about the city by the bay. "Nice try, but that ain't gonna fly here. After my visit, I checked the census—only about ten percent minorities of all colors and ninety percent white. Ain't that right?"

"Yup," Dave said. "Mostly Europeans—German, Polish, Irish, French. Nice folks, but they can't dance or jump."

"Ha ha ha ha—now that's more like it," Sam said, nearly doubling over. He reached up and slapped Dave on the back. "Come on in, guys. What brings you to Vehicle City?"

Sam's office was much different from the austere exterior of the union hall itself. His fat white leather chair stood behind a handsome oak desk. United States, Michigan, and UAW flags hung from brown metal poles in one corner. The floor was covered in thick beige carpet. The room's largest wall was lined with photos of Sam with impressive politicians and union leaders, Walter Reuther, Leonard Woodcock, Doug Fraser, Jimmy Carter, Ted Kennedy, and Jim Blanchard among them.

Nick studied the photos as Dave plunged ahead with a quick recap explaining why they were interested in learning more about Zeke Zimmer's activities with the union and his work in the auto plants.

"Brother Zeke, ah yes. A good, good man and a fine member of our union," Sam said, leaning back into the soft cushion of his chair. "But he left here many years ago, and I haven't had any contact with him since then. How is he?"

Nick joined the conversation. "This is probably not going to surprise you, but he's gotten himself into a tight spot. We think he may be the target of a hit man, so we're trying to see if we can find out who may want him dead."

Sam responded with the same belly laugh that had erupted from him in the hallway, but then he suddenly turned serious. "Brother

Zeke was always a bit of a lightning rod in the plant. A cloud followed him around wherever he went. Everybody knew him—some liked him, some didn't."

"Well, we know that he liked to gamble and carouse, but we also heard that he received an award from the union," Nick said.

Sam told the reporters about Zeke discovering the assembly line speedup device. It matched the story Nick and Dave had heard previously. What they didn't know was whether the discovery and revelation of the device were enough to endanger Zeke—especially after the passage of so much time.

"When the box was found and we saw how they used it, well, that was a game changer," Sam said. "We caught management in a big lie."

Sam told Nick and Dave that he had called his connection at *The Flint Journal* and exposed the secret device. But the *Journal* reporter had wanted firsthand proof of the contract violation before writing an article.

"So we snuck him inside the plant," the union leader said. "That was against the rules, but management was breaking the rules too, so we felt justified in bringing him inside right under the nose of plant security."

Zeke and a friend had showed the reporter how the device, which was concealed in a supervisor's office, was hooked up to the assembly line in a maze of wiring. The *Journal* reporter took photographs, and Zeke helped him create a diagram showing how the box could be activated and shut off by simply turning a dial in the office.

The result was a front-page article in *The Journal*. The scandal became known throughout the auto industry as "Chevy-gate."

At first, plant management denied that such a device existed, but soon realized that was fruitless when the union threatened a widespread strike. Negotiations began, and eventually both sides reached a settlement over financial compensation for affected workers. The company paid out more than a million bucks to three thousand GM workers.

Zeke and his pal won high accolades from the union for revealing the illegal device implemented by management, the union leader told Nick and Dave. But not everyone was happy about it.

"After a couple of months, they started getting threats—first at work and then at home," Sam said. "It all came to a head when the brakes on Zeke's truck failed on his way to work. Luckily he was able to run his truck through a ditch and into some heavy brush. If he'd been on the freeway, the outcome might have been different."

Sam said police had determined that Zeke's brakes had been tampered with. Immediately Zeke and his buddy went into hiding. Under pressure from the union, the company agreed to transfer both employees after each took long furloughs.

After a year, Zeke had showed up to work at the Chevy plant in Bay City with no fanfare. His pal went to a GM assembly plant in Pontiac under the same conditions.

"So the threats stopped?" Nick asked.

"That's what I hear, but we lost track of Brother Zeke after he transferred north," Sam said. "Me and a couple of top dogs at GM knew what happened to him, but he just disappeared from the plant here as far as everyone else was concerned."

Nick and Dave thanked Sam for his time and cooperation, and Sam asked the two to give Zeke his best regards. As the reporters walked by the front desk on their way out, Dave put a slip of paper on the front counter.

"See ya later, Becky," he said in the direction of the receptionist, who was still banging away at her typewriter. She pushed the glasses up off the end of her nose and nodded at the two.

"What was on that slip of paper?" Nick asked, following Dave to their vehicle in the parking lot.

"My phone number. She'll call."

"Right, don't hold your breath," Nick said.

On their way back to the Factory Lounge, Dave asked Nick if it was still worth stopping there to look for Big Bill Basswood.

"Sounds like we just heard who wants Zeke dead," Dave said. "If somebody was ticked enough to mess with his brakes twenty years ago, they may have just now decided to try and finish the job."

"Maybe," Nick said. "We're here, might as well see if Big Bill is around. Let's keep asking questions."

Bill Basswood, however, had not returned to the Factory Lounge since Nick and Dave had been there earlier. Nick left his card and a note at the bar for the retired union leader.

Then the reporters got on I-75 and headed north to Bay City. They both felt like their trip to Flint had given them new information and insight into the shady side of Zeke Zimmer's life.

Chapter 36

Late Saturday afternoon

Nick pulled his gold Firebird into his apartment building parking lot and lodged the machine in its usual spot. The left tire of his pride and joy pinned a piece of mesh screening, its edges frayed, against the ground, hiding all but a corner of it from view. The reporter noticed it, cursing the trash that ended up in the parking lot, when he locked up his machine.

As Nick walked to the front entrance of the building, he fanned through the pages of his notebook. The information he'd gathered in Flint was secure. He checked his mailbox and looked up the stairway.

Loud music boomed from the second floor. It made him wonder who was hosting the party. Then he thought of Tanya and her surprise visit the previous night. He smiled as he recalled seeing her sitting up in his bed, covered only by a thin sheet.

She's back, he thought. Nick took the stairs two steps at a time until he reached his apartment door. The music echoed from inside his place as he turned the key and pushed the door open.

"Hi, Tanya," he said, beaming. He looked for his girlfriend in the open living, dining, and kitchen areas of the apartment, but she was nowhere in sight. All the lights were turned on. So was the TV. An open beer stood on the corner of his dining table.

"Tanya, where are you?" Nick said as he approached his bedroom in the back. "I gotta tell you, I admire your persistence."

Still no response.

Eager not to disappoint Tanya a second time, Nick reached for the front of his shirt with both hands. He ripped it open, buttons popping and flying in all directions.

"Okay, Tanya, here I come, and I'm ready to light your fire," he said, picking up speed as he moved toward the open bedroom door.

The bare-chested reporter peered around the corner of the bedroom doorway. No Tanya. The bed had been stripped. The contents of his dresser drawers had been dumped on the floor. His eyes turned to the closet. Door open, clothes and hangers on the floor.

"Tanya?" Nick scanned the room, trying to make sense of what he saw.

The bedroom TV was on with the volume turned low. Nick approached the set. A Mackinac Island promotional video flashed across the screen. The Grand Hotel was the backdrop for a scene that focused on two horses, a carriage, and a young family on their way to never-never land. As the horses clopped along on the pavement, the four passengers in the coach laughed and smiled. The whole setting was so heavily staged that even the horses looked like they were smiling for the camera too. The reporter had never seen the video before and couldn't understand where it had come from and why it was playing.

Suddenly Nick felt as though an ice cube had slid down his spine. His eyes darted around the room a second time. Everything was out of place. He had been invaded.

Nick pulled out his handkerchief and turned off the stereo. Now he could hear the genteel voice of the announcer on the Mackinac video. He could also hear the shower running in the bathroom.

From the bathroom doorway he could see an empty shower, water streaming hard. Steam fogged the small room, making it feel warm and damp. He walked in and turned the faucets off, again using his handkerchief. Water had splattered on his tile floor. He noticed that a wad of tissue the size of a soccer ball was plugging the toilet. Why would anyone do that?

As the steam cleared, Nick spotted words smeared on the mirror. His deodorant, the cap off, was resting at the bottom of the sink. The message was simple: "Back off! You could get hurt real easy."

Nick grabbed his cell phone and punched in a number.

The response was immediate. "This is Quinn, Bay City Police. Make it fast, and it better be important."

"Dan, this is Steele. It is important. I believe somebody busted into my apartment," he said. "Gotta tell you I'm a little freaked out right now."

"I'll be right over, Nicky boy," the cop said.

Nick also called Tanya and Dave, just to make sure this was not some kind of practical joke. It wasn't. They said they had not been to his place, but they were on their way now.

The reporter went to his front door. He could not see where it had been tampered with or forced. Next he checked his windows. All seemed fine except the bedroom, where the screen had been cut out. Now, the trash under his front tire made sense. He decided not to touch the window or its frame. He peeked through the glass, noting the steel fire escape about a foot from the window.

A hard knock on his apartment door jarred Nick away from his examination of the window.

"Nick, it's Quinn."

"Door's open, come in."

The patrolman entered the apartment and immediately scanned the living and dining rooms. He was wearing gloves and cautioned Nick not to touch or move a thing.

"A detective is on the way," the cop said. "We'll get this checked out. Dust it for prints, see what we find. Best for you to just step out in the hallway. We'll get your statement. You probably should alert your landlord. Don't let your friends or anyone in until we're done, okay? And by the way, what happened to your shirt? The buttons are ripped off. Did you get into a fight with the intruder?" Quinn asked.

"Ah, no. Nobody was here when I came in," Nick said, embarrassed. "I was kind of in a hurry to get my shirt off."

Nick stepped into the hallway and went down to the first floor. He knocked on Mrs. Babcock's door. No response from her or Jenni.

A few minutes later Tanya and Dave came into the apartment building.

"What the hell happened?" Dave said. "And what did you do to your shirt, man? You get in a wrestling match with somebody?"

"I really don't know what's going on," Nick said, ignoring the question and pulling the tails of his shirt together to try to hide his bare chest. "Somebody got into my place, tore it up a little, and left me a message."

Tanya grabbed his arm and pulled him close. "You okay?"

"What'd it say?" Dave asked.

Nick recapped what he had found, telling his friends about the message written with his deodorant on his mirror.

Then he pulled a notebook out of his back pocket. He flipped it open and started writing. "Got to write it all down while it's fresh in my mind," he said. "This will make a great story for tomorrow's paper."

The reporter saw Tanya roll her eyes at him as he turned another event into a story.

"It won't take me long to bang it out, then believe me, I'll be ready to drink some beer—or something stronger," he said, suddenly realizing that he was supposed to meet with the publisher on Sunday. He still hadn't come up with a plan. "Meet you two at O'Hare's?"

Chapter 37

Sunday morning

A seagull swooped in low off the mighty Saginaw River and dropped a load of shit on Nick's forehead. As it slid millimeter by millimeter down toward the bridge of his nose, the reporter fully woke from his slumber.

First thing he noticed, after detecting that the crap was still warm, was that he was outside Hooters on the Bay City riverfront. Second realization: he was stretched out on an aluminum bench less than fifty feet from the river's edge.

Moving any part of his body made his aching head throb. He reached for a handkerchief in his back pocket. Gone. A search of his left front pocket uncovered a Hooters bar napkin. Good enough. Nick wiped at the gull goo before it spread any further.

"Wondered when you'd wake up," Tanya said. She was sitting on the next bench, sipping coffee from a cardboard cup. "When do you think you're going to be able to get past drinking all night and passing out in strange places?"

"Well, when you think about it, this really isn't such a strange place. It's a bench outside a bar," Nick said. "I'm impressed that I made it past the curb and gutter this time and actually got to a place that was not soaked in urine."

"Not funny, Nick," Tanya said. "You're killing yourself, and I'm not going to hang around and watch the train wreck you call your life. If you can't get control of this, then I'm history."

Tanya got up and tossed the Sunday morning *Bay City Blade* on Nick's lap. She turned and walked toward her vehicle in the parking lot. "Call me later. We need to have a serious talk."

"Thought we just had one," Nick muttered to himself as he sat up and looked around him.

At the side of the bench, Nick spotted a cup of coffee and a bag containing a blueberry muffin. He pulled the top off the cup and took a long sip of the charcoal-colored liquid. Still warm. So was the muffin.

"I don't deserve that girl," Nick said to no one in particular. He looked down at the newspaper, trying to focus through the fog engulfing his brain.

Nick's story about the break-in at his apartment had made the front page. The previous afternoon there had been much discussion over whether to play the first-person account under the fold on page one.

One copy editor had raised the question of whether or not the whole thing was a hoax concocted by the reporter to draw attention to his work and the Mackinac Island death—which still was classified by local police as an accident. After all, the copy editor argued, Bay City police had found no fingerprints or any other physical evidence that someone other than Nick and his friends had been in the apartment.

Drayton Clapper had made the final call on running the story, but he made two things clear during a closed-door meeting with Nick. First, he was worried about Nick being in danger, but he also wanted it understood that publishing such a story on Nick's word alone was a gamble.

"Nick, we've worked together a long time and I trust you, but this is a huge risk," the editor told him. "If you're wrong, or if you're pulling some kind of bullshit shenanigans here, then we're both fired. Do you understand that?"

"Drayton, everything I wrote in that piece is the God's honest truth," Nick had said. "I couldn't make up a story like that. Walking into my place and seeing and feeling that someone else had been there scared the hell out of me."

But he had also told Drayton that he wasn't going to stop

investigating Townsend's death. Whoever came into his place was trying to push him off the story. Printing an article about what had happened—getting the truth out—was Nick's way to push back.

The headline shouted, "Reporter in Mackinac Island death probe told to 'Back off.'" The subhead said, "'Message discovered after break-in.'" Nick's story detailed everything he'd discovered at his apartment, and noted that the police had confirmed that the screen to the bedroom window had been cut. A quote from a detective indicated that the crime lab was sifting through evidence found in the apartment.

As Nick put the newspaper down on the bench and took another long pull from his coffee cup, he heard Dave approach from the Hooters parking lot.

"You're alive, but you look like shit."

"Oh, that's bird crap on my forehead," Nick said, swiping at his eyebrows again with the napkin. He sat up straight and turned to face his friend.

"No, I mean you really, really look like shit," Dave said. "Your hair is matted, you haven't shaved, your eyes are all bagged out, and your clothes literally look like they've been slept in."

The two buddies sat quietly on the bench and watched a half-dozen small fishing boats scoot down the river out to Saginaw Bay, most likely in pursuit of walleye. Early-morning sunshine took the chill off their bodies.

Finally Dave broke the silence. "You were pretty outrageous last night. After we left O'Hare's and came down here, you got loud and feisty. Do you remember challenging Big Ben to a fistfight?"

"No kidding?"

"You're lucky he didn't mop the floor with your sorry ass," Dave said. "The two guys he was with wanted to drag you out to the parking lot, but Art Dore stepped up and kept you from getting hurt."

Big Ben, the tall, three-hundred-pound fighter who called Bay City home, had gained national notoriety when he went from being one of Art Dore's tough man competition winners to a TV boxing sensation.

"I coulda taken him," Nick said, a grin spreading across his face as his mind searched its foggy recesses for a glimpse of what had happened inside Hooters just hours earlier. He found nothing.

"I'm probably not the best person to be handing out lectures about the virtues of sobriety, but I think you are in trouble here, buddy," Dave said. "I'm afraid you're going to hurt someone, or get hurt yourself."

"You're probably right. I just got a little geeked up and carried away after my place got busted into."

"You can't let the stress get to you like that," Dave said. "This is a serious problem. You are getting too wrapped up in the island story. And then when other things—like the publisher hitting on you and your apartment getting broken into—happen, you fall apart and get wasted. I think you need to take a break from work. It's too much."

Nick sighed. He had momentarily forgotten about the publisher problem.

"Tanya already pretty much gave me an ultimatum," he said. "I'm going to work on overall self-improvement. Sorry if I embarrassed you."

"You can't embarrass me—we're buddies, and always will be. But you were very outrageous—and actually pretty funny last night."

The two friends sat quietly again, sipping coffee. Nick offered Dave a chunk of his blueberry muffin. Dave wolfed it down.

"I didn't say you could eat the whole damn thing," Nick said.

"Never try to offer a hungry man food with a string on it," Dave said. "That never works too well."

They laughed and sat together for a few minutes more.

"What am I going to do about the Castrator?" Nick asked finally. "She pretty much ordered me to be in her office this afternoon and perform."

"I've got a plan," Dave said. "Go home, get cleaned up, and take a nap. I'll be over right after lunch, and we'll put the plan into action."

"Deal. Thanks, buddy."

Chapter 38

Early Sunday afternoon

Dave pulled up in front of Nick's apartment building in his Chevy pickup truck and cut the rumbling engine. The reporter noticed Mrs. Babcock peeking through the curtains of her ground-floor apartment. She greeted Dave at the building's front door.

"Thought it might be you," the tiny older lady said, looking down the street in both directions. "Since the break-in, I'm on super patrol duty."

"Don't blame you," Dave said. He gave her a gentle hug, afraid that a good squeeze might snap her spindly bones like twigs. "I know it freaked Nick out, too."

The two walked to the entrance of the building. When Dave opened the door for Mrs. Babcock, the view inside made him do a double take. A mannequin dressed in a police uniform was propped up in a chair. The dummy sat square in front of the doorway.

Dave laughed and asked if it was an official Bay City police officer's uniform. Before Mrs. Babcock could answer, a tape-recorded voice from behind the mannequin shouted, "Freeze! You're trespassing. A patrol car is on the way."

"What in the world . . . ?" Dave looked at Mrs. Babcock, who stood in the doorway smiling, obviously pleased with her lawman's performance.

"Got him and the one at the back door from my tenant in Number Seven," she said, motioning up the stairs with her chin. "He's manager of a home security company in town. Had 'em both hooked up and running the same day of the break-in. I call this guy Bob, and the one at the other door is Tom."

"Are Bob and Tom supposed to scare intruders away?" Dave asked, moving in to inspect Bob. "How does the voice work?"

"Motion sensitive if a key is not used in the door," she said. "Pretty sweet, huh?"

"Uh, I can think of a couple of different ways to describe Bob and Tom, and sweet is not one of them. But if the boys sitting in your entryways make you feel better, I say go for it."

The reporter heard Nick come out of his apartment. "See you later, Mrs. Babcock," Dave said, moving toward the stairway.

The landlord smiled. "Have a blessed day!"

Dave followed Nick into his apartment, which looked like it had either been ransacked again or had not been cleaned up since the intrusion. Dave pushed some empty beer cans away from the edge of the dining table and sat down. He complimented Nick on his physical transformation since the early morning. The nap, a shave, and a shower had done wonders for his friend.

"Thanks. I feel a whole lot better too. So what's your plan to help me deal with the Castrator?" Nick asked, clearing his own spot at the table with a sweep of his arm. Empty cans clattered as they fell to the floor.

Dave grinned. He thought he'd come up with a great plan, and he couldn't wait to tell Nick.

"Well, the way I see it is this: with a boss as powerful as her, and no one in town to complain to about her conduct, you need leverage. So I think you get the upper hand by gathering evidence, and you do it with this."

Dave reached in his coat pocket and pulled out a handheld recording device. It was black with red and blue buttons, and just a bit longer than his hand.

Nick took the recorder from Dave and studied it a moment. "So you think I should tape her propositioning me?"

"Yup, and it would be even better if you can get her on tape threatening you if you don't comply with her demands. Then you would have the advantage in a legal fight over sexual harassment."

"Okay, but that's not what I'm after," Nick said, setting the recorder down on the table but not taking his eyes off it. "I only want her to back off and leave me alone. I just want to do my job without having to worry about her attacking me and groping me like she did the other day."

"Well, getting her on tape will either get her to back off on her own, or a judge will do it, and the company will probably can her."

Nick still didn't seem convinced. "This company would probably just transfer her to another paper," he said, his head resting in the palm of his hand as his fingers tapped at the side of his face. "And what happens if she catches me trying to record her without saying anything incriminating? Then I'm up shit creek without the proverbial paddle—fired, or sent to work on the copy desk."

"Everything we do that's worthwhile comes with a risk," Dave said, taking the recorder back into his hand. He tinkered with it to demonstrate to Nick how easy it was to use. "All you do is press the blue button to record and the red one to stop. Blue is on the right and red is on the left. You can do it blindfolded."

Dave suggested that Nick tape the recorder to the inside of the breast pocket of his sports jacket. That way, if the Castrator wanted to play rough, the recorder would not become dislodged.

But Nick said he didn't like the idea because he was afraid the boss would make him discard the jacket before foreplay was initiated. Nick also rejected the idea of taping the recorder to his bare chest, stomach, or back because the Castrator had pulled up his shirt during their first encounter.

"That only leaves one option," Dave said, pointing to Nick's pants. "We tape it to one of your legs. That way you can reach in through your fly to start the recording before you go into the office. You just have to make sure you lead her into a proposition and threat before she gets into your pants."

"Oh, God. I hate this."

After more debate, Dave finally got Nick to agree to the plan. They decided to use duct tape to attach it to the inside of the left leg so that it could be reached and activated easily with Nick's right paw.

Once it was secured, Nick put his pants back on and tested the recorder, turning it on and talking with Dave in normal tones. The device worked as finely as a European cuckoo clock. They decided to head to the office.

On the way, the two talked about getting back on the Mackinac Island story. Nick said he wanted to return to the island to meet with the police chief and the hotel manager again. He also hoped to talk with the medical examiner.

Dave, however, wanted to continue working the Flint side of the story. "I'm meeting Becky tonight. She's coming up here because she likes the bars on Midland Street."

"You dog, you," Nick said. "You got a date with her?"

"Told ya she'd call. You got your ways, and I got mine."

* * *

Nick noticed the publisher's shiny black Cadillac sitting in the management parking lot when the two reporters arrived at *The Blade.* Nick had hoped that she would have a change of heart about meeting him, or that an emergency would come up that would keep her away. He frowned. No such luck.

As the two entered *The Blade*'s side entrance, they ran into Greta Norris, who was returning from the cafeteria with a cup of coffee and a pack of Twinkies.

"Dinner," she said, displaying the packaged sweet goo in her right hand. "I'm working on a piece for Monday's paper. What are you guys doing here on a Sunday afternoon?"

"Dave's got some paperwork to do, and I'm meeting with the publisher," Nick said, heading for the elevator. "I'll catch you later."

Nick punched the elevator button and started his ascent into doom. But he stopped the elevator at the third floor. He wasn't ready for this. His chest was tight, his breathing rapid. He stepped outside into the hall and sat in a chair near the door. The hall was dark and cool. The photography and graphics departments were closed.

Conditioned air whooshed from a wall vent. Nick sat in silence and kept checking his watch.

Show time. He took a deep breath and stepped back into the elevator, pressing the button for the fourth floor. As the elevator rose, he unzipped his pants and reached in to start the recorder. Dave had told him the device would record for about sixty minutes.

Just as Nick finished pulling his zipper up, the elevator bell rang and the door opened. The publisher stood in the open doorway of her office, directly across the hall from the elevator. She was wearing a short black robe, which was held together in the front with a single sash. Her long dark hair, usually pulled back in a bun or wrap for business meetings, was mussed and fell loosely over her shoulders—clearly ready for another kind of business. Ruby-red lipstick was the only makeup Nick could detect. One name flashed in his mind as surveyed the shapely woman standing before him: Elvira.

"Hi, Nick. Right on time," she said, raising one arm and resting it on the inside of the doorframe. The movement lifted her robe to breathtaking heights. Nick tried not to notice, but his eyes betrayed him. She was hot, and she knew it. His heart pounded against his chest.

"I figured you'd be here. I've been waiting for you," she said. "You're a smart guy."

The publisher backed her way into the office, motioning for Nick to follow and pull the door shut behind him. He made sure it was not locked in case he needed to make a fast getaway.

The lights were dim, and soft music rolled across the room in waves. The air smelled of rose petals. The coffee table was missing from its usual spot in front of her couch. Instead, a long blanket was draped from the top of the couch to the floor in front of it. Immediately Nick wondered who else had been on the blanket with her.

"Make yourself comfortable, Nick. Can I get you something to drink?"

Nick steered clear of the couch and worked his way over to the front of her desk. "No, I'm good, thanks. Just had coffee. Before this goes any further, I have to tell you how uncomfortable I am right now."

"Why is that, Nick? You're not a kid. We're both mature adults. We choose how we want to live our lives."

"Well, I have to say that this is not how I want to live my life," Nick said, pausing to clear his throat. He was keenly aware that the publisher had not said anything yet that would be considered incriminating. "I've got a great girlfriend. She's bringing some stability to my life. I'm lucky to have her, and I really don't want to do anything to screw that up."

"Just don't tell Sarah anything. No one has to know," she said, turning the lights down even lower.

"It's Tanya, her name is Tanya," said Nick as he leaned back and sat on the corner of the publisher's desk. When he did, his pants pulled up and tightened around both legs. Nick looked down and noticed an unintended consequence of sitting down: his pants outlined the shape of the recorder on the inside of his leg, a bulge in exactly the wrong place.

The publisher saw it too. "Whoa there, Nick. I think I'm having a Mae West moment here. I'm pretty sure you didn't bring me a banana, and you really are glad to see me."

She loosened the sash on her robe, revealing a lacy black brassiere, both cups overflowing. As Nick tried to look away, the publisher dropped to her knees in front of Nick and lunged at the outline of the recorder. Nick grabbed at the device too, afraid that her aggressiveness would dislodge it from his leg.

The two wrestled for possession of the bulge, rocking back and forth at the edge of the desk. Nick felt like he was losing the battle—she was a tiger, and stronger than he'd imagined.

Suddenly the publisher's door opened. Greta Norris burst in. Her jaw dropped. "Ga-gosh, guess I should have knocked. What's going on here?"

The publisher sprang to her feet and pulled the front of her robe together, tying it in one quick motion. "Uh, we're rehearsing a scene from the next production of the Bay City Players."

Nick stood up straight, too shocked to speak. He looked at the publisher, then searched Greta's face to see if she was buying the excuse.

Greta clearly was not. "What's the name of the production, *Deep Throat*?"

The publisher recovered her composure, ignoring Greta's question and posing one of her own. "So what's up with rolling into my office without the courtesy of knocking?"

"The Mackinac police chief is on the phone in the newsroom," Greta said. "Chief wants to talk to Nick right away. When I saw Nick earlier, he told me you two were meeting. I thought it was a business meeting. Obviously I was wrong."

Nick thanked Greta for passing along the message and said he would walk back down to the newsroom with her.

"Did I mention that I lost one of my contact lenses and was searching for it on my knees?" the publisher asked, her voice a little shaky.

"So I guess that means you must have lost it in Nick's crotch," Greta said. "Please, I—"

Nick interrupted the two. The telephone call was his opportunity to bolt. He grabbed Greta's arm on the way out of the office, and the two retreated to the newsroom, Greta begging for information.

"What the hell was that all about? You gotta tell me."

"Fill you in later," he said. "Glad you didn't just transfer the call to the publisher's office."

"Dave took the call when it came in," Greta said. "He said you'd be so glad to hear about the call that I shouldn't bother to knock—just rush right in."

When the two walked into the newsroom, Dave was sitting at his desk with his feet up, his hands behind his head. His smile was wide enough to drive a truck through.

"You're welcome," Dave said. "I just sent you the perfect witness and guaranteed that Greta can work here the rest of her life if she wants to. From here on, neither of you will have any problems with the Castrator."

Nick gave Dave an emphatic thumbs-up as he rushed to the phone on his desk to take the call from the island. No lights were lit. "Where's the chief?"

"She couldn't wait," Dave said. "Her number is on a scrap of paper on the top of your heap."

"Thanks, Dave. You are the man!" Nick dialed the number and waited to hear her voice. She answered on the last ring before it went to voice mail.

"Calkins here. Speak!"

"Chief, it's Steele. What's up?"

"Told ya I would call if we got a break in the case. So far it looks promising, but we're still developing it."

"Please go on. Should I jump in my Firebird and run up there tonight?"

"Maybe, maybe not. Can't tell you much, and you can't print any of it at this point."

"Okay, what's the break?

"An employee of the hotel came forward with a little prodding. Got to hand it to Sylvia Shane. She's one hell of a hotel manager. Kept interviewing staff members all week. On the third round, one called in sick—said she couldn't get out of bed.

"Turns out," the chief continued, "the kid was distraught over what had happened and what she was afraid she had done. Shane went to her room and talked gently until she spit out the truth."

"And what was the truth?" The chief was spewing and Nick wanted to keep her talking. He figured he would get more information now—in the heat of the moment—than if he waited and gave the island cop time to think about what she was telling him. "What did she say?"

"Young girl gave a hotel guest a staff uniform from the laundry. Thought she was helping a customer."

"How is that a good thing?"

"Girl said the guest wanted to give her boyfriend a surprise birthday present by hand-delivering a bottle of champagne to his room—wearing the uniform made it some kind of fantasy thing. So she helped the guest get a uniform and showed her the back stairway. Worst part is, the girl accepted a hundred-dollar tip. Knew it was wrong, but couldn't turn down the cash."

Nick asked if the employee had given authorities a detailed description of the woman posing as a hotel customer. The chief confirmed that she had.

"State police are flying a forensic sketch artist up to the island in the morning," the chief said. "Once we have that, it should give us something solid, the first real good lead in the case."

Nick offered to call Zeke Zimmer and see if he would be willing to ride up to the island with him. Since Zeke may have been the original target, perhaps he could identify the woman in the sketch, Nick argued.

The chief said she liked the idea because it would give investigators another piece of information. Figuring out who the woman was and what role, if any, she had in the death of Adam Townsend could break the case open. But she cautioned Nick to proceed carefully.

"I can't tell you what to do. You can contact Zeke if you like," she said. "But Nick—I have to remind you of this—you are not a cop. You are not officially part of this investigation. I've probably told you too much."

"You don't have to remind me. You guys have too many limitations. You have to follow the law. All I have to do is chase the story for our readers. Thanks, Chief. I'm coming up, and I'll try to bring Zeke with me."

Nick hung up and filled in Dave and Greta on what Chief Calkins had told him. As he finished speaking, the publisher walked into the newsroom.

"Well, sounds like that was an important telephone call," said the Castrator, who had ditched her Elvira garb in favor of designer jeans, a tight navy-blue sweater, and a ponytail. The siren lipstick had been wiped clean. “Are you and Dave heading up there tonight?”

“Well, no,” Nick said, avoiding eye contact. “Dave is meeting a woman from Flint tonight who may have another lead for us. I was thinking of taking Zeke with me and going to the island.”

“Whatever you think is best, Nick. I’ll clear it with your editor in the morning. By the way, thanks for rehearsing with me this afternoon. Good night.”

Greta edged forward, evidently eager to tell the publisher how she viewed the rehearsal. But Nick stopped her before it got muddy. “Let it go,” he whispered. “I’ll tell you what’s going on, but you’ve got to keep it under your hat. Dave was right to send you up to her office. Now we’re both sitting pretty.”

Chapter 39

Sunday evening

The long drive to the Straits of Mackinac would give Nick plenty of time to think about where his story was heading. He was making the trip alone. Zeke had declined the invitation, indicating that he had a big job to handle early in the week. Since the electrician was officially retired, his excuse made the reporter wonder what he was up to. No telling with Zeke, Nick thought.

Tanya also had turned down the offer to ride up north; she said she planned to return to Ann Arbor on Monday. Her rejection bothered Nick more than Zeke's. He'd hoped to spend more time with her, and he knew she wanted more attention from him—but not just as his sidekick while he was out on another adventure. Nick recalled her words from their phone discussion: "Quality time, Nick. Just me and you. No distractions. No interruptions. No dashing off for an interview, no sneaking away to write passionate prose. I want you to get passionate about me."

The words rattled around the edges of his brain as he rolled north. Traffic on I-75 was thin, but headlights from weekend visitors heading south produced an almost strobe-like effect. Nick drove without music. The only sound he heard was the low growl from the Firebird's V-8 and the whoosh of wind from his open sunroof.

The list of unanswered questions surrounding the island case was long. It churned in his mind as he drove. The employee coming forward, the latest development, offered all kinds of promise. The young woman might be able to identify the person who got into Adam's room the night he died. She might know more about the mystery woman than she realized. Nick hoped he would be able to talk with her.

As Nick neared the West Branch exit on I-75, his cell phone broke his train of thought. It was Dave.

"Hey, where are you, Nick?

"Heading north, past Standish, almost to West Branch—why, what's up?"

"Turn around," Dave said. "You've got to come back right away."

"Can't. Got to get up to the Straits before I miss the last ferry. Not unless it's really, really important."

"Becky is here, and she brought Big Bill Basswood with her," Dave said. "We're drinking beer at O'Hare's."

Dave's news was so exciting that it caused Nick to swerve the Firebird over the white lines dividing northbound traffic. He quickly regained control and started looking for a freeway turnaround, the kind reserved for the police and emergency vehicles. The reporter thought he could definitely feel an emergency coming his way. He asked Dave what had led to the good fortune of Big Bill being dropped in their laps.

"When I talked to Becky on the phone to set up our date, I told her we were looking for the guy," Dave said. "Wondered if she happened to know him. Turns out Basswood is her stepdad's brother. That connection helped her get the job at the union hall. So she just brought him along for free beer."

"I'll be back in half an hour," Nick said. "Hold on to him."

"He's a character, and he's got a hell of a story to tell us."

On his way back to Bay City, Nick called Tanya and Chief Calkins to let them both know he wouldn't be traveling to the island that evening. He also called the office and left a message for his boss. He wanted Drayton Clapper to know the Mackinac story was moving and getting hot. He also thought it wise to mention that he had seen the publisher on Sunday, so the editor would not be surprised if he received a call from her Monday morning.

Rather than get tied up in southbound traffic, Nick jumped off the freeway and took the back way home through Pinconning and Kawkawlin. In no time he was looking for a bag to put over the Restricted Parking sign behind O'Hare's just off the Midland Street bar district.

When Big Bill Basswood rose to shake Nick's hand a few minutes later, it was apparent where the nickname came from. The guy was nearly as large as a sumo wrestler. At six foot six, with more than 350 pounds of mostly hardened muscle, the retired autoworker looked like he could still toss fenders and bumpers around during an eight-hour shift on just about any assembly line.

Dave handled the introductions. The thing Nick first noticed was that Big Bill did not bother drinking from a glass. He clutched a pitcher in his left hand and guzzled straight from its pouring spout.

Becky was sitting next to Dave, fighting with another uncooperative skirt that was not much bigger than a scarf. Dave did not seem to mind. He obviously enjoyed watching the struggle for modesty.

Though Nick had not ordered, Sassy Sally, the ever-popular and efficient barmaid, whisked a cold draft into his empty right hand.

"Really glad you came up to meet with us, Bill," Nick said. "We've heard that you are the man to talk with about Zeke Zimmer."

"Known the guy for the best part of thirty years," Bill said. He pushed his Chevrolet ball cap back on his head, revealing a long, sweaty curl of gray hair. Gray stubble on his face made it look like the business end of a wire brush. "Pulled ol' Zeke out of a lot of tight spots over the years, too."

Nick watched Bill's Adam's apple bob up and down while the retired union official took a long pull from the pitcher. When Bill finished drinking, he smacked his lips and swabbed them down with the top part of his right sleeve.

"We think somebody is out to get Zeke," Dave said. "We heard about his union activity and what he did with the secret button on the assembly line at Chevrolet. Wondered if that left a bad taste in someone's mouth. Bad enough to get him killed?"

"Maybe, but I doubt it," Bill said. "I think all the people in Chevy management at that time are pretty much dead now, or too senile to remember what happened."

Nick asked if Zeke's old gambling debts could be the source of his current problems. Big Bill grunted and laughed. The smile revealed a missing tooth on the right side of his jaw and two gold fillings on the left.

The former union leader finished the pitcher with three gulps that would have drowned a smaller man. He raised his arm to get the attention of Sassy Sally, who looked at Nick for approval before nodding at Bill.

"If you ask me, it all goes back to the fires," Bill said. "That World Series hero connected Zeke with some very bad dudes in Detroit."

"Do you mean Denny McLain?" Dave asked.

Nick rolled his eyes. He knew what was coming; Tigers trivia was one of Dave's hobbies, and Nick knew his friend would not let the mistake pass without full explanation. McLain was not a World Series hero. Mickey Lolich won three games for the Tigers in the '68 series and hit a home run to boot. Lolich was the hero, not McLain.

"Yeah, yeah, whatever," Bill said after Dave finished his lecture. "The ballplayer introduced him to a guy who owned a ton of rental houses in Flint's north end. He was the king of slum landlords. The guy would rent the houses to the poorest of the poor and not put a nickel into 'em."

Bill paused to let Sassy Sally place a new foaming pitcher of beer in front of him. "Want a straw?" the barmaid asked. Nick couldn't tell if she was being sarcastic.

"Naw, this will be fine," Bill said, raising the pitcher to his mouth for another massive swallow. Sassy Sally asked who had his car keys, and Becky raised her hand. She was nursing a Diet Coke.

"Ah, where was I?" Bill asked, looking back and forth between the two reporters.

"The landlord didn't put any money into his rentals," Dave said.

"Yup, that's right. No repairs or updates. When the places got so run down that nobody would rent them anymore, he would call Zeke to torch 'em for the insurance money. It was easy dough for Zeke."

"So why would anyone want Zeke killed for torching rentals?" Nick asked.

Bill turned somber, looking away from Nick and Dave. He stared into the pitcher in front of him.

Nick could see darkness rise in the old union leader's face. He decided to push for an answer. "Bill, what is it? What happened?"

"Not many people know this, but Zeke had a job go bad," Bill said. "Word has it that he burned down a house that had squatters in it. A mom and some kids died in the fire. As I recall, the dad was in the hospital when it happened. Like always, Zeke set the fire and ran. Didn't find out about the people in the house until the next day."

"Oh my God!" Nick said. The reporter was shocked. He knew Zeke had been a scoundrel most of his life, but setting a fire that wiped out a family, that killed kids? Nick sat back in his chair, his shoulders drooping at the revelation.

Dave sat motionless at the table, clearly too stunned to speak. Becky used a bar napkin to dab at the corner of her eyes. Silence hung over their table.

Finally Bill continued, telling more about what had happened. "Yeah, it was bad, real bad. That's why Zeke had to get out of town. We put word out in the shop that he was transferring because of all that shit with the secret button and assembly line speedup, but it was really all about the fire."

Bill admitted they'd never shared that information with the authorities. "Nobody I knew of had the full story about what happened—it was all just bits and pieces, lots of whispers," he said. "The whole thing didn't come out until a couple years after Zeke left town. Mostly second- and third-hand information. Just talk. Lots of hard feelings against Zeke."

"Well, that would explain why Wife Number Three said Zeke suffered from nightmares, headaches, and insomnia," Nick said. "Do you know the name of the slum landlord? And what about the dad who lost his family? Do you know his name?"

"The landlord, the guy from Detroit, was Hershel Jones—used to hang out at the Shorthorn," Bill said. "I don't remember the guy who was in the hospital. But it was in the papers. Big story. Mom and two kids got evicted, so they squatted, and died in a fire."

"Was there an investigation?" Nick asked.

Bill gulped at the side of the pitcher. Telling such a horrid story clearly made him thirsty.

"You bet, but it was declared accidental by the fire marshal," Bill said, swiping at his chin with his sleeve again. "Said it was electrical. No accelerants used. Zeke was good at his work."

Nick asked Dave if he could call his friend at *The Flint Journal* to dig back in the newspaper's clip files to find the name of the dad.

"I'll try to find out what happened to Hershel Jones," Nick said. "Maybe we can talk Drayton into giving us some help. Love to see if Greta can give us a hand."

The foursome broke up. Nick paid the tab and left Sassy Sally a healthy tip. Dave gave Becky a quick hug and said he would call her. The reporters thanked Bill for traveling to Bay City and telling his story.

"I've been wantin' to get that off my chest for a long time," he said. "Probably should have said something before now, but I figured the timing was right when Becky here told me about you guys."

Nick and Dave returned to the *Blade* newsroom to make phone calls and assemble notes from what they had learned. Neither was anxious to get home. After hearing about the horrendous fire, they knew sleep would be hard to come by.

Chapter 40

Monday morning

When Nick arrived on Mackinac Island, he walked directly to the Grand Hotel. He already planned to talk with the manager and the chief, but if he got lucky he might be able to speak with the employee who was now helping authorities or the sketch artist the state police were bringing to the island.

Tourists buzzed around the outside of the hotel like bees circling a hive. Some strolled the front porch, looking for a place to settle in and sip coffee while drinking in the view of the bridge and the lake. Others walked the hotel's heavily manicured grounds, enjoying bountiful spring flowers still wet from a thick morning dew. Fat, fluffy clouds filled the sky as the sun tried mightily to find an opening to burst through.

The hotel manager's office bristled with activity. Sylvia Shane's assistants dashed about, carrying notebooks and clipboards. They spoke in hushed tones except when addressing their boss.

Nick peered in the office door. Sylvia was on the phone. She held up her hand, which the reporter took to mean that she wanted him to stay until she finished her call.

"I wondered how long it would take you to get here," she said once she'd hung up the phone. The woman stood to greet Nick and gestured for him to take a seat. "Thought you would have been here last night."

"Me too, but something came up and I had another interview," Nick said, settling down in the soft brown leather chair. He had decided he would share what he had learned from Basswood with the island police chief because she had been so helpful to him. But he was not ready to fill in the hotel manager just yet. Perhaps later. "I hear you had an employee volunteer new information."

The manager nodded. She pulled up another chair to sit next to Nick rather than retreating behind her desk. The two were less than a foot apart. The reporter could smell her perfume, perhaps a Chanel. He also noticed that she looked fatigued. The bags under her eyes were now puffy and swollen. Thin red lines marked the edges of her eyelids against the white of her eyeballs, and she was wearing heavier makeup than the last time the reporter had seen her. Obviously it had been a tough week.

Nick asked about the employee. How was she doing, now that she had revealed what she knew about the night Adam Townsend died? He also wanted to know if she faced disciplinary action.

"We have a very strict policy here," Sylvia said in an even, matter-of-fact tone. "The rules were broken, and there will be consequences. The girl understands this. She was very shaken by what happened, and she is trying to be cooperative."

The reporter shifted in his chair and crossed his legs. "Will I be able to talk with her?" he asked.

An assistant brought a pot of coffee on a tray lined with cups and set it on a small table next to the manager's desk. The aroma of dark roast filled the room.

"May I help myself?" Nick asked.

Sylvia nodded and asked Nick to pour her a cup too.

"Of course the employee can do whatever she likes," the manager said. "I don't have to tell you about free speech, but we have advised her against it. But I don't see how the chief could allow you to conduct an interview with her at this point anyways, now that she is part of an investigation."

Nick decided to go in another direction. He asked the manager if any other employees had come forward with new information. Had other workers seen the woman when she was in the hotel that night?

Shane shook her head and repeated what Chief Calkins had told

Nick about the employee interviews. "Despite what you might think," she said, "this is a responsible company and a good corporate citizen of this community. When Mr. Townsend died on our porch, we took it very seriously. We made no attempt to cover up what happened. It looked like an accident. At first we wondered if it might have been suicide. Depression is a terrible thing."

The reporter tried not to be defensive. "None of our articles have suggested you conducted a cover up," he said, stopping to sip his brew. "But it was almost like you scooped his body up, cleaned the mess where he splashed, and then immediately moved on. I think some people believed it was a little coldhearted."

The manager seemed to think about what Nick had said. Then she spoke about resort life.

"Nick, we've got an island full of people who are here to vacation and rest and have some fun. Our guests have paid a lot of good, hard-earned money to be here. We're their hosts. We have an obligation to take care of them and do everything possible to see that they enjoy themselves and feel comfortable."

Another assistant came into the office and handed Sylvia a file. She skimmed it, signed the last page, and handed it back to the employee without speaking. As she did, Chief Calkins entered the room.

"The sketch artist is here," the chief said. "Just picked him up at the airport. He's meeting with our witness right now."

"And where might that be?" Nick asked. "Are they here in the hotel or at the police station?"

"Do I have 'stupid' printed on my forehead? I don't want you talking to either of them. This could be an important development, and I don't want to jeopardize any part of this. So please just back off a little and let us do our jobs. When we think we have a good sketch, you'll be the first to know."

Ouch. Shut down by both the manager and the chief. Nick decided to try and walk down a different path with the women.

"Okay, can you tell me what else the witness said about the

woman she met?" he asked. "Was she tall, short, fat, thin? Young, old? What kind of clothing?"

"Very ordinary," Sylvia said. "Plain features. Medium size. The woman looked fit, maybe even a little muscular. Light hair pulled back in a bun. She wore designer blue jeans and an aqua sweater. Our employee said she wore athletic shoes, like a jogger might wear."

"What about her demeanor? Bold, bossy, reserved, quiet?" The reporter scribbled notes that only he could decipher.

"Almost shy," the chief said. "I asked the same thing. Our witness said the woman did not want to make eye contact, and she was very reserved when she asked about borrowing an employee uniform. The woman smiled and blushed when she said she wanted to surprise her boyfriend with a fantasy. The witness said she had the feeling it was very innocent, and that's why she went along with it."

Apparently the employee had refused the tip when it was first offered, Sylvia said. The woman had stuffed two fifties in the employee's pocket. "That's what a lot of our guests do—even when they know about our no-tip policy, they sometimes insist."

Nick still wondered whether the mystery woman was working with a man. "How did the woman get Adam up and over the railing of the balcony?" he asked. "Was she physically strong enough to do all that, or did she have help?"

The manager and the chief looked at each other in silence. Finally the chief suggested that Sylvia give Nick another piece of information.

"You absolutely cannot print this, understand?" the manager declared in a tone that Nick took to mean she was dead serious. He nodded.

"We did a simulation on that balcony," she said. "We made a sandbag the size, shape, and weight of Adam Townsend and asked five female employees, who were roughly the same size as the woman our witness described, to try lifting the sandbag over the railing. Two of them were able to hoist the bag over just by using the railing for leverage."

The chief added that a belt buckle like the one Townsend had been wearing was strapped around the sandbag at waist level. When the sandbag was lifted and pushed over the rail, the buckle ground into the railing, spraying tiny particles of dried paint in all directions.

"That means the woman probably walked out of that room afterward with paint particles on her pants or shoes," the chief said.

"Very impressive," Nick said. "I love it. A simulation. You must have done it in the middle of the night so your guests would not pick up on it."

"We did," the chief said. "And the sandbag landed in almost the exact spot where Adam crashed."

* * *

Nick headed out of the hotel and decided to walk over to the Mustang to get something to eat—a dry lunch, he vowed to himself. On his way he passed the horse barn where he'd spent his first night on the island. Nate sat out front at a table and bench, repairing a harness.

"Hey, thanks for the tip, Nate," Nick said, slowing to chat with the horse handler he'd met a week earlier. "You were right on the nose with that info about a murder on the island."

"Oh, yeah. Almost forgot about you," Nate said, putting his tools down. "Boy, you sure are looking a whole hell of a lot better than when I found you in the barn."

The two laughed and shook hands. Nick told Nate that he was back to do some follow-up work on the death at the hotel. He asked him if he'd heard about the employee coming forward.

"Sure did," he said. "That's Suzie Alvarez. This is her third summer working on the island—and probably her last, if I was a bettin' man. It's a damn shame, too, because she's a sweetheart of a young gal. Smart, hard worker. I think she's studying hotel management back in Mexico. Wants to run one of those big resorts in Cancun."

"They got her working with a sketch artist right now." Nick said. "I'd love to talk with her when she's finished."

"Well, hell. I know where she bunks. I'll take you over there and introduce you to her a little later."

"That would be terrific, Nate. Thanks. I'll swing back by later this afternoon."

Chapter 41

Monday afternoon

Zeke Zimmer paced back and forth at the Paddock Lounge, chain-smoking Camel filter cigarettes and sipping at a rock glass filled with Johnnie Walker Black and a single ice cube.

The bar was empty except for Zeke and the bartender. Chairs still sat upside down on their tables. The smell of hot chlorine churned from the dishwashers. Bright lighting illuminated the place, including the deepest shadows of the corners. The Paddock's warts and bumps were exposed for all to see.

Ralph was carrying cases of bottled beer up from the basement cooler and stashing them by brand in the long, narrow refrigerators behind the bar. Obviously it had been a busy weekend at the Paddock.

"You want a hand with that?" Zeke asked, sipping at the scotch. "I can hear you wheezing way the hell over here."

"Naw, I got it. Almost done," Ralph said. He threw the last empty beer carton over the bar toward the basement stairway. "This is what keeps me young."

Zeke looked at the clock—1:30. Right on schedule, the phone behind the bar rang. Both men froze, staring at the ringing phone.

"Why don't you just get it," Ralph said. "That's what you been waiting for, isn't it?"

Zeke pounced on it like a cat attacking a mouse. "Zeke here." Instantly he recognized the woman's voice. It meant a payday, which he needed desperately, would be coming soon.

The woman didn't bother with small talk. "Did you check out the job?"

"Yup, just like you said," Zeke said, turning away from Ralph so the details of the conversation would not be shared. "Piece of cake. Country house. Nobody, I repeat, nobody around. Should come down real easy."

"How are you going to do it?" she asked.

Zeke told her that the job could be completed several different ways, but he thought the easiest would be a natural gas leak ignited by a candle on the kitchen counter.

"Can you do the job at two?" she asked. "We don't want any innocents to get hurt, do we? No Realtors, nobody shopping for houses. No women or children, right?"

The last remark gave Zeke a chill. Why would she say that? he wondered.

"Ah, no. We don't want anybody getting hurt," he said, stumbling over his words and pausing before continuing. "I plan to keep this a nice clean, simple job. What about payment?"

"Same as the advance," the woman said. "Check your mailbox Wednesday morning. If the job gets done right, you get paid."

Zeke hung up and finished his whiskey in a single gulp. He said so long to Ralph, leaving a twenty on the bar. "Thanks, buddy. By the way, I'll have an envelope for you Wednesday."

Chapter 42

Monday afternoon

At the Mustang, Nick worked his phone, hoping to get a lead on the current whereabouts of Hershel Jones. Big Bill had indicated the landlord had lived in the Detroit area, but that was years ago. If he was still alive, no telling where he might be now.

First Nick tried Norm Willing, an old friend from *The Detroit News* who had worked the police beat in the Motor City for years. Norm told Nick that Hershel Jones had a history of mob connections throughout the Metro Detroit area. At one time or another, he'd been charged with loan-sharking, insurance fraud, arson, auto theft, and bank robbery.

The charges never seemed to stick, Norm said, because the guy always paid big bucks for good lawyers. Plus, he was considered to be relatively small potatoes in the big scheme of Detroit crime.

"Haven't heard the name in years, but I'll make some calls for you," Willing said. "Who knows, he may be sitting fat and happy in a Florida condo. See what I can find out at the cop shop."

At the same time Nick ended his call with Willing, a call came in from Dave. His friend said he had connected with the chief librarian at *The Flint Journal*. The search for the man who had lost his family in a north-end fire would be conducted right away.

"The librarian said he vaguely remembered a horrific fire, but he would have to check the microfilm for clippings from that era," Dave said. "He hoped he would have a name for us by the end of the day."

Nick filled Dave in on his discussion with the *Detroit News* reporter. With luck, the two would be able to verify the lead Bill Basswood had given them.

"Got a call from Becky this morning," Dave said. "She said Bill slept all the way home last night—had to wake him to get him out of her car."

"The way he pounded down the beer last night, I guess I'm not surprised," Nick said. "You going to see Becky again?"

"This weekend," Dave said. "She invited me to come down to Flint, some kind of big concert at Whiting Auditorium. I figured, what the heck—why not?"

Nick asked what was happening in the newsroom. He wondered if his friend had run into the publisher. His encounter in the Castrator's office on Sunday had ended up working in his favor, but he had learned long ago to never underestimate Diane Givens, a woman who always seemed to get her way. Nick wondered what she might pull next to regain the advantage.

"No, but I did get the third degree from Drayton this morning," Dave said. "He wanted to know what we were up to. Said he got your message from last night. Also said he wanted that sketch and a fresh story from you for Tuesday's paper."

"Soon as I hang up with you, I'm going to check on the sketch," Nick said. "I may also get a chance to interview the witness later this afternoon, even though Chief Calkins and the hotel manager are dead set against it. We'll see. Think I might have a backdoor connection to her."

Nick finished talking with Dave and called Chief Calkins's office. An officer answered. He was cool to Nick, not offering much information. Didn't know where the chief was, he said, but he figured she could probably be found at the Grand.

The reporter paid his lunch tab and left Chastity a good tip. She had watched out for him the night he got out of control at the bar. "Thanks, and sorry if I was a problem," he said.

"No, well, kinda," she said. "You started out playing beer euchre with the guys, but after everybody'd had a couple pitchers and a couple shots, you decided to change the game to strip euchre. Funny, until we saw the shamrock shorts."

"And the horse barn?"

"I had a couple of the guys walk you back to the hotel, but you didn't make it," she said. "Got as far as the barn, and they put you down there, figuring Nate would get you started in the morning."

"Wow, not good. Thanks." He bought the old guys playing cards in the corner a pitcher of beer on his way out. They waved their thanks, and invited him back when he could buy more and play less.

It was starting to get late. Nick looked at his watch as he quickened his step to get back to the hotel. If he was going back to Bay City today, he would have to leave fairly soon. Catching a ferry back to Mackinaw City and driving home would swallow four hours.

When Nick arrived at the Grand, he found a beaming Chief Calkins in the manager's office.

"We've got a sketch," she said. "Our witness says it's a good drawing and a good likeness."

"You mean Suzie Alvarez?" Nick asked. "How long before she gets shipped back to Mexico?"

"Now where in the hell did you get that information?" the chief said. "We're not releasing her name. You can't use that."

"You have your job to do, and I have mine. Where's the sketch? May I take a look?" Nick asked.

The chief looked over at the hotel manager, who nodded her approval. The chief said the sketch would be released to the media after it was sent out to all police agencies across the state. But Nick could see it now and take it with him if he was going back to Bay City, because it would take him a while to get back home.

She handed Nick the paper with the drawing on it. The reporter studied it for a few minutes, pulling it up close to his nose and then pushing it out to arm's length away.

"Hmm. So Suzie thinks this is what the woman she helped looks like?" Nick asked. Neither of them responded to the question—probably because they did not want to confirm the name of the witness to Nick.

"I got it," he said, his face lighting up. A wide grin spread across his face. "You know who this looks like to me? A heavier Sarah Michelle Gellar, but with no makeup and a hangover."

"Aw, come on. It does not," the hotel manager said, jumping to her feet to look at the sketch again. The chief joined her. They stood at Nick's elbows and eyed the drawing in his hands.

The manager reached around to open her desk drawer and pulled out a recent issue of *People* magazine. She flipped through the pages until she found a photo of the actress.

"Well, maybe," the chief said, comparing the two. "I guess you could say they resemble each other a little, but only if Sarah was all fat and bloated—like she was on her period. Our sketch shows the woman with her hair pulled back. I've never seen Sarah wear her hair like that."

Nick thanked the two women for their help and placed the sketch in a large manila envelope to protect it. He told them he had to get back to Bay City to file a story to run with the sketch in Tuesday's paper.

"I want to use the background info you gave me this morning," he said. "Is that okay? Do you have a problem with that?"

"All but the sandbag simulation," the chief said. "We want to hold that back. And do not use the name of our witness, which we did not release to you."

"Sounds good," Nick said, turning to leave the office. "I'll give you a call if I have any questions, or if we turn up anything new."

The reporter scooted out of the hotel and went directly to the horse barn. Nate was still outside working on his harness. Nick asked the horse handler if there was still a chance to set up a meeting with Suzie Alvarez.

"Wish I could, but I can't," Nate said, pushing his worn, tattered Stetson back on his forehead. "Just checked, and Suzie is gone. They got her off the island soon as she was finished with the artist."

"I suppose that figures," Nick said. "She's the only witness, the only one who recalls seeing the mystery woman. They've got to protect her. Makes sense."

The reporter checked his watch. If he hustled, he could catch the three o'clock ferry going back to Mackinaw City.

"See you, Nate. I'll look you up when I come back the next time," Nick said, his voice trailing off as he started toward the main island docks.

"You do that, Nick," Nate said. "Hey, and I like you a lot better when you're not drinking so much. See you next time."

"That's what they all say," Nick called out, breaking into a trot. In no time he would be on his way home to Bay City. Finally the case was beginning to break open.

Chapter 43

Monday evening

When Nick returned to the *Blade* newsroom, he discovered messages piled high on his desk. Notes from Norm Willing, Greta Norris, Dave Balz, and Drayton Clapper implored him to call as soon as possible.

He called Willing first, hoping his *Detroit News* friend might have a lead on where to find Hershel Jones, the slum landlord who had apparently made a fortune buying, renting, and then torching homes in the north end of Flint.

Willing's inquiries had been fruitful. The cop reporter had discovered Jones living in a Bay City nursing home that specialized in care for Alzheimer's patients. Willing said he'd reached an old friend of the mobster. Jones was now so disoriented and lost that he no longer knew who or where he was. Relatives and friends had stopped visiting.

"Thanks, Norm," Nick said. "I really appreciate you digging this out for me."

"No problem. Give me a heads-up if this info takes you to a bigger story," Norm said. "You know me. I'm always looking to tap into a good piece."

Nick assured him of a return call if the lead took on a new life. The reporter created a Hershel Jones file and typed in all the notes he had on the man. If the old mobster had deteriorated mentally as much as Willing indicated, Nick wondered how much could be gained from talking with him. Nevertheless, it was a lead that had to be tracked down. Perhaps those who cared for Jones could reveal some information about him or his family.

As Nick finished his notes, Dave and Greta walked into the newsroom.

"Glad you're back," Dave said. "We think we know who the dad is that lost his family in the Flint fire. The librarian at *The Journal* sent down a handful of clippings. Greta may have already located him."

Greta handed Nick an envelope with old news articles. "You gotta read this. It's simply heartbreaking."

Nick scanned the material. It painted a dark and grim picture.

The man's name was Grant Robinson. He and his wife, Noreen, had two children, only four and six years old. They rented a home on Avenue A, just off of Saginaw Street, in Flint's north end. The clippings said the children were sickly, and Noreen stayed home to care for them.

Then tragedy struck the family. Grant, a roofer, fell from a two-story building while on a job. He suffered a closed-head injury and a broken back from the accident. Fortunately shrubbery had broken his fall, or it would have been worse for the tradesman. Grant had good health-care coverage through his skilled trades and union connection, but his recovery was painful and slow. Soon it became obvious he would never walk again.

After a year, Noreen and the children were evicted from the home they rented. With no family members in the immediate area, and friends who had also fallen on hard times, Noreen moved their kids into the second story of an abandoned house on Avenue B. The news stories indicated that the family became squatters, hoping to survive through the summer and then find relief before winter returned.

Late one night at the end of July, the articles said, an electrical fire ignited on the first floor of the house. The family that had previously lived in the structure had stuffed old newspapers in the exterior walls of the house to help insulate against the cold. When fire reached those walls, the house exploded in flames. Noreen and the children were trapped upstairs. Firefighters discovered their charred bodies while the house was still smoldering.

Nick threw the handful of clippings across the room. He rested his head in his hands. Throbbing pain crept up his spine and pounded at the back of his head. A sudden urge to vomit sent him running to the men's room. The tragedy brought back the memory and pain of losing his wife in a car accident.

Nick doused his head in the bathroom sink, hoping to cool the rage that coursed through his body. It didn't help.

Dave and Greta were silent when he returned to the newsroom.

"How does it get any worse than that?" Nick asked, his voice rising to match his anger. "Can you believe it? This was Zeke's fire. I feel like killing him right now myself."

"Hold on, hold on," Dave said. "I got a call in to the register of deeds to see if that house on Avenue B was owned by Hershel Jones. If it was, then we'll both help you kill Zeke."

Greta said she had found a Grant Robinson residing in an assisted-living facility near a Saginaw hospital. She handed Nick the telephone number for the home. The reporter could not bring himself to make the call right then. He stuffed the number in his pocket.

Twenty years was a long time to carry a grudge, but Nick knew the need to settle a score—especially when someone had lost his family—could be a very powerful motivator. The loss of his wife to a car wreck and his son's departure had left Nick alone, turning his life upside down. Only now, with Tanya coming into his life, was he starting to recover from the losses.

"I can't think of a better reason for wanting revenge," Nick said. "And if Mr. Robinson never was able to walk again, like the clips suggested, then why not hire a contract killer?"

He pulled out the envelope with the sketch in it. "Here's what our mystery lady looks like."

Greta peeked over his shoulder. "That's it?" she asked.

Dave grabbed the drawing and held it at eye level, turning it sideways as if to see if it looked different with more lighting. "Looks like Sarah Michelle Gellar, only whacked out on steroids."

"Yup, but heavier and in need of some makeup," Greta said.

"That's exactly what I thought," Nick said, retrieving the sketch. Clapper would want it for the next edition. Plus he would want a good story, which Nick needed to bang out right away.

"What have you two got going in the morning?" he asked, pulling the slip of paper out of his shirt pocket. "Either of you want to call Mr. Robinson? We've got to find a way to talk with him. We need to know if he's the Grant Robinson who lost his family, or another guy with the same name."

"I'll do it," Dave said. "I'll come up with some pretext and ask for an interview. Should at least confirm if he's our guy. Then either he'll see us, or he won't."

Nick suggested that Greta drive to the West Side nursing home in the morning to check out the lead he'd received from his pal at *The Detroit News*. The reporter thought Greta's youthful appearance would not be threatening to nursing home staff. If Dave showed up at the front desk, Nick was afraid the cops would be called to haul off a scary intruder.

"How do I get in to see him?" she asked, looking back and forth between Nick and Dave.

"Well, figure it out," Nick said. "Talk to some of the nurses or orderlies to see what they know about him and his condition. Take your hanky, weep a little. Show how concerned you are for ol' Hershel."

"Right, weep a little. Turn it on and off, kind of like a faucet," Greta said. "Guess I missed that class at J-School. "

"Hey, go get the story, or don't come back," Dave said. "You do what it takes. We're working for the greater good here."

"Is that what Nick was doing when he was involved in the Battle of the Bulge in the publisher's office Sunday?"

Nick decided to let it pass. Too much to do, too little time.

Chapter 44

Tuesday morning

Greta Norris pulled into the parking lot of Rest Haven Nursing Home on Bay City's West Side. Her research had indicated the home specialized in caring for patients with severe cases of Alzheimer's disease. The reporter hoped to find Hershel Jones among the home's 150 residents. She also hoped he would be in good enough physical condition to talk with her about his past. She wanted to know if he was the same man who used to own rental units in Flint.

The front entryway of the home was her first surprise. It contained a visitors' waiting area, a reception desk, a water fountain, and restrooms. A staff directory and listing of services swallowed up a whole wall. But the other wall was covered with a huge photograph of the sun setting on Saginaw Bay. It was as big as a picture window and gave the otherwise barren room and tile flooring a warm feel.

The reporter approached the reception desk slowly. She knew how lucky she was to catch an assignment like this fresh out of college. The opportunity to work on a big story with award-winning reporters like Nick and Dave was a break she could not screw up.

"Hi, Marilyn, my name is Greta Norris," she said, reading from the nameplate on the desk and smiling. The reporter leaned over the desk toward the receptionist.

"Ain't me. Marilyn is on break," the woman said, not looking up from her screen. "I'm Kaye—that is, if you really want to know." Kaye appeared to be in her mid-thirties, Greta guessed, and she looked as serious as a mathematician. She wore no makeup and her hair was in a tight ponytail that kept long brown hair out of her face. Her desktop was empty except for a nameplate and her screen.

Greta tried to be friendly, though she had the distinct feeling that Kaye didn't care and was just filling in for the regular receptionist. Hopefully that might work in the reporter's favor.

"Why yes, Kaye. I'm here to visit with one of your patients, Hershel Jones," Greta said. "What room is he in?"

"You a relative?" the receptionist asked. She glanced up from the screen without moving her head.

"No, I'm a reporter from *The Blade* and I was hoping to meet with Mr. Jones," Greta said. Before going into the building, she had decided to play it straight. That's what she had learned in journalism school—be up front and honest about who you are and what you are doing.

"You have to be related, or designated as an authorized visitor," Kaye said. "Can't let you in or give you any information about patients without written permission."

Greta decided not to protest. She would wait and give the reception desk another shot when Marilyn returned.

After sitting in her car for a few minutes, Greta moved her vehicle so that she could see the reception area through the front window. Soon another woman approached the desk and replaced Kaye. Must be Marilyn, Greta thought. The reporter figured she would watch and wait for a few minutes before trying again.

Ten minutes passed. As she reached for the door handle of the car, Greta noticed the woman behind the desk standing up. Marilyn stretched, looked around the entryway, and walked into the ladies' restroom.

"Screw J-School," the reporter said out loud. "I gotta get this story."

Greta scooted through the front door and shot straight for the patient-wing hallway. She had no idea where to find Hershel Jones, but figured a blind search would bear more fruit than sitting in her car or conversing with Marilyn.

Each room off the hallway was numbered. All doors were closed. Patient names were neatly printed on nameplates that were attached to the doorway wall above plastic filing trays. Greta walked slowly, trying to read the names on each side of the hallway. They were not alphabetical.

"May I help you?" a young man said—an orderly, she thought. She tried not to make eye contact or look lost, but the effort failed. He was dressed in a colorful smock and matching pants, each loose fitting and held together with cloth strings. The reporter thought he looked pleasant, almost handsome, with dark features and hair.

Greta thought fast. "Guess I got confused after talking to Marilyn at the front desk," she said. "These hallways all look the same."

"Takes awhile to figure out which way you're going here," he said with a warm smile. "Who are you looking for?"

"Hershel Jones," Greta said.

Instantly the orderly's smile faded. His face turned somber, furrows cutting across his forehead. "Oh, I'm so sorry," he said, his voice barely above a whisper. "Mr. Jones passed away last week."

"Oh no." Greta covered her mouth with her right hand and blinked furiously, as if to fight back tears. She remembered what Nick had suggested: take your hanky, weep a little. "I knew that he was doing poorly, but I had no idea."

The orderly explained that Mr. Jones had died suddenly, apparently from natural causes.

"I was on duty when he passed—it was last Tuesday," the young man said. "Very peaceful, lying in bed under his covers. He was holding a pillow to his chest."

The reporter asked if anyone was with him when he died.

"No," the orderly said, "but we all thought it was kind of funny that he died on the same day that he had a visitor for the first time in three years."

"Who was the visitor?" Greta asked, placing her right hand on the orderly's left arm. "Must have been a relative."

"Signed in as his granddaughter," he said. "Check with Kaye or Marilyn at the front desk. Either of them would have her name."

Once in her vehicle, Greta called Nick with the news.

"Natural causes, my ass," Nick said. "Now we've got two dead. Good job, Greta! Way to go. When you come back to the office, write down everything you learned and how you learned it."

He also urged Greta to go back into Rest Haven with the sketch from Mackinac Island.

"It's on our front page today," he said. "See if they think the woman in the sketch is Hershel's granddaughter. Let me know what you find out."

Chapter 45

Early Tuesday afternoon

A single phone rang near the entryway of Tri City Airport, a medium-sized facility located near Freeland. The airport served Bay City, Saginaw, and Midland.

Charlie grabbed the receiver on the second ring. It was precisely one o'clock.

"Yes?" She looked around the terminal to detect anyone who might be listening.

"You all set to finish the job in Bay City today?" the raspy voice asked.

"You bet. My traps are set. Ready to go."

"That reporter you tried to scare off is on his way here," the man said. "He's a ballsy SOB, I'll give him that."

Charlie was surprised at the news. The hired killer had thought breaking into the reporter's apartment would push him away from her trail—at least for a few days. She asked the man if he still wanted the job finished. If things were too hot, she could wait until they cooled.

"Oh no, proceed as planned. The sooner the better," he said. "You already got Jones, now finish it with Zeke this afternoon—then move on. After this call, I don't ever expect to speak with you again."

"My pleasure. I'm eager to wrap it up," she said. "I'll be out of Michigan in no time."

The man offered a final word of caution. "Be careful—your face is plastered all over the front page of *The Bay City Blade*," he said. "Don't know your name or anything about you, but I finally got a chance to see what you look like. You kinda look like Sarah Michelle Gellar, only higher than shit on mushrooms."

"What? I don't look anything like that Hollywood vamp," Charlie said, taking great offense at the notion.

The man laughed until his rasping turned into a hacking cough. When he regained steady breathing, he said, "Good luck, and good hunting. Now go bag your prey."

Chapter 46

Tuesday afternoon

At one o'clock, Nick pushed his Firebird onto the Veterans Memorial Bridge after momentarily waiting for a Great Lakes freighter to pass under the bridge's open span. In twenty minutes, he would be sitting in a Saginaw Township facility to interview Grant Robinson. Dave had set up the interview, suggesting that the newspaper was reviewing devastating fires in the region. But Clapper had pulled Dave off the story to work on a piece developing at the city commission, so Nick was taking over the interview.

Inside the facility, the common area hummed with afternoon activity. Some residents were watching a large TV in one corner of the cafeteria-like room. Others played cards or board games. Four ladies knitted, their wheelchairs forming a small circle.

Grant Robinson was waiting for Nick in an area off to the side, behind a short privacy wall. Nick towered above the large man in the wheelchair, who leaned slightly to the right. His lifeless legs dangled at the front of the chair, held still with a single strap. The introduction was quick and friendly, both men shaking hands and smiling.

Nick put his notebook down and placed a copy of that day's *Bay City Blade* on the table in front of the man. The main headline above the fold asked, "Who is this woman?" Under it was the sketch from Mackinac Island. The headline with Nick's story declared, "Police search for mystery woman tied to Adam Townsend death." The sketch, headlines, and article made a package that swallowed almost half the front page.

"Thought you might like a copy of today's paper," Nick said, settling into his seat and reaching for the ink pen in the breast pocket of his coat. While there, his fingers searched for the top of the recorder for the on button.

"Thank you, but I already got it when it landed on our front step an hour ago." Grant said, studying the front page. His voice was raspy and wheezy. "So you're the guy writing the stories from Mackinac Island? Interesting, very interesting. Just a damn dirty shame what happened to that Townsend fellow. But then, you're aware that I am very familiar with the concept of innocents dying."

Nick studied the man. Grant was dressed in a blue sweater and gray work pants. Slippers and socks covered his feet. A bald spot peeked out from the top of his thinning Afro. His ebony skin had a charcoal cast to it. He wore wire-rimmed glasses. He smiled frequently, but did not look comfortable.

"Yes, I covered Mr. Townsend's funeral last week," Nick said. "Lots of people from Bay City were very hurt by what happened. He was loved by many."

Nick asked if Dave had explained the reason for the interview request. Grant nodded, narrowing his eyes and focusing on the reporter's words. He said he'd agreed to the request because he wanted to be helpful with such a sensitive subject.

"Lost my family in a house fire—never really got over it, even after twenty years," Grant said. "I'll never forget the feelings I had when they told me what happened."

"I understand that you were in Vietnam."

"That's right. First Marine Division. *Semper fi*, man," Grant said, the smile returning to his face. "Two years of combat in 'Nam and the only thing that happened to me was a dousing with Agent Orange. I didn't get a scratch. Came home, got a good job with a future, and then I end up in a wheelchair for life. Hard to figure."

"The articles said you had a home on Avenue A in Flint," Nick said. "But your family lost the house when you got hurt. Is that correct?"

"We had a lot of bills to pay," he said, turning his head slightly. "When I found my wife after getting back from 'Nam, she was buried in debt. My kids were sick—they said it was from lead poisoning. They'd gotten into lead-based paint in that shithole we lived in on Avenue A. I got the house on a rent-to-own deal, but when I got hurt my wife couldn't pay."

Nick jotted notes as quickly as he could, but he also wanted to monitor Grant's facial expressions and mannerisms. He tried to slow the pace of the interview.

"That must have been a terrible burden for your wife. Did she ask for help in the community?"

"Oh yeah. Our church helped. The neighborhood groups pitched in, but it wasn't nearly enough," Grant said, growing quiet. His voice lowered to an almost whisper. "Not nearly enough. You have to understand that we lived in a dirt-poor part of town. People gave what they could, but their pockets were empty too."

"What happened when the house was lost?" Nick paused to see how the question settled on Grant, who shifted in his chair.

"My wife did the best she could," he said. "I was no help to her, and she didn't want to put it all on me while I was in the hospital. She just moved the kids one block over to a house she thought nobody cared about. It had sat empty for a while."

Nick asked Grant if he knew who owned the house. The reporter watched Grant's face, trying to see how the question affected him.

The former roofer responded calmly. He explained that the owners of most rental properties in the north end of Flint were absentee landlords. "They just pick up the rent checks. They don't fix nothin'."

"Did you ever find out who owned the house?" Nick asked.

"You're goddamned right I did," Grant said, his voice rising, his body stiffening in the chair. "Took me a while, but I also found out who burned it down."

Grant's face had filled with rage. He leaned forward in his chair and his fingertips turned white from digging into the cushioned arms. His eyes focused on Nick like they were lasers, burning holes through the reporter.

Nick decided to press ahead, but with caution. "The news articles indicated that the fire was electrical and that it was declared accidental. Is that incorrect?"

"That is bullshit, and those news articles were bullshit," the elderly man ranted. "Nothing accidental about what happened on Avenue B. The slum landlord cashed the place in for insurance money.

"It was all about money!" Grant slapped his right hand on the table. The resulting bang caught the attention of the others in the common area. All eyes turned to the two men. "I lost my family, my babies, my wife, and it was all about money. Those sons of bitches."

Grant, fueled by roiling anger, bounced up and down in his chair and slapped the table again. "And nobody, I mean nobody, gave a good goddamn about it."

An attendant of the facility ran from across the room to Grant's side. "Mr. Robinson, are you okay? Is this man disturbing you?"

Nick rose from the table and saw a water fountain on an adjacent wall near an interior door. A paper cup dispenser hung just above it. He told Grant he was going to get them some water.

The break eased the tension in the room. The reporter could hear a low murmur as he filled the cups and returned to their table.

"Sorry for losing my cool," Grant said. He shifted in his chair again, seeming to regain composure. The fire was gone from his eyes. Small droplets of perspiration beaded on his forehead. "Is this going to take much longer?"

"No. I just have a couple more things I'd like to ask," Nick said, picking up his pen and jotting down a few more notes. He cleared his throat to ask the next question calmly and clearly. "If you knew who owned the property and who burned it down, did you take that information to the authorities?"

"Oh, come on. Are you kidding? Did you just fall off the turnip truck, or what?" Grant asked, laughing and grunting at the same time. "We lived in the north end of Flint. The authorities didn't give a shit what happened up there. It's all black families. We didn't matter. We didn't count. Our children were disposable.

"When white people saw the story in the paper about my family burning up in that fire, you know what they thought? Deep down most of them were thinking, yeah, that's a shame, but it just means two less kids going on welfare or heading for prison. That's the real truth that nobody wants to admit to."

Nick did not respond. The words cut deeply, but he had to stay cool and neutral while conducting the interview. The reporter shifted in his chair and jotted down more notes.

After a moment, Grant continued. "I had the state fire marshal take a look, but it didn't matter," he said. "If a woman and babies had burned in a house in Davison, or Grand Blanc, or Fenton—or one of the lily-white areas of Flint—you can bet your ass there would have been a big-time investigation." His voice was even and matter of fact. "But the north end of Flint? We're not worth it. A professional set the fire. It looked like an accident. The authorities had the only answers they needed, and they moved on."

Nick had one more question. "For the purposes of this article, are you willing to share the names of those responsible for the fire?"

The question hung over Grant like a heavy cloud. He shifted in his chair again, not taking his eyes off Nick. Leaning to his right, he tugged at the bottom of his chin with his right hand as though he were trying to pull out the correct answer. Nick waited. He thought it best not to push any harder. He let the question linger, hoping the silence would work in his favor.

"No," Grant said. "They are well-known criminals. Cops been aware of them for years. They have been scamming, screwing, and harming people, and the big wheels of justice let them continue to operate.

"But I know who they are, and God knows who they are," Grant said. "I have full confidence that God will make sure these despicable human beings get what's coming to them. In fact, I know they are going to pay for what they did to my family. I have faith."

The reporter stood to close his notebook. Grant pointed to Nick's coat pocket and asked if the recorder was still working. "I ain't no fool. Figured you were taping me, and that's okay. You got nothing on me, and you never will."

Nick shook his head, pulled it out of his pocket, and showed it to the elderly man. "Thank you, Mr. Robinson. Appreciate your candor," he said.

As Nick left the facility, he looked at his watch. It was 2:45. He decided to return to the newsroom and tell his boss what Grant Robinson had said about getting revenge. He also believed he should alert Zeke, just to make sure he watched his step.

CHAPTER 47

Tuesday afternoon

Charlie parked her car in a farm field behind a fencerow on Three Mile Road in Monitor Township. She surveyed her surroundings. No kids on bikes. No joggers. No farmers on tractors getting ready to plant spring crops.

The country setting was quiet except for a barking dog off in the distance. It was cloudy and cold, and a light breeze made her zip her jacket. She walked to the farmhouse that Zeke was scheduled to torch in one hour.

Once inside the house, she would wait for Zeke. Charlie punched the code into the Realtor's lockbox to get the door key. It didn't open. She tried the code again. One-nine-five-two. Still no luck. A third try ended the same way.

"Damn it!" she said out loud, though no one was listening. "Mary Rose—that bitch changed the lockbox code."

Charlie shook the steel box on the doorknob, but it would not yield. She stepped back and examined the door. Too tough to kick in, she thought. The killer vowed that Zeke was not going to slip the hook again. She walked around to the back of the house to find a different way in.

A quick scan of the backyard revealed a burn barrel sitting on cement blocks in a clearing at the back of the property. Charlie tipped the barrel over on its side and rolled it to the base of a first-floor bedroom window. Then, after checking to make sure no one had approached the property, she grabbed one of the cement blocks and hurled it through the window.

Within minutes the contract killer was inside the building, opening the front door. Nothing had changed. It all looked the same. Satisfied, she checked the basement and second floor to make sure the place was empty. Nothing. Charlie looked at her watch. Still thirty minutes before Zeke would show.

Charlie walked back to her car and pulled a gas can out of the trunk. She also picked up the leather case containing a syringe that was already loaded with a paralyzing dose of Ketamine. Carrying both, she returned to the farmhouse to wait for Zeke.

* * *

At 1:50 p.m., the electrician's car turned the corner at Three Mile Road. Zeke drove to the old house slowly, his head swiveling back and forth to check for activity.

Three double whiskeys at lunchtime had given Zeke a warm glow and liquid guts. He pulled into the driveway and looked over the premises from behind his steering wheel. No one was in sight. He turned his vehicle around in the driveway and left it running so he could pull away from the property quickly.

When Zeke had previewed the job, he'd calculated that once he cut the natural gas line to the fireplace in the house, he'd have seven to ten minutes to light the candle on the counter and get off the property before the house filled with gas and blew to smithereens. As long as it happened after he left the house and it was in his rearview mirror, it didn't matter.

Chapter 48

Tuesday afternoon

Charlie waited just behind the door, ready to strike when Zeke cleared the doorway.

The electrician stopped just short of the door. Charlie heard him take a step back—hesitating at the open door, no doubt. The house was dark and quiet.

She heard Zeke sniff the air. His breathing was heavy. The assassin could smell whiskey on his breath. She didn't move, barely inhaling and exhaling.

Zeke stepped forward on the porch. The wooden decking creaked. Charlie saw the door move an inch. She could tell he was nudging it with an outstretched hand. She knew he was going slow, being cautious. Finally the door's hinge squawked as the door swung open and the torch eased forward, sticking his head into the doorway. Charlie watched him look around the dark room and check his watch. She checked her own: 2:15.

Charlie watched as Zeke inched forward, steadying himself by grabbing the doorframe. Then he stepped inside, one foot at a time. He took a deep breath and seemed to relax slightly. The smell of warm whiskey was even heavier now.

Zeke looked around, finally focusing on the fireplace in the living room. "Okay, let's do this," he said out loud, moving past the doorway.

As soon as his head cleared the door, Charlie stuck the needle into his neck and jammed the plunger down, forcing the animal tranquilizer into his body. Zeke clutched at his neck. He tried to turn away, but it was too late. Charlie kicked at the back of his knees. He staggered two steps and went down. The assassin jumped on top of him, pinning his head and shoulders to the floor.

Slowly the drug took effect, rendering his arms and legs useless. She could tell that Zeke was still able to see and hear, but he was now struggling to breathe, gasping for air.

Charlie grabbed her gas can and doused the floor, the walls, the drapes, and the wooden cabinets in the kitchen. Then she soaked Zeke, who was twitching on the floor.

"You're getting just what you deserve," she said. "You're going to go out the same way you killed those kids and their mother in Flint twenty years ago. You've got about five minutes to think about that. Better say your prayers."

Charlie splashed the remaining gas in a trail leading to the bedroom window where she'd gained entry. Carpeting soaked up the liquid. She tossed the cement block back outside.

As she passed Zeke's sprawling, soaked body one last time, she saw terror in his eyes. She raised the volume of her voice to make sure he could still understand what she was about to say. "It's my pleasure to bring you to this conclusion, compliments of Mr. Grant Robinson, the husband and father of the people you killed. Hershel Jones is already gone. Now it's your turn."

The killer walked around to the back of the house and rolled the barrel away from the window. She pulled a pack of matches out of her pocket, ignited it and let it flare up, and then tossed it into the bedroom window. Flames shot up from the carpeting.

Charlie quickened her pace, jogging to her car. She jumped in and turned the vehicle to the south, heading for Ann Arbor. Soon she would pick up her money, gather her things, and catch a jet out of Michigan.

The house erupted in flames. In minutes, it was completely engulfed.

Chapter 49

Tuesday afternoon

As Nick headed back toward Bay City from the assisted-living facility outside Saginaw, he could see smoke billowing on the horizon just to the north. The reporter in him screamed, "Chase the smoke, find the fire." He did, wheeling the Firebird in the direction of what looked like a growing blaze.

As he turned onto Three Mile Road, Nick spotted firefighters spewing water from a pumper truck onto an old farmhouse. The flames had not been brought under control. Smoke continued to fill the sky.

A familiar vehicle was sitting in the driveway, still running. The reporter had seen the electrician driving it on many occasions. No doubt it belonged to Zeke Zimmer.

Nick stopped the Firebird on the side of the road. Township police had set up a roadblock to keep motorists away from the burning building. The reporter felt sick to his stomach. He watched the house burn. He thought about Zeke.

The electrician, it turned out, was a horrible human being who had hurt many people. But Nick still thought this was a terrible ending to a wretched life. In the reporter's view, Zeke's fate should have been determined by a jury and a judge, not a vigilante.

Nick called the newsroom to update Drayton Clapper. As he waited for his boss to pick up, the fire raged even hotter. Popping, perhaps from exploding paint cans inside the home, erupted as the reporter sat on hold.

Finally Nick heard the editor's voice. Drayton was clearly excited. The editor said that Greta had come back from Rest Haven.

A receptionist at the nursing home had confirmed that the sketch of the woman on the front page of that day's paper was indeed the same woman who had signed herself in as Hershel Jones's kin.

Clapper said the sketch and Nick's story had already caused a stir around town. A clerk at Keit's Flowers had called the newsroom to report that the woman on the front page had bought a plant for Adam Townsend's funeral. But the woman had paid cash and had not offered a name or address for her receipt.

"Right now I'm at a fire," Nick said, his breathing labored. "It looks bad. I'm sitting here watching a house burn to the ground, and Zeke's car is in the driveway, running. He might be inside. I'm going to wait here to find out."

Nick clicked off his phone and got out of his car. Flames were still shooting out from the guts of the farmhouse. The reporter showed his identification to the cop blocking the road. "Anybody inside?"

"Think so, but I don't have many details," the officer said, looking back at the burning wreckage. "One of the firemen said a firebug—a torch—got caught in his own fire. He's stretched out on the kitchen floor. Looks like he almost crawled out of the place, but couldn't get through the doorway. An ambulance is on the way. Fire is still too hot, guys can't get inside yet."

That was enough for Nick. He did not want to be around when the electrician's body came out of the house.

As he drove away, all he could think of was Zeke's brother Jake. In just over a week, the Zimmer family would again get word that Zeke was dead—this time for certain.

Chapter 50

Late Tuesday afternoon

After it was confirmed that the fire at the house on Three Mile Road had consumed Zeke Zimmer, Nick decided that he needed to talk with Grant Robinson again.

Too much had happened, and Nick sought answers to questions he was afraid would not get resolved.

In eleven days, Adam Townsend, Hershel Jones, and Zeke Zimmer had died under mysterious circumstances. The two threads that tied them all together were Grant Robinson and a mystery woman who might never be identified.

The reporter did not call the assisted-living facility to arrange another interview. He just decided to show up and see if Grant would speak with him again. Nick waited in the common area as the Vietnam vet rolled across the room to the area they had been in earlier that afternoon. Grant was dressed in the same clothing, but a blanket covered his legs.

"Thanks for seeing me again without notice," Nick said. The reporter did not have his notebook or a recorder with him this time. Nick was upset by the developments of the day. "I need some answers to questions that I'm struggling with. You may not want to answer, and that's your choice, but I've just got to ask them. I need to know the truth."

"Are we on the record? Are you taping this or recording this discussion in any way?" Grant asked.

Nick shook his head and sat down at the table.

"Well, I am recording it," Grant said, pulling back the blanket.

A recorder the size of a paperback book was resting on his legs. The red light on the top indicated that it was running. "When I heard you came back to talk with me again, I figured I better protect myself. I don't want to be misquoted or be misrepresented in any way. Now what are your questions?"

Nick studied the hardened man who sat before him. No point in trying to sugarcoat it, he thought. Nick cleared his throat and began. "Are you responsible for the deaths of Zeke Zimmer, Adam Townsend, and Hershel Jones?"

The response was short. "If those men are dead, I did not kill them."

"Did you hire someone to kill them?"

"There is nothing—no notes, no records, no letters, no telephone calls—that would connect me to a person or people who might have killed them," he said. "You can search. The police can search. The prosecutor can search. But you will find nothing connecting me to their deaths."

Nick shifted in his seat and pushed ahead. "Is it just a coincidence, then, that Zimmer and Jones burned down the house that killed your family, and now they have died under unusual circumstances on the twentieth anniversary of that tragedy?"

"Must be," Grant said, his face expressionless. "Isn't it odd how things happen in life that simply cannot be explained. Life is funny like that—some things just work themselves out over time."

"What about Adam Townsend? Is his death just one of those things that happen?" Nick asked, his voice rising with indignation. The man who had died on Mackinac Island had nothing to do with what had happened in Flint twenty years before.

"As I mentioned to you when we spoke before," Grant said, "what happened to him was very unfortunate. It is a terrible thing when innocents die. Are we done here?"

Nick nodded, and Grant turned off his recorder. For a second time that day, he motioned for Nick to come close. The reporter bent over and leaned in toward the veteran.

"Nick, we can't expect God to get involved in every little dustup that happens on earth. Obviously He's got His hands full with the big picture," Grant said. "Let's just say that what got done was what needed to happen. The world is a better place now without those scumbags."

Chapter 51

Late Sunday morning

Nick walked into the newsroom carrying five copies of that day's newspaper, which he had just picked up in the pressroom. He tossed four copies in a basket. They would be clipped and put in story files.

The fifth copy landed atop his desk. He scanned the front page. Most of it, complete with photos and graphics, was devoted to the Mackinac Island piece.

> **Assassin Kills 3 Local Men, Disappears, *Blade* Probe Shows**
>
> *By Nick Steele, Dave Balz and Greta Norris*
>
> Three Bay City men died during the last two weeks at the hands of a contract killer, an investigation by *The Bay City Blade* has revealed.
>
> Zeke Zimmer died in a house fire last Tuesday. Hershel Jones, originally from Detroit and later Flint, died in a Bay City nursing home on May 11. Adam Townsend died on Mackinac Island on May 8.
>
> Immediately before their deaths, witnesses say, all three men had contact with the same unidentified woman in three different locations. The *Blade* investigation found that the woman is believed to be a paid assassin who executed each of them, then vanished without a trace.
>
> The killer was so professional, police said, that they have not been able to develop any direct evidence linking her to the men.

"The trail is cold," said Charles L. Wilson, Bay City police chief. "No fingerprints, no footprints, no record of communication. We're still developing leads and working the case. We're asking any individuals with information about these deaths to come forward."

So far, the only solid evidence uncovered is the identification of a drug that was used to incapacitate two of the three victims.

Extensive toxicology screening by the Michigan State Police Crime Lab reveals that two of the men, Zimmer and Townsend, were injected with Ketamine, an animal tranquilizer, before they died. The third man, who suffered from advanced Alzheimer's disease, died from suffocation, the autopsy showed.

Authorities in Bay City and Mackinac Island are investigating the ties between the men to discover who might have ordered, and paid for, the contract killings.

The *Blade* investigation suggests that a Saginaw man, who is a native of Flint, had motive to hire a contract killer. Local authorities are aware of the man and his connection to the case.

The first death occurred at the Grand Hotel on Mackinac Island. At first it was believed that Zimmer had fallen to his death from a third-story balcony room, but it was soon revealed that a case of mistaken identity had occurred.

Zimmer was alive and gambling in Traverse City that weekend. He had allowed a good friend, Adam Townsend, to use the room. It was Townsend who went over the railing, not Zimmer.

"Initially, it looked like Mr. Townsend's death was accidental," said Lucille Calkins, Mackinac Island police chief. "But evidence shows that a woman entered that room and the victim was injected with a double dose of Ketamine and was boosted over the railing, where he fell to his death."

After several days, a hotel employee came forward, the chief said, because she was so distraught about the death. She worked with a state police forensic sketch artist to create a rendering of the woman who had sought access to the room where Townsend was staying.

"That was our first big break in the case," Calkins said. "Later, when the advanced tox screen came back showing Ketamine in Mr. Townsend's blood, we knew we had something—a homicide, and possibly a contract killing."

Since then, a receptionist at Rest Haven Nursing Home has identified the woman in the sketch as the same person who claimed to be Hershel Jones's granddaughter and visited him the same day he died. Later, a check of nursing home records showed that Jones did not have a granddaughter.

A Bay City Realtor also came forward with information after seeing the sketch in *The Blade*. Mary Rose Hayden said the woman in the drawing identified herself as Barbara Fowler and asked to see four homes listed for sale. One of the properties Hayden showed the woman is the house that burned and ended Zimmer's life.

"I am just sickened by what happened. I had no idea," Hayden said. "The woman was very friendly and professional—I never would have suspected for a minute that she was a cold-blooded killer." The woman had given Hayden a card with her name and telephone number, both of which turned out to be fake.

Police checked the card for fingerprints, but found only smudges. Investigators reported that the card also contained specks of a dark, creamy substance believed to be Mackinac Island fudge.

In addition to the main article, *The Blade* also published background sidebars on Mackinac Island, each of the three victims, and how contract killers operate. Nick was proud of the work. It was what he lived for.

As the reporter admired the publication, Drayton Clapper came into the newsroom and approached Nick's desk.

"Good work, Nick," Clapper said. "Of course we'll chase the follow-ups on this. But I wanted to ask you about Grant Robinson. Now that the police are involved, I'm a little concerned that they may come in here with a warrant, looking for info."

"Don't worry. There was nothing incriminating on the tape," the reporter said. "He was very smart and coy about it. And, in accordance with our policy, I already got rid of it as well as the handwritten notes. The police can do all their investigating on their own."

Nick felt confident that the newspaper had done its job by investigating the case and making its findings public. Now it was up to law enforcement to determine what crimes had been committed and mete out justice.

The reporter asked Clapper about continuing to follow the case as the police investigation continued. The editor agreed as long as Nick did not run up any more expensive hotel tabs.

"Speaking of the hotel," the editor said, "I wanted to get your read on how all this was handled by the big wheels on Mackinac Island. Should they have done more early on? If they had acted differently, could the assassin have been caught? Should we do some more reporting on how it might have been handled better?"

Nick leaned back in his chair before responding.

"Given the circumstances, with the thousands they have coming and going every day, I don't know what else they could have done," he said finally. "Chief Calkins—I really like her. Tough and smart. She really pushed the case hard. And the hotel manager—very diligent. She kept pressing for answers and talking to her staff. Professional all the way. The employee coming forward and helping with the sketch was the key. That's really what broke it open."

Clapper said he felt satisfied with Nick's answer. The local news editor was about to take his wife to Sunday brunch, he said, but he had an order for Nick that he wanted accomplished right away: "I want you to take some time off. Get out of town—rest and relax."

The reporter smiled and nodded. He didn't need to be asked twice. Nick had been under tremendous pressure and wanted a break. His life, and what he was doing with it, needed sorting. He'd already made plans for a two-week vacation.

As the two talked, Dave and Greta came into the newsroom. They both carried their own stacks of papers fresh from the pressroom. The damp odor of ink and newsprint filled the office. Dave wanted them as keepsakes to add to his long history of work at the newspaper. Greta wanted them to send out with her resume if she decided to job hunt.

"Thanks, you two," Nick said. "I think it turned out very well. Couldn't have done it without you. Now what's next?"

Dave did not hesitate. "Two words," he said. "Darrin Appleton. We've got unfinished business with the pervert."

Before Nick could respond, Greta pushed her way into the discussion. The young reporter said she wanted to work on the piece.

"I've got history and insight to bring to the story," she said. "My high school softball coach was the same kind of predator. He hurt a lot of my friends. I was a victim too. I really, really want to help you with this one."

"Holy shit, Greta. Well, let's talk with Clapper about it," Nick said, looking at Dave, who nodded his approval. "I also promised Tanya that we would chase after Appleton. And that reminds me to call her. I picked up something for us yesterday, and I've been dying to share it with her."

As Nick grabbed his phone to place the call, Dave and Greta left the newsroom. The reporter was eager to hear her voice. He was convinced that their relationship had strengthened in the last two weeks in spite of her ultimatum. And he was certain that his love for her grew each day.

Finally she answered on the fifth ring. “Hello, this had better be Nick Steele on the phone, or I’m hanging up,” she said.

“It is,” he said, smiling. “Been waiting to talk to you all morning.”

“Wait, I’ve got great news to share with you,” she said, almost sounding gleeful. “Joe is coming home to visit. He will be here for the Fourth of July—that’s always a great time in Bay City.”

Nick was jubilant. He said he thought Joe coming home was fabulous news. He thanked Tanya for making it happen. Then he asked her what she had on her schedule for the next two weeks.

“That depends,” she said. “What for, and who’s asking?”

“I’m asking you to run off with me for two weeks—just you and me,” Nick said. “No stories, no interviews, no calls in the middle of the night. The two of us completely on our own to do whatever we want. It’s time to get serious.”

“You’ve got a deal on one condition. I’ll go with you as long as we’re not going to Mackinac Island.”

Nick laughed at her response. As much as he liked the Great Lakes jewel, he had his heart set on another destination that was surrounded by water and immense beauty.

“Nope. I want to bake in the sun and hear the ocean roar every day,” he said. “We’re leaving for Key West in the morning. Pack your bags!’

CPSIA information can be obtained
at www.ICGtesting.com
Printed in the USA
LVHW021211240523
746432LV00023B/370